GOLIATH

RUSS WATTS

SEVERED PRESS
HOBART TASMANIA

GOLIATH

Copyright © 2016 Russ Watts
Copyright © 2016 Severed Press

WWW.SEVEREDPRESS.COM

ISBN: 978-1-925493-09-2

In an insane world I'd like to thank my family and friends for keeping me sane. The monsters in this book are for you. Now you know what dreams are made of...

CHAPTER 1

"Norman, what are you doing?" whispered Melanie. She looked at her colleague as the bus ran over another pothole, throwing her back into her seat.

Norman Livingstone cast his weary eyes around the school bus, and then slowly back to Melanie. A bead of sweat ran down the side of his forehead. God he felt old. He had been teaching twenty-four years, and instead of it getting easier, he felt like it was getting harder. The classrooms got larger, while the budget got smaller. As Vice Principal, he shouldered a lot of responsibility, and though he hadn't discussed it with anyone but his wife, Joan, retirement was a distinct possibility in the next couple of years. He wanted to be able to spend some time with his wife before the job killed him. He had no doubt that fate would somehow find a way of bumping him off on a Friday afternoon, just before summer vacation.

"Norman. Hello? What are you doing?"

Melanie was only in her third year at Saint Joseph's and still enthusiastic about everything. Literally, everything. She volunteered for anything going: netball practice, co-ordinating dance class for the lower grades, and organizing the annual Christmas Dinner for all thirty teachers. Now, she was helping him take a class of delinquents out into the Mojave.

"I'm thinking," he replied. He wiped the bead of sweat away with the back of his hand. They had chosen May to visit, as it was cooler at the start of summer. It was only in the nineties instead of over a hundred if they had come a month later. Unfortunately, it was proving to be a very hot start to the day, and inside a cramped crowded bus with almost thirty boisterous children, it felt like an oven. Norman was counting down the minutes until he could get off.

"What are you thinking about? I thought we were going over the schedule for later. You kinda...tuned out there. I thought you might be having a stroke or something."

Norman offered Melanie a weak smile at her equally weak attempt at humor. She meant well, but her bubbly personality and enthusiasm was beginning to grate. She was attractive with short blonde hair and always had a long queue at parent-teacher evening, mostly from the single fathers. Norman doubted if she would ever wake up one day to the reality that this was hell. Teaching had been rewarding at times, but mostly at the start of his career rather than the end. Now, he just found it to be completely and utterly draining. Inner-city schools in Los Angeles tended to rank low on the list of 'Top Fifty Places to Work' list. It wasn't just the kids either, but the red tape and bureaucracy, the tick-boxes and forms that constantly had to be done. He hadn't signed up to spend half of his day looking at revenue-streams, expenses and attending urban school facility planning forums.

Norman looked at his colleague and leaned over to her conspiratorially. "I was thinking how nice a day it could be to be out here all alone, just wandering through the desert with nothing but the sky above me for company. Then I remembered I have thirty delightful children to look after for the next twelve hours. I was thinking, how many of the precious little darlings will I have to send home with a detention slip today? I was thinking, how many of them have smuggled alcohol or drugs on board?"

Melanie laughed. "Norman, you're such a joker. They're only ten years old!"

Exactly, he thought. He returned her laugh with a deadpan smile. "You're right, Melanie, I'm joking."

The bus turned a corner in the dusty road, and Norman felt his stomach go as they jolted over another pothole. Christ, hadn't they heard of asphalt out here? It wasn't just the heat or the noise he had to contend with, or Melanie's constant never-say-die chirpy attitude, but the cheap rust bucket the school had provided for them. It had most likely last been serviced when Nixon was facing off against Kennedy.

"So, you think we should—"

The bus lurched and came to an abrupt halt, and everybody was flung forward in their seats. Some of the children joined Melanie in screaming, and Norman wondered if they had hit something. As long as it was a skunk and not a hitchhiker, he could live with that.

Norman reached over the aisle and touched Melanie's arm. "Are you okay?" He turned around to see dozens of scared faces looking back at him. "Is everyone okay? Settle down, and stay seated please, I'll check what is happening. Miss Sykes is here if any of you need anything."

Norman unpeeled his legs from the worn leather seat, and approached the driver. Other than a cloud of dust, the view through the front window was unimpeded. As the dust cloud settled, Norman saw sparse scrub, and the burgeoning Joshua tree forest ahead. He could see no reason for an emergency stop.

"What's the problem?" Norman asked the driver. "We just add to the roadkill count?"

The driver was an old man who had been driving school groups and tour groups to the area for as long as he could remember. He was an employee of the bus company and cared little for pleasantries. Norman had been on plenty of trips with drivers just like him and knew full well that the drivers loved children about as much as they did potholes.

"Goddamn roads out. See? Shit, if I hadn't seen it when I did, we'd be ass over teakettle now."

Norman looked to where the driver was pointing, trying to ignore the peculiar expression emanating from the old man's mouth, and noticed the subsidence in the dirt road. To the left, it fell away into the scrub narrowing the already constricted road down to barely a single lane.

"Can we get through?" Norman asked.

The driver shifted in his seat to look at Norman and turned up his nose. "No. I've barely enough room here to turn around. If you want to carry on, you'll have to go on foot. The parking area is about a hundred feet up ahead. You'll find the gift shop, bathrooms and signs pointing out where the path is through the forest. I suggest you head on in. Just retrace your steps when you're done. I'll back up and find some place to turn us around, and wait here for you. I'll have to call it in too. We can't bring any more tour groups down here with the road like this."

"What happened?" Norman knew there had been no rainfall in the area for a couple of weeks, and precious little before that. Perhaps it was just old age that had caused the road to collapse. He could identify with that very well. Norman knew the roads out here often suffered from poor maintenance. They were low down the list of priorities compared to the network in LA. *Just like Vice Principals*, he thought.

"We had a good jolt three weeks back, that could've done it. There've been a few shakes lately, more than is usual for here." The driver shrugged his shoulders to indicate he wasn't interested in discussing the condition of the road any further. "Anyways, you want to get off here?"

"Thanks, yeah. Let me and Melanie get the kids ready, and we'll see you back here in, what, about two hours?"

The driver nodded and opened the bus door, letting the warm air inside. Norman felt the heat envelope him, cuddling him in its arms like an overly protective mother. It felt like he was slowly suffocating, and he wished he was back at home sipping a cold Chardonnay with Joan in the spa pool. Instead of enjoying some down-time, he was walking through a hot desert with a group of future petty criminals. It was going to be a long day.

Sighing, Norman turned back to Melanie and explained what was happening. Together, they herded the excited children off the bus and outside into the sunshine.

"Oh, I do love the drama," said Melanie. "Isn't this just fascinating? This may be old news to you, Norman, but I've never been here before. I don't know who's more excited, me or the children."

Norman smiled, and when Melanie turned away from him to wave the driver off, he rolled his eyes. *Give it twenty years, then see how exciting you find it*, he thought. Norman pulled the backpack around his shoulders tight, feeling the weight of it press against his back. Rivulets of sweat were already forming, and he was going to need more than a shower when he got home. Joan would probably hose him down in the back yard. The backpack was essential though, full of medical supplies and water, just in case one of the precious children decided to fall over and scrape a knee. He also had thirty candy bars tucked away at the bottom of it, a little bribe to make sure they all stayed in line. The threat of denying them their sugar fix would soon see all but the most delinquent of them follow orders.

A slender pale hand reached up and took Melanie's. Sparkling blue eyes looked up into hers. "Miss Sykes, I need to go to the bathroom."

"Okay, Robert, we're going now. We'll be there in a few minutes. You can stay with me until then."

As Melanie held little Robert's hand, Norman felt guilty for being annoyed by her. She could be a bit over-the-top, but she meant well and always put the kids first. If he was twenty years younger, he would probably have had a crack at her too. He occasionally overheard some of the other younger teachers discussing how hot she was. He hadn't failed to notice, but the days of chasing skirt were long gone. He was happy with Joan and had no desire to find himself a young plaything to ruin things. He was quite happy with how things were, and Melanie could screw her way through the entire teaching staff if she so wanted. He doubted she would even think about such things. Her private life remained private, and all he knew about her was that she had been brought up on a small farm close to Fort Worth with two dogs, a brother, and a regular visit to church on Sundays. She had been the perfect teacher since arriving and hadn't had a single grievance raised about her performance.

"Right, stay in your pairs and follow me," Norman shouted to the disorderly line behind him. "The bathrooms are right up ahead so *try* to control yourselves, please? Do *not* leave the road. Do *not* touch anything. And do not even think about... Benji, what are you doing? Now is not the time for dancing. Back in line, *now*. Right, follow me."

Shaking his head, he led the line of children away from the bus and into the forest. He heard the bus reversing slowly, knowing the driver would ensure he found time to take a good nap whilst they were gone. He was lucky he didn't have to accompany them on the field trip. Norman had come to this spot a few years ago, but it had been a while since the school's last visit to the Mojave. After the Joshua tree forest, they were going to head on to Kelso Depot for a history lesson and some lunch at the only café for miles in a nearby store. Then it was back to Baker to the wildlife park before the long journey back to the city. Norman hoped that the kids would be able to run around at the park and tire themselves out. He could do with a quiet journey home, and the only way that was going to happen was if he could get the children tired. He knew he was going to be shattered, and tomorrow morning promised no respite, just meetings and classes, followed by more mundane meetings. He looked over at Melanie holding Robert's hand and smiled. The boy trusted her to look after him completely. Norman knew he had to shake off this mood he was in. It wasn't all bad. Joan often told him he was turning into a grumpy old man. Now that the bus was out of sight, he looked around and remembered why he liked coming here. It was so different from LA. There were trees for a start, and he could actually see the sky. The air was clearer, fresher, and the kids were more engaged. So many of them would never get the chance to do this with their families, and it was good for them not to be cooped up inside in a stuffy classroom for a change. Norman decided he was going to try to find some of that excitement that Melanie and the kids had, to feed off it and use it.

As they walked down the road, Norman noticed the trees were sparse, but thickening quickly. Occasionally, a small cluster would cast a shadow over the road, and he could feel the temperature drop just a few degrees. It was still very early in the morning, so the sun was just low enough to throw them a few shadows. It was a welcome respite from the sweltering heat. As they approached the parking area he realized that there was nobody else around. With the road out and the early time of day it was hardly surprising, yet it was a little unnerving to be so alone. He was used to people being around all the time in the city. If it wasn't for the chatter and laughter of the children, he would probably be able to hear his own heartbeat.

At the sight of the concrete toilet block, the children splintered. Some of them ran straight for it. They had been on the bus for a couple of hours. Small bladders and long bumpy journeys were not a good mix. As the giddy children swamped the toilets, Norman approached Melanie.

"The gift shop's closed. Maybe we'll give them a few minutes to look around it after we've been into the forest and done the trail?"

"Yeah. It's too early to be open yet," she said, watching Benji raise his hands above his head and then perform a pirouette in the dust to the laughter of the crowd around him. "I'll give them five minutes to do their business, then round them up. You want to check out the sign and make sure you know where we're going? I can't wait to get in there, it's just so—"

"Fascinating? I know." Norman winked and grinned. Melanie chuckled, and then went to gather the children as Norman examined the sign. There was a small map of the area with blue arrows indicating the best path through the forest. The circuit they were doing took almost an hour to walk, though Norman knew it would be a lot longer with nearly thirty excitable children in tow. There were the usual warning signs about snakes and coyotes, and a reminder not to touch anything or be tempted to take it home. The desert was precious and there for everyone to be a part of.

He couldn't explain it, but he had an odd feeling. Shouldn't there be other tourists here by now? It was approaching nine thirty and it wasn't that unusual for tour groups to get an early start out here, to avoid the midday heat. The shop was supposed to open at nine too. Norman shrugged it off. Enjoy the day out, he told himself. It beats sitting at a desk and marking tests all day long.

As they walked through the trail, Norman blocked out the sound of the children's chatter. He stayed at the front, frequently turning around to make sure they were all following him. Melanie was busy pointing out various plants and describing the Joshua trees to them. Most of the class were enthralled by her, captivated by the way she spoke fervently about the native trees. Some of the children though were more interested in entertaining their friends or playing the fool. Benji was still busy dancing, Aaron was picking boogers and flicking them at Brooke, while little Lizzy Morrison was pulling Ophelia's pigtails. The two girls were giggling away, and Norman knew they weren't interested in the desert. They would be when they got back to class tomorrow and had to write about their experience.

Norman suddenly stopped and held up his hand. "Hold on, everyone, just hold it." They had been walking for half an hour, pushing further into the forest, and Norman knew he hadn't deviated from the track. He had walked this path before, and definitely had not gone wrong. So what lay ahead of him was very odd, very odd indeed.

The children behind him ceased walking immediately, and Melanie told Jessie to quit punching Liam in the arm.

"He started it," muttered Jessie, before Melanie gave her a glare that told her to shut up while she was still ahead.

"Melanie, can you come up here a second?" Norman turned around and beckoned her forward.

"What is it?" Melanie swept the blonde hair from her eyes and peered at the track. She knew they couldn't carry on. The trip was turning out to be a failure. First the awful road, and now this? "Oh...shoot. Norman, what happened?"

"My guess is the same quake that took out the road back there. Who knows? The driver said they'd had a few lately. Looks like the path has been taken out. There's no way we can get through. The Joshua trees will have to wait for another day." Norman saw the disappointment in Melanie's eyes. He knew it wasn't for her own sake, but for her class.

The path was gone. It looked like it had been torn from the ground, ripped up into pieces, and then thrown back down. Broken chunks of rock scattered the forest, and some of the trees had been uprooted, exposing their dark innards. It was quite impossible for even an experienced walker to carry on, and certainly there was no way to take the children through. That look of sadness in Melanie's eyes punctured Norman's thoughts. He felt like a bully, bursting her balloon for no good reason.

"Look, we can turn around, go back to the bus, and carry on to Kelso Depot early, or we can have an adventure," he said, an idea suddenly popping into his overworked mind.

"An adventure?" Melanie looked at him, as if he were mad. "Norman, I don't think the children are quite ready to go rock-climbing just yet."

Norman dabbed at his forehead with a soggy tissue. "Look, the path has slumped away to the side here, and the ground is firm. You can see a clearing down there, so let's just take the kids down there for a few minutes. They won't know any different, and you can still show them what we came here for. It's better than getting back on that big old yellow bus, right? Come on, just give it a few minutes. It's perfectly safe."

"Yeah, okay, it does look quite interesting."

Norman smiled. "I'd say it looks fascinating."

"Okay, let it go, old man." Melanie turned around to face the children who were still lined up in their pairs. "All right, we're going down here to a clearing in the forest. Mr. Livingstone has a treat for you all, *if* you behave. That includes you, Lizzy. You pull any more pigtails, and I'll give your candy bar to Liam."

The children squealed with laughter, and then Norman walked down the gentle slope through the forest. There were only half a dozen trees, and the ground was easy to navigate. The clearing appeared, although it wasn't quite how he had expected it to be. The ground was firm, yet there was another opening through the forest, where the trees had been pulled apart as if by a giant.

"Miss Sykes, perhaps you would like to hand out their treats?" asked Norman, as he removed the heavy backpack from his shoulders. "I just need a few minutes."

"Why? Where are you going?" Melanie told the children to be quiet and saw Norman looking at what she could only describe as a chasm. "You don't want to go down there, surely? Look, we really shouldn't leave the path, and the kids are quite safe here. We head off any further, and who knows what we'll find. There could be snakes, sinkholes, anything down there. Look at the way the trees are bent out of shape. If an earthquake has—"

Norman sighed, knowing Melanie was right. It was dangerous. Tomorrow, he had to go back to work, back to the mundane reality of running a school. Rarely did he get an opportunity to do anything more exciting than ordering pay-per-view these days. There was every likelihood that he'd be retired before they came back here, and he couldn't face the prospect of getting back on that bus just yet. It had taken them hours to get here, and it was time to put common sense to one side.

"Melanie, just stay here with the kids, please? I'll be fine. Five minutes, that's all. I'm curious as to what sort of earthquake leaves damage like that. Why isn't this clearing damaged too? The ground is perfectly fine, yet all around it is a mess."

"Norman, wait…"

Ignoring Melanie, Norman knew he just had to look. The ground at the edge of the clearing was scuffed and rough, and as he put a foot on a boulder, he peered down the chasm. The ground had been split open, and it resembled a dry riverbed. The area was strewn with rocks of all sizes, and Norman carefully clambered over a few in order to get a better view. The twisted roots of a tree tried to trip him up, but he had every intention of going home to Joan when this was over. If Melanie really needed any help, he was only two minutes away. He wasn't about to go digging his way down into the ground, or go caving, he just wanted to see what was going on.

He could still hear the children in the background, and he sat down on a smooth piece of rock that was sheltered from the direct sun by an overhanging tree stump. Looking further down the track, it appeared as if the ground gave way into a black hole. There was a cave down there, although he had not read of any caves in the area, or seen any on previous trips. It was thirty or forty feet across and pitch black. Despite the overwhelming sun above, the opening of the cave was shrouded in darkness.

"What is it, Mr Livingstone? A den?"

Norman turned to find a small boy standing behind him.

"Matthew O'Leary, you're supposed to be with the others. Did Miss Sykes give you a candy bar?"

Matthew shook his head. "I don't eat sugar. I need to look after my body. Mom said if I eat too much junk, my brain will rot, and then I won't get into Harvard."

Norman suppressed a laugh. Matthew was a good kid, and one who actually might make it all the way through school without getting a criminal record. He could be a bit of a nerd, but Norman would rather have thirty nerdy children truly interested in investing some time and brain power into what they were learning today, instead of unruly kids who were just eager to get home so they could fester in front of the all-powerful, all-consuming demagogue that is TV.

"It could be a den, but it looks a little too large, don't you think?" asked Norman. "Besides, the ground around here seems to be a bit...unstable. I rather think the mother would choose somewhere safer to raise her pups, don't you think, Matthew? A little more private?"

The young boy looked puzzled. "But I can see the coyotes."

Norman looked down at the cave, and saw no coyotes anywhere. "Matthew, I think you must have been out in the sun too long." He clambered back up the rocks and stood beside the curious boy. Norman could see the rest of the children all sat in a circle around Melanie. She would be telling them about the dangers of wandering off in the desert, or perhaps about how many deadly snakes there were nearby. Nothing like a little fear to ensure they followed orders.

"There, sir, can't you see?"

Norman looked at Matthew. He held out a long arm in the direction of the cave, yet was not pointing directly at it. Norman let his eyes follow along the line of sight where the boy was pointing.

"See? They're asleep, right? I guess it's too hot for them now."

Norman felt queasy. Suddenly, being back on the bus seemed like a great idea. There were three coyotes, no doubt the remnants of a pack, lying on the ground just to the side of the cave. Norman could tell they were dead, and he was thankful that Matthew had such poor eyesight. Two of them were smaller and lay next to each other. They did look like they were sleeping, but there was just too much blood, and no movement from their bodies. The largest of the three had a leg missing, and its head was cocked to one side. Its neck had clearly been broken, and Norman knew this could not be the work of another pack. Maybe hunters, he thought, but unlikely.

Norman had never seen anything like it. The bodies were lying out in the sun, and it wouldn't be long before their intestines swelled up and exploded. The fact that the bodies were, for the most part, still intact, suggested that they had been killed recently, perhaps even only earlier that morning.

"Matthew, let's leave the coyotes to sleep it off, what do you say? I think it best we don't tell the others, they may be frightened. Just keep it between you and me, huh?"

Norman caught sight of another coyote as he went to take Matthew's hand. Its body lay halfway up a boulder, its corpse mangled and torn apart, as if something had been angered by its very existence and thrown it there. It was possible that the earthquakes had injured some of the coyotes, maybe even killed one, but these bodies weren't trapped between the rocks, or buried in the ground. It looked very much to Norman as if something had been feeding on them.

And that thought made him very nervous indeed.

As Norman looked closer, he thought he saw movement at the entrance to the cave. Something shifted in the shadows. There was a stirring of the dense air within, a whisper that could become truth, and finally common sense kicked back in. He decided to get back to Melanie and herd the children back toward the bus. Whatever had taken out the coyotes wasn't part of today's agenda.

A cold, low moaning sound came from the cave, echoing off its rocky walls and drifting over the harsh terrain to Norman. It was deep and mournful, and worryingly close, as if it was coming right from the cave's entrance. It made him shiver, and he felt Matthew grab his hand. The moaning sound continued for a full ten seconds before abruptly stopping. It was followed by a series of short, sharp barks.

"Matthew, let's go," said Norman firmly.

As Norman helped Matthew up over a large rock, the ground began to tremble. At first it was barely perceptible, just a quivering that shook the loose grains of dirt and made his already shaky hands grip Matthew's even more tightly. Norman felt the vibrations increase and they traveled through his shoes, up through his body to his head. This wasn't right. He looked across at Melanie. Her expression was one of confusion. Was this another quake?

"Matthew, I want you to—"

Norman never finished his sentence. The ground exploded in front of him, throwing rocks and boulders up into the air, blocking out the sun. The Joshua trees were lifted up, their roots pulled up from the earth like a baby being reluctantly pulled from the womb. There was a deafening boom, and then Norman felt himself falling. His feet had nothing to stand on, and he felt Matthew being wrenched from his hands. There was a short, high-pitched cry of horror from the boy, and then more sounds of children screaming in terror. As Norman fell into the hole beneath where he had been standing, he saw the flying boulders falling down toward him, and the last thing he thought of was how nice it would be to have one more glass of wine with Joan. The earth swallowed Norman greedily, and then he was sucked into the cold dark underground.

CHAPTER 2

Time seemed irrelevant, yet very important. Something bad had happened. Something had gone wrong. Had it been mere minutes, or hours? He was on a bus, on a hot, uncomfortable bus, and then…

Something *very* bad had happened.

Norman tried to open his eyes, but he realized they were already open. He was in complete and utter darkness. How could he be? It wasn't night, he was fairly sure of that. He reached a hand out in front of him and it touched soft dirt. Where the hell was he? Panic began to grip him, spreading out over his body like a network of cobwebs, slowly wrapping him tighter and tighter in their tense web. It was as if he had been buried alive, but that wasn't likely. He had been on a bus. What happened to him? What happened to the children?

The children!

Suddenly, Norman remembered: the school trip, the dead coyotes, Miss Sykes looking at him confused, Benji dancing, the bus driver cursing, the ground trembling, and the sound of boulders falling all around him.

Norman knew he had to find a way out of whatever hole he had been buried in. There was no light to see by, so he had to go by instinct and touch. He couldn't sense if he was upside down, or what way he was facing, so he summoned up a saliva ball and spat. The spit went only a few inches in the air and then landed back on his chin. So he was on his back, on a slight incline. At least now he had something to start with.

He wriggled his fingers and was pleased to find they all responded. Then he ran his hands over his body and waited for the inevitable pain. At some point, he was going to touch an exposed nerve, or a piece of bone. He ran his fingers over his chest and arms, but found nothing. Feeling more confident, he sat up so he could check his legs, and immediately banged his head on a sharp rock.

"Damn it," Norman proclaimed, and he winced as he touched the fresh cut on his temple.

Continuing with his quest to check if he was seriously injured before he attempted to stand up, he ran his hands down his legs. They were covered in dirt, but there were no wounds and he tentatively moved his feet. Though his body ached, and his head was now throbbing, he seemed to have survived whatever had happened relatively unharmed. Norman put his right hand down on the ground, ready to get up, and found it touch something warm and soft. It felt disturbingly like another person's hand.

"H…hello? Are you okay?"

Damn it, he thought, *if only there was some light in this hell hole.*

Norman traced his hand slowly from the hand on the ground up to the arm and squeezed. The arm was small, definitely a child's, so it didn't belong to Melanie. It could be Matthew, and Norman hoped the boy had just been knocked out alongside him.

"Hello?"

He tried shaking the arm, but there was no response. The darkness surrounded him like a blanket, and the silence was disquieting. He would rather have someone cry out in pain than suffer this interminable, insufferable silence. He ran his hand up the arm further, and then found his fingers sinking into dirt where the blood had soaked in. The arm wasn't attached to anything, and Norman shuddered as he touched a piece of bone.

"Matthew?"

Norman knew the boy was dead. It had to be the boy's arm. Nobody else had been close to him. The others were in the clearing, sitting around Melanie. Christ, what had happened to them all? Had it been another earthquake? The bus driver had said they had experienced more lately. Norman knew that smaller tremors could be a precursor to a major event and often followed by a larger one, yet there was something unusual about it. He had felt earthquakes before, admittedly only small ones, but this had been different. In his experience, the ground usually swayed or rolled gently when a quake struck LA. This had been much more violent, more like a bomb going off than a simple ground tremor.

In all his years of teaching, he had never had a child die on him before. The worst he'd had were broken arms and black eyes. Yet there was every chance Matthew was dead, probably crushed beneath the rocks and the dirt. It was an odd feeling. Norman didn't feel particularly sad, didn't feel like grieving, but he was upset that this horrible event had happened on his watch. He was undeniably responsible. It didn't matter if it was an accident, Matthew was under his care; it was as simple as that. He should have listened to Melanie and stayed with the children instead of going off exploring like that. Matthew was dead, and who knew how many of the other children were injured, or worse. He had to find a way out of here, to make things right. He had a duty to the children.

Norman cautiously pushed himself up, and felt the rock above his head. He ran his fingers across it carefully, worried about unsettling it. For all he knew, it was perched right above him, just waiting to be dislodged so it could fall and crush him. When he brushed against it, it seemed to move slightly, and he held his breath, gently removing his fingers from it. When nothing came crashing down on his head, he breathed out slowly. The air was cool, but thick with dirt, and he needed fresh air to fill his lungs.

"Anyone there?" he called out.

His voice bounced back to him, and he was met with nothing but more silence. Norman stood up and began creeping forward slowly. He kept his arms outstretched, trying to feel his way around blindly. The ground was uneven, littered with stones, and he tripped frequently. Every time he stumbled, he was worried he would find himself falling again, falling into nothing but a big black hole where he would lie for days dying in the darkness. Trying to keep a lid on his growing panic, he kept moving, trying to find a way out of the cold, lightless tomb.

Abruptly his hands came to a rock wall, and he stopped. Was he imagining it, or was there a chink of light coming from above? It was barely a spot, no bigger than a button, yet it was definitely there. He tried to find its source, unwilling to start pushing aside the rocks in case they fell. Brushing his hands over the rocks above, he found himself getting caught in tangled tree roots. He took it as a good sign. Maybe he could use the tree to pull himself up, if he could just find an opening. As he scuffed around in the dirt, his feet kicked something solid, yet soft. It wasn't just another rock, and he bent down to examine it. It could be one of the children, so he knew he had to investigate.

As he crouched down over whatever he had kicked, a disgusting odor reached his nostrils. It was the same festering smell that permeated the hall when the school toilet block got backed up, and he wondered if he had stumbled across one of the dead coyotes. Reaching out warily, he braced his back against the rock wall, and groped around in the darkness.

"Matthew? Melanie? You there?"

His hand found hair, matted together with what he guessed was blood. It was long and stringy, more like the hair on a human head than a coyote, and he ran his fingers up over the cranium of the skull, onto the person's forehead. He found the eyes, closed, the nose, and then the mouth with the small lips slightly parted. Whoever it was, they were staying awfully still. The features on the face were small, and he guessed it was one of the children. Perhaps Matthew, but it was impossible to tell for sure in the darkness.

"Wake up. Please, come on, I'm here now." His voice bounced off the walls, and Norman didn't know what else to say. He tried to pinch the person's cheek, to wake them, but there was no response. He leant closer, and ran his hand down the child's jaw, over their chin, until he reached the neck.

That was when he screamed.

Norman's fingers plunged into the severed neck, coating themselves with gore and blood, still warm and wet and sticky.

"Jesus." Norman recoiled from the severed head, his heart pounding. He wiped his hand on his chest, and stood up, desperate to get away from whoever it was that lay dead at his feet.

"Jesus," he said again as his breathing became faster.

Norman was so eager to get away from the dismembered corpse that he forgot where he was, and as he stood up his head became entangled in the roots of the tree. They coiled around his neck, wrapping themselves in his thin gray hair. Norman screamed again. He tried to pull at them, to extricate himself from their grip, but they seemed to grab onto him and pull him in tighter to the mesh of roots. Unable to pull himself free, he began to pull the tree down instead, sucking it toward him, hoping to create an opening from this death trap that had imprisoned him in the never-ending dark. The tree began to move, inching down toward him, bringing with it dirt and soil. As Norman howled and pulled at it, the tree dislodged itself, and then it tumbled down on him, bringing a torrent of dirt with it. Suddenly, Norman saw daylight, but it was all too brief. A flash of blue sky, and then it was gone, replaced with brown dirt and rocks, falling down to replace the tree. It was like standing in a sandpit, and Norman felt like he was being suffocated. He managed to break free from the tree roots and discard the Joshua tree to one side, only to find himself stuck in a growing pile of dirt that clawed at his legs and body. As he called for help, dirt entered his mouth and nose, clogging his throat and burning his lungs. He kicked and scrambled upward, his fingernails digging into the ever-growing pile of dirt that threatened to submerge him.

"Help!" Norman blurted it out, just as the last of the blue sky disappeared. He knew this was his only chance. If he let the whole thing cave in on him, he wouldn't be able to get out. This was his last chance to get back to Joan, his last chance to help the children topside, and his last chance to live. Being buried alive was a horrific prospect, but it was all he could think about. It felt like he was swimming against a strong tide, and every time he managed to pull himself up, something sucked him back down. He reached up a hand and grabbed a boulder, wedging his hand into a small crack in it. Norman roared and tried to find a surge of energy, not wanting to join the dead body buried beneath him.

Suddenly a hand grabbed his, and he looked up. His eyelids flickered, protecting his eyes from the dirt falling down on his face. He couldn't see the owner of the hand, but it was help. They were pulling him up, and he kicked as hard as he could, digging out of the sand and soil that was swallowing him.

Seconds later, and he was free. It seemed to be over so quickly. One second he was drowning, and the next he was lying on his back, staring up into a clear blue sky, the blazing sun warming his cold skin. He rolled over, and spat out a lump of saliva choked with dust. He coughed and then sat upright, brushing the dirt off him, catching sight of the blood on his shirt, trying to forget about how it had got there.

"Melanie? Thank God."

Her face was streaked with tears, her eyes sad, yet full of fear. She embraced Norman, and he could feel her shaking. This wasn't the same happy woman he worked with. Her enthusiasm and love had gone. Her eyes were full of desperation.

"How long was I down there?" Norman guessed from the position of the sun in the sky he hadn't been down there long. It was not yet above them, so it was still morning. He had only been down there for perhaps a few minutes, yet it had been an agony, and felt like years.

"Are you okay?" he asked her. "What about the children?"

"Quiet," she whispered. Her eyes darted around from side to side, and she gripped his shoulders tightly. She leant into him, so her face was barely an inch from his, and she lowered her voice to almost nothing. "It'll *hear* you."

Norman glanced around, but saw nothing that Melanie could be referring to. What was *it*? There was nobody around. "Melanie, calm down. The children, where are they? Did you manage to get them back to the bus? We need to—"

She put a bloody hand over Norman's mouth. It was then that he noticed the scratches and blood on her face. Her shirt was torn, and her shoulder was badly scraped too. When Norman looked into her eyes, the eyes that he had so fondly looked into over the last few years, he didn't recognize her. It was as if she was possessed and had taken on the aura of a crazy woman. Maybe she had suffered some sort of breakdown? Perhaps the earthquake had shaken her up? He was beginning to feel physically better, now that he was free of the tomb below. How he was going to explain this to the school board he didn't know, but he was focussed now on helping Melanie and the children. They were his priority. He had to get the situation under control.

Norman gently removed her hand from his mouth. "Melanie, listen to me, the earthquake is over. We're fine, okay? We need to make sure the children are—"

Melanie looked at him with bewilderment. "Earthquake? Is that what you think? An earthquake?"

Her lips curled up into a smile, and then she began to laugh. She tried to hide it behind her dirty hands, but it erupted forth like a geyser, her giggle soon turning into a maniacal laugh that Norman had only ever heard in bad horror films on late night TV. She had lost it. Norman could tell that she had truly lost her mind.

"Melanie, I know this is a traumatic time, but we *have* to get out of here. Come on." Norman stood up, and held out his hand to her.

As her laughter died, she stood up and looked at him. She shook her head. "That wasn't an earthquake."

Exasperated, Norman looked around for help. He couldn't see any children, nor hear any, and the clearing had gone completely. The whole ground seemed to have been blasted apart. Many of the trees were scattered around with boulders the size of cars, as if something had picked the ground up, shaken it around, and dumped it back down forcefully. The area had been destroyed, and Norman hoped the quake had been confined to the desert. If anything that strong hit LA, the damage would be off the chart.

"Okay, here's what we're going to do," Norman said, taking Melanie's hand in his. "We'll slowly find our way back to the bus, and take it from there. Remember the bus?" He had no idea if the bus was still there, but it was all he could think of. The driver would be able to relay a message for help so they could get someone out here to look for the children. They had probably run, scattered into the desert, terrified.

"It's too late for that," said Melanie. Her voice was devoid of hope, and dropped when she spoke. "They're gone. They're all dead."

Norman shivered. Despite the unbearable heat, despite Melanie's psychosis, he didn't doubt for one second that she was telling the truth. Christ, surely not all of them? Surely at least some of the children had gotten to safety?

"Miss Sykes, you need to think *very* carefully about what you're saying. Those children are in our care. There's no way they can all be…"

He couldn't bring himself to say it. He couldn't imagine going back without them. Benji, Lizzy, Liam, Lisa, Robert, and all the others; he would give anything to have them back, to have them annoying him and pestering him, singing loud songs on that hot stinking yellow bus, farting and giggling incessantly, rather than face the awful thought that they were all gone. He needed to get Melanie back in one piece. He couldn't do this alone. He needed her as much as she needed him.

"Look," he said forcefully, trying to muster up as much confidence as he could, "I expect you to—"

A noise interrupted him, a bellowing sound emitted from somewhere close by that seemed to fizz through the air and across the desert. Norman whirled around. There was nothing there. No children, no animals, nothing; yet that noise had been loud, wondrous and terrifying all at the same time. It had to have been a coyote, he told himself, perhaps injured and scared.

"I told you," whispered Melanie. "*It can hear you…*"

"Miss Sykes, let's—"

The ground rumbled again, making the loose dirt jiggle and jump as if on hot coals. He could feel something underneath the ground building up, like a pent-up pressure steamer ready to explode. The vibrations were growing stronger.

"Melanie, run!"

Norman grabbed her hand, and together they ran across the desert. Norman tried to lead them back to the bus, but any sign of the path was now long gone. He was running blindly, hopefully, just running anywhere that was away from whatever was going on. The earthquake and the noise seemed connected somehow. Had he been mistaken? Was that noise not natural, but a sound made by the earth's crust below? He knew a little about how earthquakes manifested themselves, and the damage they could do to the surface, but he hadn't read anything about them making a noise like that. A slight rumble, maybe even a bang, yes, but a bellowing sound?

Melanie yelped as she fell, twisting her ankle as she collapsed to the ground.

"It knows we're here. It knows." Melanie began to cry, clutching her foot. The ground still shook, and she looked from left to right, scanning all around.

Norman had never seen her look so scared. Something had gotten to her. Something had scared her so much that she had left the realms of reality. She was babbling something about monsters as he tried to lift her, when he saw movement ahead: a figure running toward them, then another. Two small children came bounding towards him, their faces a picture of horror. As they came closer, he recognised them: Rachael and Kelly, two sisters who were amongst his brighter students. He could see their clothes ripped and torn, their hands and arms covered in blood and deep cuts. They ran hand in hand. Rarely did they leave each other's side, and Norman was glad they had stuck together.

Norman left Melanie and began running toward them. "Rachael, Kelly, where are all the others?"

As they came nearer, the ground jolted once more beneath his feet, sending Norman down to the hard ground. He wasn't sure what came first, the sound or the explosion. There was fifty feet between him and the two girls, and as he looked at them running toward him, the ground exploded upward sending huge lumps of rock into the sky. They began to shower down around him, and he tried to see if the girls were all right. As the ground shook around him, he heard the same bellowing sound again, and something emerged from underneath the ground, something huge and monstrous and terrifying. Norman watched in disbelief as two massive claws appeared, swiftly followed by the creature's back, its skin covered in what looked like scales, its flesh a dark black color, jarring with the blue sky. Its spine was rippled, as if the bone was protruding through the thing's skin. The appearance of the monster, whatever it was, shocked Norman to his core. He couldn't identify what he was looking at. This couldn't be, couldn't exist. He was hallucinating, he had to be. The animal was like nothing he had ever seen before, certainly nothing that lived in the Mojave. Hell, it was like nothing that he had ever seen living on Earth. Except, maybe…

Norman saw Kelly trip, the girl falling face first into a boulder. She was knocked out instantly, and her sister paused, caught between running for help, and stopping to help her sister. Norman saw Rachael look up at the monster, her mouth open ready to scream, her face bewildered. He had never seen her look scared before, and it broke his heart.

"Rachael, run to me!" he shouted. There was still a chance she could make it. Maybe they could find a way back into the underground cave, find some place to hide. He had to get the girls to safety. He had to...

The monster towering above them raised a huge foot in the air, and Norman watched as it swung toward Rachael. The beast had to weigh several tons, and as it moved, the ground churned with it. Its foot came down right in front of Rachael, smashing the boulders there into dust. Norman thought it had missed her, and that she would still be able to make it, but then he saw the raised claw protruding from the center of the thing's foot. It was like an eagle's talons, razor sharp and poised to strike. The single claw had to be six feet across at least and as soon as the foot was planted on the ground before Rachael, the monster stabbed the claw forward. It struck her right through her chest, shattering her ribcage and pinned her to the ground. A fountain of blood erupted from her body as Norman watched her struggle and fight.

"No!" Norman got to his feet. "Leave her alone!" he shouted, hoping to distract the animal. There was still a chance for her. She was in trouble, but she wasn't dead yet.

Norman watched as the claw retracted from Rachael's body, and it seemed to have worked. The monster was going to turn on him now. Norman began to run toward her, but no sooner had he started than the claw smashed down again, this time obliterating Rachel's head. One second she was there, the next she was gone. Her body convulsed before going limp. The monster flicked her battered body up into the air deftly, using the claw on its foot like a fork. Norman watched as it caught her in its mouth, and swallowed her whole.

"Yakazar-yakazar!"

The giant monster roared its satisfaction at the meal, sending shivers down Norman's spine. There were no words to express what he felt. Fear, paranoia, horror and the urge to run all swept through Norman. But then he remembered he wasn't alone.

Kelly.

Norman saw the girl still lying near the thing's feet, unconscious and immobile. He had to get her away from here, away from whatever this nightmare vision was, away from the beast. It wasn't a hallucination, that was for sure.

As if anticipating Norman's thoughts, the monster turned quickly to Kelly. That was when Norman saw its arms. They had been tucked down by its side, but now Norman saw them extended fully. The forearms were thick and muscly, and they ended abruptly with three fingers on each hand. Each finger had to be the size of a man, yet with more of those razor sharp claws on each one. The monster reached down and scooped Kelly up with ease, lifting her high into the air.

"No, don't," pleaded Norman.

Kelly appeared to regain consciousness just as the monster brought her up to its mouth. Norman saw her eyes grow wide, and then she uttered a short, terrified scream that was abruptly cut off as the monster threw her into its jaws. The upper half of her torso was ripped away and swallowed, and Norman watched in amazement as it chewed on her body. The thing's arm swung down loosely, still holding the girl's lower half, with blood pouring copiously from the dismembered legs. Norman felt dizzy. It wasn't the heat, or the terror at standing beneath the shadow of a hundred foot monster that was causing him to stumble, but the sheer disbelief of what he was seeing. His brain couldn't comprehend what was going on. After the earthquake, the disappearance of the children, and Melanie's erratic behavior, he somehow had to accept this thing standing in front of him: a giant monster in the Mojave Desert, eating his children, a fantastic creature that couldn't, *shouldn't*, exist.

As it devoured Kelly's lifeless, warm body, the monster turned slowly until Norman could see its face. It swallowed Kelly's legs quickly, and let out a series of short barking sounds, almost as it if were coughing. Norman looked the thing over. The nearest he had seen to anything like it was in picture books, when he had taught the third grade about how the world was formed. The class had studied the dinosaurs, and one in particular jumped to the front of his memory now: Dromaeosaurus.

"No," whispered Norman as his brain tried to accept what he was watching. Had it done the same to his other children? Had they all been devoured? Surely some of them had got away. As Norman watched the creature swallow Kelly, he thought back to the picture books. This was different. To begin with, it was standing in front of him, whilst Dromaeosaurus had been extinct for 100 million years. Then there were the others things. Its body mass was different: thicker, muscly, and more robust, as if it spent a lot of time building up those muscles. The toe claws were different too. He had never read about those on any kind of dinosaur. As he ran over the options in his mind, one of his pupils sprang to mind and he heard John's voice in his head.

"Coelophysis, sir? One of the best killers of the Triassic period."

Norman looked down at his hands, covered in blood and dirt. The sun was already drying them out, and the semi-dry blood was caking his fingers like cement. "Quiet, John, it'll *hear* you."

He could still see John standing in front of class, reading aloud from the book proudly, whilst the rest of the class looked on bored. He was a good kid, but he was wrong about this. It wasn't like a Coelophysis either. It was some kind of rogue mutant; it had to be. It couldn't be a dinosaur, it just couldn't. Norman saw Matthew's decapitated head again in the darkness, smelt the fecund death that had almost driven him insane, and realized he was losing it like Melanie. John was gone, like all the other children. He had no time to wallow in grief now and certainly no time to lose his mind. He had to find some survivors. Rachael and Kelly had hidden so perhaps there were more out there, hiding amongst the rocks. There may be more still alive, hiding in the shelter of the Joshua trees. He had to get home to Joan. He had to find Melanie. He had to...

A shadow fell over Norman, and he looked up into the creature's red eyes. They were a deep crimson, and in the center of each a jet black pupil stared at him. The non-dinosaur seemed to stare at him for a while, unblinking, sizing him up, probably deciding whether he had enough meat on him to eat. Norman stared back, a cold sweat breaking out across forehead despite the heat. Maybe he could play dead. Maybe this was like a bear attack. As Norman saw its hands reaching down for him, he knew that playing dead wasn't going to work. Norman waited for the inevitable. There was no outrunning this thing. There was no hiding from it. That didn't mean he wanted to wait to be eaten though.

Norman looked around and noticed the blood; a splash here and there, the leaves of a nearby Joshua tree red instead of green, and pools of it at the monster's feet. How many had it killed? All of them? Had any of the children escaped? Melanie had said they were all gone. Rachael and Kelly had managed to hide, but only for a short while. Melanie would know. He had to make her tell him. If he could get through to her, and avoid this monster, he might be able to find some of the others. He might still be able to save some of his children. Even if only one, even if he died trying, he *had* to do something.

Norman dodged the advancing claws and whirled around to see Melanie where he had left her nursing her ankle. He rushed to her, scattering up stones and dirt as he ran. When he reached her, he skidded to a halt, and hoped that the cloud of dust would give them some cover, maybe just enough to hide them from the beast and get away.

"Melanie, get up, we need to get the hell out of here." Norman quickly dragged Melanie to her feet, aware of the monster following him. He could hear the thudding noises it made as it walked and felt a vibration run up his spine every time it planted one of its feet on the ground. He would have no more than a few seconds under the cover of the dust cloud. Shaking Melanie's shoulders, he started to drag her away. "We *have* to find the children."

"They're all dead," she said softly, letting him lead her. Melanie's moist eyes looked at Norman. "I'm sorry, I…"

A puzzled look spread across her face, and blood began to drip over her lips. Her body seemed to jump, as if hit by an electric shock. Norman reached for her, waving away the spurious dust he had thrown up into the air around them. "Melanie…"

She slowly shook her head and looked down. The tip of the monster's claw was sticking through her chest. She reached out a hand to touch it, pressing on the tip of the claw as if she could push it back in. Her fingers traced a line through her own blood, and she looked up at Norman curiously.

"But…"

Norman took a step backward as Melanie was suddenly flung to the ground face first. Her face smacked into the ground, and Norman heard her nose break. The sharp corner of a jagged edge of rock sliced through her skull. When she looked up at Norman, he could see a piece of bone sticking out of her skull. It was glaringly white against the blood on her face and the dark tissue of the monster's claw. The monster was stood right behind her, its foot inches away. Norman watched in shock as it retracted its claw from Melanie's back. It was coming for her now. It was leaning over them, reaching for the wounded woman, preparing to finish her off.

Without thinking, Norman leant forward and grabbed her outstretched hands.

"Melanie, hold on to me, I'll…"

Melanie was wrenched from his grasp easily. The giant monster threw her up into the air, and Norman heard her scream before it caught her in its jaws. Her body became wedged between its front teeth, and then it began to chew on her, breaking her bones like dry sticks. Norman collapsed to the ground, feeling tiny droplets of Melanie's blood rain down upon him. Her body was tossed from side to side as it ate her alive. An arm suddenly dropped on to the ground beside him, mangled beyond recognition, resembling a chewed piece of meat that that even a butcher would discard. Norman rolled over and threw up.

It was over. This nightmare wasn't going to end. He wasn't going to find any of the children. Melanie was right. There was no way they could have escaped. This aberration, this demon spawn, this thing, a pet of the devil himself, had taken them all. Wiping his face, Norman looked up into the thing's red eyes. If the creature had any emotions, if it could express anything, then Norman knew it was content. It had eaten, and eaten well. Its mouth was dripping with blood, and there was no more Melanie. She was in its belly now, dissolving in its stomach acid.

Dirt and grime were plastered to the sweat on Norman's face, and tears finally began to fall as he watched the monster turn to him. He didn't want to die out in the desert, not like this. He always thought he would simply fade away, perhaps in his sleep, with his wife at his side. As he listened to the monster utter another victorious bellow, he thought of how good it would be to share one last bottle of Chardonnay with Joan. And as the monster began to bend down to him, he knew he had drunk his last.

"I love you, Joan," he said, and Norman closed his eyes. There was no point in praying. God wasn't present here. There was nothing left to do now except hope it would be over quickly. Norman shivered as the monster came closer, opening its jaws wide. Their eyes locked together one last time, and Norman braced himself.

This was going to hurt.

CHAPTER 3

"It's not poisonous is it? Should we kill it?" asked Laurel as she climbed onto the bus quickly. The spider sat motionless on the pavement beneath the wheel arch, yet to Laurel it almost seemed to watch as she hopped past it. Its brown, hairy legs were almost three inches long and its body fat and dark. Laurel half expected it to jump up at her, although its eyes remained fixed on the ground where a tiny ant was passing in front of it.

Akecheta slowly shook his head and brushed his thick, black hair behind his ears. "Nothing to worry about, Mrs. Brown, she's just a little lost," he said smiling. "Probably looking for some shade."

Laurel scurried toward a pair of seats midway back and waited for her husband Mackenzie to follow. Realizing he wasn't behind her, she looked down the length of the bus and saw he was beside the guide, bent over and studying the spider.

"I've never seen one this close," said Mackenzie slowly, fascinated. "We don't get anything like this in Milwaukee."

Akecheta slowly reached out and cupped his hands around the spider. Very carefully, he scooped it up and walked across the pavement away from the bus.

"What type is it?" Mackenzie followed and watched Akecheta release the spider into the grass verge behind the bus stop. He simply let the spider walk off his hands and onto the ground, as if he were doing nothing out of the ordinary at all. Mackenzie's heart was pounding the whole time.

"Tarantula," said Akecheta watching the spider disappear under the fallen brown leaves of a Desert Fan. "Didn't want her to get run over. She was minding her own business, so best to let her get on with it, don't you think?"

Mackenzie followed Akecheta back to the bus. "I guess so. Say, how'd you know it was a 'she'?"

Akecheta shrugged as if it was obvious. "She's pregnant."

Mackenzie looked amazed and then laughed. "Maybe don't tell my wife, okay? She's already had two cups of coffee this morning, and news like that might just push her over the edge."

Akecheta laughed politely and then introduced Mackenzie to the driver, Mr. Stepper, who was waiting for them.

"You haven't got any more eight-legged critters on board have you?" asked Mackenzie as he shook hands with the driver.

"Mr. Brown, you have nothing to worry about. Our friends rarely come into town and are very particular. They show very little interest in my tours."

Mackenzie laughed once more. "Good to know."

Mr. Stepper got behind the wheel as Mackenzie climbed on board the bus. "Look, seriously, I clean our bus every day. We do have a first-aid kit in case of emergency, but you have nothing to worry about. You and your wife just sit back, relax and enjoy the ride. You'll get plenty of opportunity later to see more of 'em if you want to. We'll get on our way although we've a couple more stops to make this morning. From there on it's about an hour's drive before our first stop." Mr. Stepper closed the door as Mackenzie went to sit down beside his wife, nodding and saying hello to the others who were already seated. Akecheta sat down right behind the driver.

"Don't you get any funny ideas, Mac," said Laurel. She let her husband slide over to the window seat and then sat back down beside him. "We're here for the scenery and the history, *not* the creepy crawlies."

"Just making friends." Mackenzie put an arm around his wife.

"Well don't make friends with anything that bites." Laurel rested her head on her husband's shoulder and rubbed her eyes.

The coffee was yet to kick in and it had been an early start. Still, she was eager to get going. She had never been to the desert before, in fact never to any desert, and there was something captivating about the Mojave. She had read so much about it, and watched so many documentaries, that being here was a real thrill. She knew she was going to have to put away her dislike for bugs for a while if she was going to get the best out of this trip. She was hoping to see an eagle, ideally a Golden Eagle. Spiders she could take a pass on.

Mackenzie looked around the bus. There were two young men sat at the back who said hello before burying their heads back behind their cellphones. He guessed from their accents they were European, but having only got one word from them, wasn't sure exactly where yet.

Sat right at the back in one corner Mackenzie noticed a man who had a briefcase on his lap. He looked oddly like an old Indiana Jones, minus the Fedora. The man had combed graying hair and wiry spectacles and was tapping away into a tablet or netbook of some sort. Mackenzie had avoided being caught up in the technology race, settling instead for keeping his battered old Nokia which was still going strong, despite approaching ten years old. He had a desktop computer at work, but that was Laurel's domain. He kept away from it, and it kept away from him. That was how he liked it. If Laurel wasn't there to keep an eye on things, the dealership would still be run with pen and paper, and a heap of luck. He would never be able to cope without her. Mackenzie was lucky to have her and he knew it.

The bus lurched onto the road and Mackenzie watched the Wills Fargo Motel slip away quietly. Baker was a small town, very small, and they had arrived yesterday. Mackenzie had driven them over yesterday from Vegas in a cramped rental. With a busted stereo, its only saving grace had been the working air-con. Their vacation had been planned with military precision. It had been years since they had all been away together as they hadn't wanted to interrupt Amy's school-work, and in the last couple of years, the business had been struggling. This year, though, things had been going well and it had all just seemed to come together.

After flying over from Milwaukee with Amy, they had spent three days in Vegas soaking up the delights. Laurel had taken Amy to a Celine Dion concert, whilst Mackenzie found a sports bar showing the Brewers playing the Cubs. Mackenzie hadn't missed a game all season and saw no reason to let a vacation ruin things now. Unfortunately, the Brewers hadn't been on the same page and had lost in the final innings, going down seven to six. The Brown family had then spent much of their allocated spending money in the huge malls rather than the casinos, despite Mackenzie's insistence he could handle it. The hotels had sucked up the rest of it. From there, they had headed to Baker, before going their separate ways.

Earlier, they'd said goodbye to Amy, who had mumbled a goodbye through her sleep. Instead of sitting on a bus with them, she was taking a charter across to LA from where she would get a connecting flight to San Diego and spend a week with her biological father, John. Laurel and Mackenzie were to spend two nights in Baker so they could get out to the Mojave and explore, before heading west and staying two nights in LA. The plan was to pick up a rental from there, driving on down to San Diego at a leisurely pace before picking up Amy and then all flying back to Milwaukee together. That was the plan, anyway.

Mackenzie closed his eyes as the bus ponderously wound through Baker, picking up the last of the tourists. They had eaten in Baker last night and there was little to see that they hadn't already, so it wasn't long before Mackenzie drifted off. The day was warming up nicely and after yesterday's long drive, he was tired. They had been up since six making sure Amy was okay, and it was some time later that he woke with a jump.

"What was that?" he said as he awoke and rubbed his eyes.

"You awake now, sleeping beauty? You're missing out." Laurel gave her husband a nudge and Mackenzie straightened up.

He tried to stretch out his aching legs, but only succeeded in knocking his knee against the metal seat in front of him and he winced. The rattling bus was small and hot, and he was feeling the need for a cigarette. He looked at his watch. They had only been traveling for forty minutes, yet it had felt like hours. Through the dusty window next to him, he saw the sky was a perfect deep blue and the sun illuminated the desert road, lighting it up like a landing strip. It was probably pushing ninety degrees out there and it wasn't even nine a.m. The dry land was heating up with every minute and so was the bus. It had been an early start, but Mackenzie knew it was best to avoid the sun in the middle of the day out here. The brochure had promised a long lunch in a shady Joshua tree forest and he was already looking forward to a cold beer. He could feel the power of the sun beaming in through the windows and wondered if they'd made the right decision to visit in early summer. Winter might have been better. He looked over at his wife, Laurel, who was gently waving a tour pamphlet in front of her face. A faint sheen of sweat covered her skin, but she was smiling. Her upper body was leaning out into the aisle so she could see forward. She had been talking about this trip for months and to see her happy face now meant he forgot all about the cramped seat, the sweat trickling down his back and the jarring pain in his knee every time they went over a bump in the road.

As they continued south, he looked around the tour bus. There had been three other people on board when they had been picked up in Baker, but there were not many spare seats left now. Mackenzie counted eight in all, excluding the driver and guide. Mr. Stepper seemed pleasant enough and Mackenzie estimated he was in his fifties, but he looked like he kept in shape. His head was shaved and he wore a loose-fitting blue-collar shirt, crisply ironed over neat slacks. Mr. Stepper was probably a retired postman or something, filling in his retirement years as a local bus driver. As Mackenzie looked around the bus, he tried to work out who else he was going to be spending the day with.

The guide, Akecheta Locklear, had introduced himself and shaken hands warmly with a spry grin on his face as he did so. Mackenzie had almost wanted to go up and give the man a hug. He had a big, kind face shrouded by long black hair, and Mackenzie had warmed to him immediately. Akecheta was from the local Fort Mojave tribe and lived on the Reservation there, according to the brochure. Mackenzie saw no reason why they should lie. One of the reasons Laurel had picked this tour was because of the 'expert local guide' who would be able to tell them all about 'the fascinating wildlife and rich cultural history of the area.'

Mackenzie noticed the two men, who had been on the bus first, were whispering to each other and sniggering. They were young, skinny, fair-haired and pale-skinned. He couldn't tell what they were laughing at, but they were huddled low down in their seats and sat very close together, even closer than he and Laurel were now. Something told him they weren't just friends. Despite being first on the bus, they had chosen to sit at the back and Mackenzie wondered why they were on the trip. If they had come all the way over from Europe to see the Mojave, then sitting at the back of the bus was by far the worst place to be right now.

Of the others on the bus, there was a young black couple at the front with a child. They must have been picked up in Baker too. More tourists, like him and Laurel, probably passing through on their way to or from LA. Whilst the couple were pointing out of the window and chatting, the young girl was sat opposite her parents and very calmly stroking a golden Labrador puppy on her lap. Mackenzie was a little surprised it had been allowed on the bus, but as long as it was kept controlled and on a leash, there shouldn't be a problem. He had never seen the point in getting a pet, and thankfully Laurel agreed with him. He had enough going on at work to keep him busy and didn't want to have to walk a dog when he came home.

Laurel turned her face to Mackenzie and whispered in his ear. "I hope those boys at the back aren't going to giggle their way through the whole day. They're starting to get on my nerves."

"I'm sure they'll settle down once we get there. They're just excited," he said, not thinking anything of the sort. Glancing over his shoulder, he saw one of them holding up a cellphone and frowning. Mackenzie turned back to his wife. "Should get quieter now. I think they just lost reception."

Laurel smiled. "No more Instagram? Shame. Now they'll have to learn something." She put her lips on Mackenzie's cheek and gave him a damp kiss.

Mackenzie rolled his head around, feeling the muscles in his neck stretch out. He tried to sit upright, but his legs felt stiff and his lower back was cramping up. "We should be there soon, right? I don't think they planned for people my size when they designed these seats."

Laurel smirked and put a hand on her husband's leg, clenching her fingers together and softly kneading his thigh. "Oh, poor Mac, are your legs aching? Do you need a massage?" She leaned in closer and ran her hand up to the top of his thigh. Her warm breath flowed over his ear and a tingle went down his neck. "When we get back to the hotel, I'll give you a good rub down."

"You gonna start that now? Like I'm not hot and sweaty enough?" Mackenzie gave his wife a wink and they laughed.

It was going to be a good day. Mackenzie had made solid figures this year at the dealership and sold well over a hundred cars in the last six months. He couldn't remember how long they had been planning this vacation for. Now they could actually afford it and were here it was unreal. He wished Amy were with them, but one of the problems of inheriting a child meant having to share them with the other half. She only got to visit her real father a couple of times a year, so he couldn't complain. Still, he missed her. He had helped raise Amy and felt like *he* was her true father, not like the part-timer from San Diego.

Laurel resumed looking forward at the road stretching ahead, and Mackenzie held her hand as he looked out of the side window. The desert was flat and seemed to be devoid of any life. He knew it wasn't really and that the desert was full of life *if* you looked in the right places. There were probably a dozen deadly animals only feet away, but they weren't visible from the bus. God, he was looking forward to getting off the bus.

There was little to see beyond the barren land, other than the blinding white sun and hazy sky above. Only colorless scrub and cacti decorated the arid plains. Mackenzie suddenly saw a shooting flash of black as a snake or lizard darted off the road under a rock, away from the deadly wheels of the bus to find cooler sanctuary. It left a jagged line behind in the sand, an indentation of where it had been just seconds before, and Mackenzie remembered how they had to be careful in the desert. They hadn't been before, but he had read up on the creatures that lived here: bobcats, scorpions, sidewinders and even coyotes. None of which he intended to take back home to Milwaukee. He thought of telling Laurel about what he'd just seen and then stopped himself. She didn't need to know.

Mr. Stepper turned the radio off as the signal began to fade into a buzzing static. Instead of a fresh silence, Mackenzie heard somebody loudly singing the last phrase of the song that had been playing.

"California, rest in peace." The man at the front sheepishly turned around and smiled as his wife gave him a disapproving stare. "Sorry everyone, what can I say? Karaoke's my thing." The man shrugged and his wife rolled her eyes but laughed sweetly.

Akecheta let out a deep laugh. "Okay, we're going to stop for just a moment. If you haven't seen a Joshua tree before, you're about to see your first one. We'll just pull up for five minutes and then be on our way to the Kelso Depot."

"Yes," said Mackenzie. "Sweet freedom beckons!"

Laurel nudged him again. "Shut up, loser."

"Do you think I've time for a quick smoke too?"

The look on Laurel's face told him the answer was no.

"You didn't even move your lips. You're getting good at this game." Mackenzie let Laurel stand up as the bus pulled onto a clear strip of land at the side of the road.

Everyone filed off the bus, stretching and yawning. The warmth of the sun hit them as they got out. There was no other traffic around and Mackenzie found the stillness and quietness of the desert strange. He was aching for a coffee and a smoke, but intrigued as to what they were going to see. "There's never a Denny's when you want one," he said to Laurel before marching off behind Akecheta.

"Mac, honestly." Laurel sighed as her husband walked down the path behind the guide and the others.

"Yours too, huh? Mine's been bitching about missing the Dodgers game at the weekend. I told him, they'll still be around next year, and the year after that. We get one vacation a year. It's only one game, but you'd think he'd missed a front row seat for the end of the world."

Laurel shook hands briefly with the woman who was holding a knapsack over her shoulder.

"I'm Michele. We're vacationing from LA. Just need a few days out of the city, you know? That's my husband Myles up there with Alyce." The man who had been singing in the bus was introducing the young girl to Akecheta.

"Laurel Brown, and that's my husband, Mac," said Laurel. She leaned in to Michele and winked conspiratorially. "For now. Any more complaining about the bus, and he's going to find himself spending a lot more time in the desert than he planned for."

They laughed and began walking after the others as Mr. Stepper closed up the bus.

"You stop in Baker last night?" asked Michele. She was wearing a cotton blue dress with thin white stripes and sandals. Laurel looked at her enviously, wishing she hadn't worn jeans on what was clearly going to be a hot day. The dress was slimming too and she guessed the couple were still the right side of thirty.

"Yeah, just on vacation too. We came over from Vegas yesterday."

Michele looked surprised. "Vegas? You don't sound like you're from Vegas."

Laurel smiled. "Milwaukee."

Michele nodded, as if that explained everything.

"How old is your daughter?" asked Laurel. "Alyce, was it?"

"Yeah, she turned seven last month," said Michele proudly. "Want to guess what her birthday present was?"

"Let me see," said Laurel innocently. "Something cute and furry that likes going for long walks?"

They watched as Myles tried to take the leash from Alyce, but she refused to let the puppy go. Alyce picked her new pet up and held it tightly as Myles gave up trying to take the dog from her.

"She called it Beers. Lord knows why. I tried to convince her that there were far better names she could pick. I personally wanted to go with Pup."

Laurel laughed.

"Okay I know, not very original. But Beers?" Michele shrugged. "Don't ask me what goes through my child's head."

They joined the rest of the group and began to listen to Akecheta talking about the native flora of the region.

"Now this tree here is somewhere between fifty to seventy-five years old. It is very difficult to determine exactly how old they are, and they often live for hundreds of years. Later on, we'll take you to a forest where you're going to see a lot more. Some of you probably passed some on your way here without even realizing it. Wherever you've come from, you won't find one growing in your back garden. These trees are exclusively—"

Akecheta was interrupted by an eagle crying out high overhead. He turned to look up at it and was surprised to find there were two more flying side by side, not far from the leader. He pointed up into the brightening sky with one hand whilst shielding his eyes with the other.

"Folks, that is most likely a family of Desert Eagles. It's rare you will see them out in the open like that all together. In fact, I don't—"

"Look," said Alyce tugging at her father's trousers. "More eagles, Daddy."

Everyone was squinting up into the sky, marvelling at the eagles that soared high above them and didn't see the frown spreading across Akecheta's face. There were two more eagles, and then another cluster of four. Following the direction of the first, all the birds were headed inland in a direct path.

"I didn't think we'd get shots like this," said Laurel to her husband as she snapped away with her camera. "I didn't think we'd be lucky enough to even see *one* eagle."

Mackenzie looked down and rubbed his eyes. The sun was wickedly hot and so bright he was tearing up. "Get some good ones, honey. We can get some blown up at K-mart when we get home. Maybe we can put one up in the garage? It'd look cool on the wall, wouldn't it? Be something to talk about to the customers?"

Laurel looked at her husband as the birds flew out of sight. Her blue eyes sparkled with excitement. "Can we really? Oh Amy is going to be kicking herself. She's missing out."

"Yeah, but somehow I think cruising the malls in San Diego is preferable to sitting on a hot bus in the desert with us," said Mackenzie. Whilst Laurel looked back over her photos on the viewfinder, and the others chatted about the eagles, he noticed Akecheta and Mr. Stepper in conversation. Neither looked happy and they were keeping their voices low so as not to be heard. Mackenzie wondered what wrong. He hoped there wasn't a problem with the bus already. The nearest garage was in Baker which was a long way back.

"Jesus!"

An exclamation broke the party up and everybody looked to see who had said it. A thin man dressed in tight jeans jumped up in the air and scrambled behind his partner. "Jesus fucking Christ, look at that!"

Mackenzie recognised him as one of the two men who had been laughing together at the back of the bus. His accent was undeniably English and Mackenzie saw the man's face was contorted into a mask of fear. He was pointing at the ground near the Joshua tree.

"Now wait up," said Myles. "My daughter does not need to hear language like that. Think about where you are."

"All right, calm down," said Mr. Stepper. The driver could see the anger in Myles' eyes and needed to calm the situation down before it boiled over. He approached the young English man. "Calm down and tell us what you saw."

"A snake! Right there, I saw it. Vic, tell them, you saw it too."

The other young man, confusion written across his spotty face, licked his lips before his spoke hesitantly. "Well, there was definitely something, but I'm not sure exactly what it was. James, are you sure it was a snake? I mean, it might've been a branch or something."

"A fucking branch? Please Vic, I know a fucking snake when I see one."

"James, stop pulling on my arm. What are you going to do, rip it off and the beat the snake with it?" Vic tried to shrug off the excitable James who was clinging on to him and using his friend as a barrier between him and the snake.

"Okay, boys, that's enough horsing around. James, just relax," said Mr. Stepper. "You're in the desert so there's a chance you did see a snake. There's more than a few out here. But there's no need to react like that, and in case you hadn't noticed, we have a seven-year-old girl with us today. Keep your voice and the language down or the tour will be over for you and your friend *very* soon." Mr. Stepper spoke with authority and both James and Vic immediately quietened down.

"Everyone, step back slowly toward the bus," said Akecheta. He was looking at the Joshua tree and walking backwards himself. "Just a few feet please. I think it's time to go. No need to run or panic."

Mr. Stepper opened his palms and began ushering the tour group back slowly. He didn't need to see what was going on behind him. The tone in Akecheta's voice told him that James hadn't just seen a branch.

Everyone obeyed Akecheta and no one spoke. They stopped walking and an uncomfortable silence spread amongst them. After a few feet Myles stopped, and one by one the rest of the group did the same. Curious, they all looked at the base of the tree, trying to spot the snake. Laurel had her camera poised and Mackenzie assumed a position beside Akecheta so he could find out what was going on.

"Sidewinder?" asked Mackenzie quietly. He had no idea what a Sidewinder actually looked like, but he wanted to get some information out of their guide.

Akecheta shook his head slowly whilst staring at some scrub a few feet to the left of the Joshua tree. "Kingsnake."

Mackenzie couldn't see it and assumed it must be dangerous if Akecheta had made them back off. "It is poisonous? Should we get back to the bus?"

"I can't see anything," said Myles. "Maybe it's gone?"

"A bite would hurt, but it's not venomous," said Akecheta to Mackenzie.

"Honey, I can't see it either," said Laurel. "I think it's gone."

"Is it?" asked Mackenzie. Their guide seemed overly worried about a non-venomous snake. Surely there was no need to get everyone worried like this. Mackenzie glanced at the little girl next to Myles. Her face was a mixture of excitement and concern.

Akecheta slowly shook his head and then lifted his gaze from the scrub. He turned around to face everyone, ignoring Mackenzie's question. "I want everyone to listen to me. You need to stand completely still. Do not move. Do *not* run. Trust me. It will be over soon."

Mackenzie shivered in the heat as he felt the sand shift by his feet. He looked down and saw a snake about three feet long pass within inches of his left foot. His eyes widened as he looked across to his wife and saw the terror on her face. A snake, beige in color and twice as long as the one at his feet was winding its way through her legs. Her eyes were fixed on the creature and he willed her not to move. Scanning the rest of the desert around the group, Mackenzie saw more snakes, all making their way east, the same direction as the eagles. He counted six or seven and then gave up. He looked around the tour group and saw the same mix of fear and panic on everyone's faces. To their credit, they were all doing just as Akecheta had told them to. Not a single person was moving. Even the excitable James, who had panicked when he'd seen the first one, was standing still. His eyes were screwed up tight and his hand firmly holding Vic's. As soon as the snakes appeared, Myles rapidly swept Alyce up into his arms, telling her not to worry and to just close her eyes for a minute. Mackenzie locked eyes with Myles, yet neither man knew what to say. They were both amazed as the swarm of snakes, long and short, dark and light, all literally snaked past them. After two minutes that felt like two hours, the snakes disappeared. Mr. Stepper let out an audible sigh and nervous chatter broke out amongst the group once more.

Mackenzie was still standing beside Akecheta and spoke first. "Akecheta, what the hell was *that*?"

Laurel ran to her husband's side and he could feel her trembling. "You're not going to tell me that's normal. Did you see how they were all going in the same direction? It was like they were all running to something."

"Or away from something…" Akecheta glanced up into the sky and then began walking back toward the bus. He raised his voice so everyone could hear him. "We should go now. Back on the bus, please. *Now.*"

Mackenzie took his wife's hand and marched toward the bus, frightened. The look on Akecheta's face was as alarming as the swarm of snakes they had just experienced.

"Daddy?" Alyce tugged on her father's trousers again. "Beers is sick."

"Alyce, I told you…" Myles saw their puppy lying on his side as urine began to pool into the sand. The little Labrador was trembling and whining. He picked the dog up as Michele grabbed

Alyce's hand. "Let's do what Akecheta said and get back to the bus. Beers will be okay."

"Very interesting, eh?"

As they made their way back to the bus, the old man who looked like Indiana Jones passed Mackenzie. Until now he had not said a word.

"You could say that," replied Mackenzie. "Any idea what's going on? Mr…"

"Chris Olsen. Pleased to meet you." He held out a thin hand which Mackenzie awkwardly shook as they hurried back down the dirt path toward the bus. "And no, I haven't the faintest idea what's happ—"

It was then that the ground started shaking. What started as a gentle rolling soon turned into a violent shaking as the group tried to get back to the bus. The ground around them opened up with a booming, cracking sound and clouds of sand and dust billowed up into the air.

"Mac!"

Mackenzie felt his wife's hand pulled sharply from his and he found himself alone, suddenly showered by blinding sand. "Laurel? Laurel!"

He was unable to stay on his feet as the ground bucked and rocked beneath them, and he fell down in a heap. He heard his wife scream and then more shouts from up ahead, which he assumed to be the others. It was like a bomb had gone off. Even though it was daylight, the swirling sand puffed around in the air, making visibility almost non-existent.

"Laurel, where are you?" Mackenzie crawled around on the ground, but found it impossible to get anywhere as it constantly moved and shifted beneath his body. It was like trying to surf a wave and he was not able to control where he went. He banged his head suddenly against a sharp rock and a terrible moaning sound filled the air; he heard a low boom echo across the desert that could not have come from any human being. Mackenzie called out frantically, "Laurel, please, where are you? Laurel!"

CHAPTER 4

"Can't you go any faster?" shouted James. He clung to Vic in the back of the bus, willing the bus to go faster. He kept trying to text his friends back home, but couldn't find any signal. There was no Wi-Fi on the old bus they rode, and his cell was as much use out in the desert as jelly in a sandstorm.

"I got nothing either—looks like there's no reception out here," said Vic as he nervously tried to access the internet. He had hoped he would be able to access the news sites and found out what had happened. It felt like a bomb had exploded, but the nearest army testing range was miles away. The tour brochure had said they would be completely safe. The brochure had said they would enjoy a relaxing day out in the desert. It hadn't mentioned anything about swarms of snakes or bombs going off.

Akecheta stood at the front holding onto the seats for support as Mr. Stepper drove as fast as he dared. The bus was speeding down the rough road and Akecheta was being thrown from side to side. He wanted to stand though so he could keep an eye on the tour group, in particular the Browns.

Myles and Michele Connell sheltered in their seats, trying to quieten their crying daughter and whining dog. Alyce had her face buried into her mother's chest which muffled her sobs. None of them had sustained serious injury, but they were all terrified. Myles was forcing himself to calm down, knowing that whatever had happened out there in the desert hadn't just happened to them. Whatever eruption or event had taken place had to have been felt for miles away. The sooner they got back to Baker, the sooner he could make arrangements to get home.

Chris Olsen had sprained his ankle when running blindly through the desert, but had eventually found his way back to the bus, its metallic exterior now coated in a fine layer of sand. Gleaming in the sun, the bus had shone out like a beacon and he had limped back on to find he was the last on board. He sat in his seat now, tenderly rubbing his ankle and willing the swelling to go down. He glanced up at Mackenzie and Laurel, and was thankful he only had a sprained ankle.

Mackenzie suffered a sharp blow to his temple and the deep bleeding cut on the side of his head was testament to that. He was holding a bandage to it now, grabbed from the first-aid kit by Mr. Stepper and thrust into his hands as he'd boarded the bus. Laurel had been thrown into a crevice in the ground and suffered several cuts to her arms and legs. Rolling around in the desert, she had suffered severe scratches to both hands, and now back in the safety of the bus, she was resting on her husband. They had come off the worst in the group and Akecheta wanted to keep an eye on them to make sure they didn't go into shock or pass out.

Mackenzie felt sick. He had lost sight of his wife back there and for a moment wondered if he would find her again. The thought of losing her was too much to bear and he felt himself welling up. He cast aside his thoughts and decided to focus on the here and now. "Akecheta, how long before we get back to Baker? My wife needs medical attention."

"Yeah, I need to get my family home," said Myles. "I don't know what that was, but we want off this bus ASAP."

"Seriously, can we not go any faster in this piece of shit?" James got to his feet, ducking to avoid hitting his head on the low roof. "If I was driving, we'd be in Baker already."

Akecheta pointed at James. "You. Sit down. *Now.*" He leant back and whispered something to Mr. Stepper then turned to face the group again. This was not going to go down well, and he braced himself for the barrage of complaints that was about to come when he told them the plan. "Here's the situation. Baker is too far away, so we are going to the Kelso Depot. It's much closer and we will be there in a few minutes. We can get much better medical attention for Mrs. Brown there."

"Hey Akecheta, the tour is over. We don't want to go to Kelso anymore," said Myles, frustrated. "We just want to go home. All our stuff is back at Baker." He lowered his voice. "My daughter is upset, you can understand that, can't you? She just wants to go home."

Akecheta nodded as the protestations amongst the tour group rose. Everyone wanted to go back to Baker, to go back home. It was only natural to head for home given how scared they all were. He could understand what they were thinking, of course. His own family were at home too, at the Fort. He hoped that they were safe. At this time on a Saturday morning, the kids would probably be playing games around the house whilst his wife would usually be baking or cooking up something for dinner. He longed to go home, but he knew he couldn't just leave these people to fend for themselves. They were his guests and his responsibility.

"Listen up," said Akecheta as he waved down the voice of protest. "Mackenzie and Laurel need medical attention, more than what we can offer from our small first-aid kit. Chris Olsen too. I know you're all shaken up right now, we all are, but there's a store next to the Depot where we would usually stop for some morning tea. Maria is the owner and she is a trained nurse. I know her well, and she'll look after us. There's a landline there, so we can find out what's going on. With the cells not working, you can all use it and call whoever you need from there."

It had been a full two minutes before the ground had stopped shaking. Once the dust and sand had settled, Mr. Stepper had made sure everyone was back on the bus, bleeding or not, and started them off as quick as he could toward Kelso Depot. It was the next stop on the tour, but today was going to be a little different. He didn't want to push the bus too much or it was liable to overheat. The roads were dangerous too, and if they had a blow out here, they could end up stuck for hours. He'd agreed quickly with Akecheta that instead of making the long journey back to Baker they should head to Maria's first. She could help the walking wounded and hopefully know what was going on. A rest, some cold drinks, and *then* they could start thinking about getting back to Baker.

In recent years, with the tours growing more popular, a store had been set up next to Kelso Depot, selling a range of souvenirs. It also doubled as a gas station and grocery store. Campers and hikers often passed through and so Maria Johns had taken over the running of it. She was a retired nurse with a quick mind, and she had helped Akecheta many times in the past. Too many times people forgot how unforgiving the sun could be and so most of the time she just attended to tourists for sunstroke and minor complaints.

Akecheta remembered how a few months back he'd had to bring in a Canadian man to Maria. The man had decided that when nature called he would just drop and go in the desert. Unfortunately, he squatted right over a Barrel Cactus and got more than he bargained for. Once she had stopped laughing, Maria had sent him away with some ointment and a red face to match his red ass.

"How about calling 911?" said Mackenzie. "I mean, what the hell was that?"

"My guess is a large earthquake, most likely along the San Andreas fault. We're pretty much at the tail end of it down here, and we would almost certainly feel anything that was centered somewhere along it." Chris's ankle had begun to go numb, and he had got his brain back into something like normal working order. "I wouldn't like to guess at the magnitude right now, but it was certainly a big one."

"Centered *somewhere* along it?" Mackenzie shifted in his seat to try and face Chris. "It felt like we were right on top of it."

"An earthquake? Jesus." James clasped his hands in front of him. Already pale, his face grew paler and he tried not to throw up.

"I could be wrong," said Chris, "but it's more likely that the earthquake was centered further north. All we felt were the…side effects."

"Nausea, sweating, headaches; yeah, I'm feeling the side effects all right," said Mackenzie. He turned back to face the front and held Laurel's trembling hand. Her cuts weren't deep, but they covered much of her arms and legs, and he knew she was in pain.

He gave her cold hand a gentle squeeze. "Don't worry, honey, they'll look after us. Once we get to this Maria's place, everything will be fine."

As the bus continued on, Mackenzie wondered. *An earthquake?* He had never felt one before, and if that was what they were like, he could live happily if he never experienced one again. It was as if the ground had turned to mush. Laurel looked in bad shape. She hadn't said a word since getting back to the bus. Her hand was gripping his firmly and her eyes were cast down to her feet. He hadn't seen her look like this before. They led a happy, simple life. This kind of thing didn't happen to them. It happened on the news, miles away in countries you never visited, to people you never knew. There was something else too that was bothering him: that sound.

Whilst Mackenzie had no experience of earthquakes, and his knowledge was limited to the occasional documentary on the Discovery Channel, he didn't think they should sound like that. That moaning sound that had echoed across the desert. It had been like a thousand cows all bellowing at once. He couldn't even explain to himself what it had sounded like, but that was a close as he could think. He hoped to never hear it again.

The bus began to slow, and Laurel let go of her husband's hand. "We're here. Mac, let's just get out of here as fast as we can. I want to see Amy. Let's just go get her and go home." She looked across at her husband, tears filling her eyes.

"We will, I promise. Let's get you attended to first." He reached up and felt his head. His fingers came back with blood. It was congealed and thick. The bleeding had stopped, and although his head hurt, he could deal with a little pain. He was more concerned about Laurel. "Let's go see if we can find you some help."

"Wait," said Laurel as Mackenzie went to get up. "I was thinking about what Chris said about the earthquake."

"What about it?"

"If it wasn't centered here, then wherever it was is going to be in a hell of a lot worse shape than us."

Mackenzie nodded. "Well true, but my concern right now is you and how we're going to get out of here. So—"

"So what about Amy? What if San Diego got it worse than us? Oh God, if she—"

Mackenzie took Laurel's hands in his and stared at his wife. "Listen here, she is fine. You got that? John will look after her, you know he will. I promise, once we get out of here, we are going to get her. I wouldn't let anything hurt you or her. So calm down, get off the bus, and let's get you fixed up."

Laurel nodded as they got up. She leant into her husband briefly. "Thanks, Mac. I know, I know, but I'm just worried with the phones being out. I don't like being out of touch with her."

"Well okay then," said Mackenzie, as his wife grabbed her bag from the spare seat opposite. "We'll give her a call from the landline and you can talk to her yourself, tell her we're fine and we'll bring the vacation forward. We'll pick her up tomorrow. John will understand given the circumstances."

Laurel proceeded to get off the bus and as the bus emptied out, Mackenzie waited for Chris who was last off.

"Thanks," said Chris as Mackenzie leant him a shoulder to lean on.

"You want some painkillers?" asked Mackenzie as they departed the bus and planted their feet on terra firma.

"I'd rather have a cold beer," said Chris wincing as he put his foot down.

As Mr. Stepper closed the door and locked the bus up, Akecheta slung a bag over his shoulder and shouted instructions at everyone. "Follow me. The store is right over there. We're a little ahead of schedule, but Maria was expecting us anyway."

Alyce put Beers down and he immediately began barking out small high-pitched yips aimed in the direction of the bus. Myles took the leash from Alyce, who didn't argue this time, and watched as her father dragged Beers away from the bus.

"What's with that fucking dog?" asked James as he took a photo of the dog with his phone.

"Search me," said Vic. "She's just stressed out probably. Aren't you?"

"Well they need to shut it up. I'm not putting up with that for long." James began to walk toward Maria's store behind the others and glared at Myles as he overtook him. Myles chose to ignore him and concentrate on controlling Beers.

"Go ahead, Laurel, just follow Akecheta. I'm right behind you." Mackenzie put an arm around Chris to help him to the store and looked around at where they were. He recognised the Kelso Depot from the brochure and pictures his wife had shown him. It was quite a large building, and he recognised the arches and colonial style roof easily. It was unmistakeable, not least as it was one of only two buildings around. The other, the store they were heading for across the road, was a small one-storey brick building with a glass façade and flat roof.

The bus was parked across the road from the store, and looking around, Mackenzie couldn't see any other buses or vehicles. They were clearly the first ones to arrive for the day. There was a rail track running away from the Depot building, but other than that, just endless blue sky that touched the desert's horizon. There was no sign of any damage to either building, and Mackenzie hoped that meant things would get back to normal soon. Perhaps Kelso had escaped the quake. The store they were headed for was cute, its windows decorated with a variety of posters and adverts, and a silver bowl outside. Mackenzie watched as Myles tied the dog up to a bike stand outside the store. Beers inquisitively poked his nose into the water bowl, and then resumed barking at the bus.

Mackenzie's head was throbbing, but he could feel the adrenaline receding. It was over now. The quake had literally shaken everyone, but now that they were approaching the store, people were relaxing. He saw Mr. Stepper holding the store's front door open whilst Myles entered behind Michele and Alyce. James was next, barging past Laurel on his way in, forcing her and Vic to go behind him. James was pushing his luck and if he pushed one too many times, he was going to find himself in trouble. Mackenzie was rapidly running out of patience with the young man, and he was quite sure Myles felt the same. Akecheta was nowhere to be seen and Mackenzie assumed he was already inside talking to Maria, getting things organized. They probably had to report it before they could turn the bus around. There was going to be a long queue for the phone too, so they may as well take Maria's hospitality and get some food inside of them. Now they were safe, Mackenzie felt his stomach rumble. He was ready for some of that morning tea the tour had promised.

As he helped Chris to hobble over the dusty road, he couldn't help but notice that Beers was still barking. Something had gotten into the dog that was for sure. Mackenzie remembered then how the dog had wet itself right before the earthquake. Along with the eagles and the snakes, it was as if it could sense something coming; something bad. He hoped the barking was not indicative of anything else and just a way for the little pup to release its nervous energy and fear.

Inside the store, everyone found a seat. Maria had set up a few small tables and chairs to one side where she served morning tea to pre-booked tour groups and casual visitors. Mr. Stepper had been coming here regularly for a couple of years and Maria had tea and fresh coffee ready to serve, as well as cold water. The dining area was decorated with old pictures of the Kelso Depot, stunning aerial photographs of the desert, and various wall charts of spiders and snakes. Alyce was looking up at one of the charts as her mother poured out three glasses of water from a jug on the table.

"We saw some of them earlier, didn't we, Mom? I remember that big brown one." Alyce's tears had dried up, and the pictures on the wall were a useful distraction for her. She was clearly more relaxed now too. She liked shops and restaurants, and this place was both all in one.

"We sure did, honey." Michele popped a bright red straw into a glass. "Alyce, drink some water, please. You remember how we have to keep drinking in the summer, don't you? It's real hot today."

Alyce took a sip of the water, turned her nose up and pushed the glass away. "I don't like it. Can I have some milk? Please, Mom?" She curled a few strands of hair around her finger, and cocked her head to one side as she asked.

Michele got up and saw two refrigerators on the back wall full of bottles of water, soda, beer and finally cartons of milk. "Sure, Alyce. Strawberry, right?" Michele could see Alyce nodding eagerly as Myles stared out of the window.

Over at the next table close to Alyce were James and Vic, deep in a hushed conversation.

"Tweedledum and Tweedledee are at it again," said Laurel as Maria dabbed her forearm with antiseptic and a cotton pad.

"You know them?"

"No, only just met them. They're a charming couple," Laurel said sarcastically. "I don't think we'll be exchanging email addresses when this is all over."

Akecheta pulled a chair up beside Maria and Laurel, and sighed. "No good, Maria, your phone's out. Guess the quake probably took down the line."

"Figures," said Maria shrugging, still dabbing at Laurel's cuts. "It's iffy on a good day. Soon as I felt the quake, I tried calling my sister in Baker, but I couldn't get through. Phones are probably jammed now anyway. I'm sure she's fine, but I worry you know, ever since Bobby passed. She forgets things."

"Mr. Stepper asked if he can get up onto the roof. He wants to see if he can get a signal on his cell." Akecheta watched as Maria lifted up Laurel's left leg and began to run a fresh cotton ball over it, wiping away the blood so she could get to the exposed cuts and clean them.

"Sure, though I don't think he'll get one, not for a while at least. There's a ladder around back he can get up there on. Just tell him to watch his step. I ain't been up there in a while so I don't know what state it's in."

Laurel inhaled sharply as the alcohol touched a fresh wound. Myles was standing beside a rack of faded postcards, and through the small doorway next to him, Laurel could see Mackenzie and Chris halfway across the street.

"Sorry," said Maria, noticing Laurel wince.

"I'll check on the rest, then help Mr. Stepper," said Akecheta as he left them.

Laurel was pleased Akecheta had brought them to Maria's. The woman was sweet and had a good bedside manner. All the while she attended to Laurel, she was muttering soothing words and making sure she was okay. Laurel had discovered Maria was pushing sixty, but she didn't look it. Her hair was still a dark brown, and she could easily pass for ten years younger than she was. She wore a long flowing dress tied back in a bow and dressed younger than her age too. Laurel noticed a golden locket that hung from her neck.

"That's a beautiful necklace, Maria."

"It was a present from my Tony on our thirtieth anniversary," said Maria without looking up. She smiled when she spoke. "And the great thing is that it goes with whatever I wear."

"Is he here?" asked Laurel, wondering if he was perhaps out back. "Does he help with the store?"

"Oh, he helps me all right," said Maria. "He gives me the strength to carry on every day. Without him, I wouldn't be half the woman I am. Unfortunately, he passed a few years back." Maria gently touched the locket. "I just like to have him as close to me as possible until we meet again."

"Gosh, I'm sorry, Maria." Laurel drew in a sharp breath as Maria placed a Band-Aid over a particularly sore cut above her knee.

"Never you mind about that," said Maria as she stood up and folded her arms. She looked Laurel up and down, smiling as she did so. "I think we're all done here. Where's that husband of yours? Pretty girl like you, I wouldn't be leaving your side if I was him."

Laurel grinned. "It looks like Mac's deep in conversation with a new friend out there."

"Well, you make sure he comes to see me when he finally drags his ass in here. I'll give him the once over, make sure he's okay. I gather you all took a bit of a beating out there." Maria frowned suddenly. "It's a worry, that's for sure. Seems odd I didn't feel much here, but I guess that's the way it goes. Hey, look, I'm no scientist. I'm much better at looking after people. Least I was."

"You were a nurse, right?" asked Laurel remembering something Akecheta had mentioned.

"*Was* is about right. I quit that after Tony moved upstairs. I needed a change of scene, you know? Bought this place and started looking after people in a different way. We get a lot of tourists pass through. It's a living, and it's quiet. I like it. It's not often I get a bus full of people needing medical attention, but in this job you never quite know what or who is going to turn up. Anyway, I should go check the others. You sure you're feeling okay, honey? There's some fresh coffee in the pot. You just help yourself."

Laurel was worried about Amy. If San Diego had suffered from the earthquake, she could be hurt or worse. Her biological father, John, would take care of her, as long as he was capable. A voice interrupted Amy's thoughts, followed by the sound of chair legs scraping over the floor.

"Where the hell are we? You've brought us to the middle of nowhere. Do you even know the way back to civilisation? I should sue you for this."

Laurel turned to see what was going on. James was standing toe to toe with Akecheta, pointing his finger in his face, and practically shouting at him. His chair had fallen over, and James was red in the face, clearly angry. Akecheta appeared to be calm, and Laurel could tell he wasn't reacting to James' threats.

"Why are we sitting around here when we should be going back to Baker?" asked James. "Tell me that, at least."

"James, come on, calm down," said Vic standing behind him. "Let's just—"

"No, why should I calm down? Look at this mess. Answer me, Akecheta. How are we getting back to Baker?"

Akecheta rolled his eyes and sighed. "Fine. Head west and the Pacific Ocean is a few hours' drive away. North is Death Valley. Go south far enough and you'll eventually make the Mexican border. East – ish – and across the state line you'll find Vegas, eventually. Of course, without a vehicle you won't get far." Akecheta could tell James was scared, but the priority now was to make sure everyone was safe. If Baker had been hit hard by the quake, there would be nothing to go back to. "You're better off staying right here with us. It's safe and secure, and I'm sure this *mess* will be sorted out soon. Maria is fixing up everyone's scrapes, so until everyone is comfortable, we're not going anywhere. My job is to make sure everybody is safe. Mr. Stepper is shortly going to head outside to try to find some cellphone reception. Once we know what is going on, we'll get you home as soon as we can. As you're my responsibility though, I can't take you anywhere without knowing that it is safe."

"Awesome. I'm going to die in some backwater tacky tourist shop surrounded by rednecks and red Indians." James looked at Vic and then to the useless cell in his hand. "What's the point? You gonna tell me there's no signal out here either in Hicksville?"

Akecheta had dealt with a few irate passengers in the past, with people who didn't like the tour or made nothing but sarcastic comments the whole time which spoilt it for the rest of the group. Usually, he could keep a lid on his emotions, but this was turning into something different. The tour was over and something was happening out there, something far more important than this whining racist tourist realized. Akecheta had heard taunts before, name-calling occasionally happened, but he wasn't about to take it now from a jumped-up, foul-mouthed little kid. "Listen up, James, the phones usually work fine. I would expect that the earthquake is causing the outage. If the power's not been knocked out, the phones will be down because the system's overloaded. A million dumb people like you are all trying to use their phones at once. How about you stow that cheap piece of made-in-China crap and help out? Otherwise, your attitude is not helping anyone and it's certainly not helping you get any closer to home."

James' mouth fell open. He looked back at Vic in shock, and then back to Akecheta. "You're crazy. Who do you—?"

"I don't have time for this, kid. If you're not going to help, be my guest and see how close to Vegas you get. Get walking now while you still have the energy. You can handle the heat, of course, so I assume you can navigate by the sun as well? Naturally, you know how to avoid the scorpions, rattlesnakes, and tarantulas, yes? I'll be sure to send out the search party just as soon as you give me a call."

Akecheta marched past James to the front door so he could tell Mr. Stepper how to access the roof, leaving James dumbfounded. James scurried back to Vic and sat down, his cheeks still red except now flushed with embarrassment instead of anger. He had been put in his place, and worst of all, it had been done in front of the whole group.

Laurel glanced at Maria and suppressed a smile. Both of them knew Akecheta had handled it well.

"What a dick," muttered James as he slumped down in a chair.

"Just leave it," said Vic as he rubbed his hand across James' back. This was supposed to be a fresh start, a way for James to forget the past and his troubles. "We're on vacation, just try to cool down, okay? I'll go get us some water."

Vic went to find a bottle of water, leaving James on his own. He felt like a child who had been scolded in front of class. Couldn't they see what was happening? They were going to get stuck here, all because of some arrogant prick. James stared with hatred at Akecheta. Who did he think he was, telling James what to do? That was something he could not allow to happen. It was something he never allowed to happen back home and being overseas was no different. James picked up the cutlery that had been set out on the table and ran a finger along the serrated edge of the knife. It was a little blunt, but it would do the job. "I'm going to teach him a lesson," whispered James. He knew he would have to bide his time, but there was no way he was going to let him get away with it. James tucked the knife into his jacket pocket and sat back as Vic returned with two bottles of water. James said nothing to Vic, but stared at Akecheta. He would wait, and when he got his chance, James was going to let Akecheta know exactly what he thought of him.

CHAPTER 5

"Beers, can it!" Myles tried to soothe the puppy but was having no success. The dog was ignoring the bowl of water, and still yapping in the direction of the parked bus as Mackenzie and Chris reached the store.

"Something's got her spooked," said Mr. Stepper from the doorway.

"Yeah, beats me. She's normally so placid. I guess it's the quake. Must've shaken her up." Myles gave Mackenzie a hand as Chris sat down on an old wooden bench under the shade of the overhanging roof. Two rectangular freezers chugged away quietly beside him as he rested.

"Head on inside as soon as you like," said Mr. Stepper letting the door shut. "Maria will sort you out, Chris. Hopefully your ankle's not too bad, but she knows what she's doing, so let her take a look at it. Everyone else is inside. There's plenty to drink and I suggest you get some water on board. Mr. Brown, your wife is being taken care of. I've known Maria for a while now and she's a good sort. You can rely on her. I'm just going around back. I need to find a way up to the roof, see if I can't get a signal there and found out what the hell is going on."

Mackenzie thanked Mr. Stepper who disappeared back into the store leaving the three men alone with Beers. Mackenzie took a seat beside Chris. "Think there's any beer in those freezers?"

"Only one way to find out," said Myles, lifting one of the freezer lids. As he did so, he heard a low thudding sound. The sound slowly increased and the beats thumped regularly, the pauses between the thumps lessening as the volume increased. He pulled out a can of Bud Light. It was then that he noticed Beers had stopped barking, finally, and became aware of the silence apart from the thudding noise.

"Mac, Chris, you want one?"

Before either of the men could answer, the bench started shaking, followed by the whole store. It happened quickly, as if someone had flicked a switch.

"Shit, another quake?" Myles dropped the freezer lid with a bang. The can in his hand fell to the ground and rolled out into the road, the condensation instantly coating the cold metal with gritty sand.

Suddenly, the ground began shaking more violently, and Myles was thrown to the ground. He saw Mackenzie and Chris holding onto the wooden seat as it tossed them around, and the store swayed from side to side behind them. Through the large windows, Myles saw things falling from shelves and heard screams coming from inside. Shelves were being wrenched from the walls and anything not anchored down was tossed around like a feather in a hurricane. He trusted Michele to take care of Alyce, but still wished he was inside with them instead of outside rolling around in the dirt. He had to admit he was scared. There was no way of knowing when it was going to end, and the ground just kept rolling and rolling as if it had turned to water. The noise, too, was terrifying. It wasn't just the sound of the store being torn from its foundations, or the endless screams of the terrified people inside, but the other sound. The moaning sound that accompanied the quake; the bellowing that sounded organic, as if made by an animal rather than the churning ground. Myles knew it was madness, that is was just panic making him think like that, yet he couldn't help but imagine some kind of monster beneath the crust of the planet causing the earthquakes.

Mackenzie's knuckles turned white as he gripped the wooden seat. It was like riding a rollercoaster, but there was nothing fun about it. The quake felt as big as the one earlier, if not bigger. He desperately wanted to get inside to Laurel, but there was no way. Walking was impossible. Myles wasn't even able to stand, and as Mackenzie watched him, the dirt beneath Myles began to twist and turn, the surface rippling and bending as if it were the surface of a bowl of milk. Small stones bounced up and down, and then they turned back on themselves, rolling toward the center of the disturbance. The dirt was slowly sucked backwards, and then the ground behind Myles began to collapse in on itself like a black hole, draining all the life around it away into a dark recess. At first, the concentric hole was small, no larger than a fifty-cent piece, but soon it was spiralling out of control, becoming as large as a manhole, then a truck, and then…it stopped.

The quake stopped so abruptly that Mackenzie thought he was imagining it. He looked at Chris next to him, and his expression returned the same thought: what was going on?

"Laurel. I have to get to Laurel," said Mackenzie plainly. He stood up and watched as Myles did the same, brushing the dirt off him, wiping the sweat from his face.

"I'm not sure we should be inside," said Chris. "It might be safer out here, in case the structure of the store has been compromised. We need to—"

The ground behind Myles erupted violently, the road's broken asphalt thrown up into the air as what appeared to be a sinkhole emerged right underneath the road. Tons of dirt filled the sky, and Mackenzie looked up in wonder as concrete and rocks began to fly through the air. There was no shaking of the ground to accompany it, just a faint vibration, followed by that noise; the bellowing sound was back. Mackenzie's mouth fell open when he saw a shape in the dirt. A shadowy figure was emerging from the hole in the ground, climbing out of it like some sort of underground behemoth. Huge slices of earth, boulders of all shapes and sizes obscured his vision, but there was definitely something there.

"Myles!" Mackenzie beckoned the man over, and Myles began running away from the cascading rocks that threatened to shower over him as they rained down.

Grabbing Myles and pulling him under the shade of the store, Mackenzie felt a hand grab his shoulder.

"I was wrong," said Chris quietly. "We should go inside. Definitely go inside now."

Mackenzie's eyes were open now, and as the dirt fell down revealing the blue sky once again, he saw what the shadowy shape was. Something had crawled out of that hole, something unnatural, inhuman, and horrible; a sort of goliath that was now towering over them with a snarl on its face, and a glint in its eyes that told Mackenzie he should listen to Chris and get inside. Yet he couldn't quite believe it. There was the tour bus, there was the Kelso Depot building across the street, the desert behind and the railway track; so what was this monster doing here? Was he awake? Had he fallen asleep on the tour bus and dreamt this? Why wasn't Laurel waking him up from this nightmare?

The monster took a step forward, and the ground shook. Its head was huge, almost as big as the bus, and it had a row of teeth that glistened with saliva. The thing's leathery skin shone in the sunlight, and as it moved, the color of it seemed to change, from a brown to a green to a silvery copper. There were talons on its feet and Mackenzie could only imagine what they were used for. Its bulky body suggested it didn't go short of food and its two muscular arms, though short, had enough power in them for Mackenzie to know this would be a very one-sided fight. As he looked slowly up, taking the creature in and trying to comprehend what he was looking at, he reached its head. Those eyes that looked back at him were like fiery orbs that burned into his very soul. This was an animal, no doubt about it. He wasn't hallucinating or dreaming. This thing was real. He had seen eyes like that before on the National Geographic Channel, when lions and tigers stalking their prey were about to pounce. He had seen enough documentaries about the hunters in Africa to recognize the signs. This thing was about to strike.

"Inside, now!" hissed Mackenzie as he pushed Myles toward the door.

"Inside…yeah, right," replied Myles in disbelief. His feet shuffled slowly, scraping across the sand as he approached the doorway. He couldn't believe what he was seeing, and his body was resisting Mackenzie's efforts at getting him to go inside.

"Myles, hurry your ass up. We need to get inside," whispered Chris. "I don't want to be out here any longer than we have to be."

A noise seemed to come from the creature's throat, a bubbling sound like a kettle boiling. A low hiss escaped the creature's jaws, and Chris noticed its rear legs tensing up. It was getting ready to strike.

"Myles, fucking move it!" shouted Chris, and he began pushing both Myles and Mackenzie forward.

Falling through the doorway into the store, Mackenzie immediately saw Laurel and ran for her. Myles tripped, but was picked up swiftly by Akecheta. Chris heard the monster behind him and felt the ground trembling as it came at him. He practically flung himself through the doorway but was not quite fast enough.

The monster's outstretched claw caught hold of Chris' leg, and instead of tumbling into Maria's store, he found himself flung against the doorway. His body slammed into the wooden frame, and three ribs cracked instantly, such was the force of the monster's attack. The claw scraped across the back of his leg, gouging out a deep line that immediately filled with blood. Chris plummeted to the ground and was knocked unconscious as his head struck the frame of the door.

Ignoring the screaming, Mackenzie pushed Laurel back into the arms of Michele.

"Wait here," he told her, and rushed to Chris' aid. The man was lying in the open doorway, unable to move, half of his body across the threshold and the other half out in the open where the monster could grab him at any second. Mackenzie could see its powerful legs standing close by, but strangely the monster wasn't making any movement. It was just standing there. Was it waiting to pounce? Why hadn't it dragged Chris off already? Mackenzie didn't doubt that if he left Chris like that, inevitably it would strike again, and he just couldn't wait around for that to happen. He had to get Chris inside. There was a small part of him, a selfish part that realized he had an ulterior motive for getting Chris inside. The door was still open and wouldn't shut with him lying there. If the door stayed open, then they were all in trouble.

Mackenzie put his hands underneath Chris' shoulders and began to pull him into the store. He dare not look up in case the monster was watching. He didn't want to see it coming, didn't want to look at it in case he had to admit that it was real. He was terrified enough, and he thought if he looked into those red eyes right now, he might not keep it together. He kept pulling Chris into the store, and Akecheta closed the door behind him. The monster didn't attack, and Mackenzie slumped onto the floor, relieved when Chris was finally inside.

"Are you insane?" Laurel rushed to Mackenzie and held him to her. "What the hell were you thinking?"

Mackenzie shrugged. Laurel didn't need an answer, and frankly, Mackenzie wasn't sure that if he opened his mouth to speak that he might not just vomit up all his horror and terror over her. He let her hold him and looked around the store. Everywhere he looked he saw shock, fear and destruction. The store's windows were shattered, large cracks running through all of them, but they still held together. The rest of the place looked as if someone had ransacked it. It had been trashed, and all over the floor Mackenzie saw the result of the quake: sunglasses, hats, cans of Raid, boxes of candy bars, tables and chairs turned upside down, and photographs on the wall now lying in their broken frames on the floor. A postcard stand had fallen over, and the cards were strewn everywhere like bizarrely colored tiled flooring, smiling faces beaming from the lurid pictures of a time when the Kelso Depot was more than just an out-of-the-way tourist attraction. A fizzy drinks machine had been ripped from the wall, releasing some of the cans inside before crushing them and causing them to explode. Sticky, brown liquid oozed out from its crevices and was mixing with some spilt milk cartons to make a dirty brown sludge that covered one half of the room.

A woman that Mackenzie assumed to be Maria came over to see Chris. With the help of Mr. Stepper and Akecheta, they picked him up carefully and took him into the back room where Maria could attend to him. Mackenzie noticed that Myles was with his family now, talking to Michele, trying to placate her whilst dabbing at her tears. Alyce was cowering behind her father's leg, and he had one protective hand resting on her head. Mackenzie looked around for the others, finally spotting James and Vic behind the counter rummaging through the boxes that had fallen. He hoped they were looking for something useful like a radio, matches, or water, and not just plundering Maria's store for a freebie whilst nobody was watching them. Each and every one of them looked terrified.

They all spoke in hushed whispers as if afraid their voices might lure the monster outside in, and when Mackenzie finally summoned up the courage to speak, he too spoke quietly.

"Laurel, we should check on Chris."

"Jesus, Mac, what is it, what is that thing? This is…this just can't be real. It *can't* be."

Laurel was staring past him and didn't register Mackenzie's statement. Her eyes were fixated on the thing outside, drawn to its magnificence, transfixed by its fantastic size.

"Laurel, look at me," said Mackenzie. He stared at her intently, forcing her eyes to focus on his. "Laurel, I don't know what it is, but I know we're not safe here. They took Chris into a back room, a store room of some kind, right?"

Laurel nodded. Her eyes were glazed over, but finally she settled them on Mackenzie. "Mr. Stepper was going to try to find a signal and…I guess…" Laurel shook her head. "Oh, Jesus, I feel sick, I—"

"It's all right, honey, I've got you," said Mackenzie, feeling Laurel lean into him. "Just let it pass. It's the shock. Just ride it out, honey, I've got you."

They stayed like that with Mackenzie holding his wife as the others began to move out into the back room. James and Vic, Myles, Michele and Alyce, all eventually finding their way back there, to where it felt safer, away from the windows; away from the thing outside. Mackenzie felt uncomfortable with it being so close and wondered if it was watching them. It hadn't moved since narrowly missing out on taking Chris. When Laurel raised her head, he was relieved to see she was back with him again.

"Sorry, I just thought I was going to pass out there for a minute."

"Forget it," said Mackenzie as they got up. "Let's just head on back and see what's what."

Mackenzie cast only the briefest of glances back as they left the front of the store. The building was shaking slightly and Mackenzie was pleased to see that it looked like the monster was backing off. The monster was still out there, but it was retreating toward the bus, back to the hole in the ground from where it had emerged. Perhaps it was leaving, he hoped, going back to hell.

* * *

"We can't stay here, that thing is right outside! We don't know what the hell it's doing. For all we know, it could come crashing in here at any second."

Mackenzie heard James' voice before he saw him. The back room was crowded now that everyone had settled in. The little room had no windows and nothing but a yellow fluorescent light overhead, which only served to highlight the tiredness and worry on everyone's faces. Chris was laid out to one side of the room, with Maria and Michele tending to him. Maria was wrapping his leg in bandages, and Mackenzie noticed a first-aid kit by his side.

"You want to go outside? It's safer in here." Vic rubbed his chin nervously. "James, we need to stay with the others. Safety in numbers and all that."

"Piss off, Vic, you might be a good fuck, but you're a pussy. You just want to—"

Mackenzie watched as Myles calmly left Alyce opening a packet of chips and strode over to James. Myles grabbed the Englishman by the arm and thrust him backward until he was pinned against the wall.

"I warned you. I told you not to talk like that around my daughter." Myles was ready to explode, his anger all too obvious.

"Get off me," demanded James. Their eyes locked together in battle, neither of them willing to back down. "Vic, make yourself useful for once and knock this bitch out."

"James, I'm not going to do that," said Vic, clearly afraid. "Just apologize and we can discuss this calmly, yeah?"

James fought to free himself from Myles' grip, but the man had him pressed up against the wall and there was no way out. Mackenzie watched them, knowing that his wish for the argument to dissolve was only going to remain that way if he didn't intervene. He looked at Alyce who was nibbling on some chips, her head down, too scared to look at what was going on around her.

"Laurel, can you look after the girl for a second?" Mackenzie gave Laurel a gentle nudge in the direction of Alyce. "This can't go on."

"Myles, let him go," said Mackenzie as he reluctantly joined the fight. There was anger in Myles' eyes that he could identify with. He would do anything to protect Amy too, and Myles was only doing what felt natural, defending his family. "Myles," said Mackenzie again, resting a hand gently on his shoulder.

Myles took his arms off James, and stepped back, leaving a little space between them.

James knew he could pull the knife out and cut Myles quickly, but he had been saving it for the guide. It felt like they were all ganging up on him, and he was going to have to be careful. He was still outnumbered and couldn't rely on Vic for support. James pointed a finger at Myles. "You'll keep, old man. You'll fucking keep."

Mackenzie stepped between them, knowing another outburst from James would only rile Myles up more. "No, James, this stops now. Like it or not, we *are* all in this together. That thing is right outside the door. One step outside and you're history. Take a moment." Mackenzie turned to Myles. "We all need to take a moment, okay? Chris is hurt, and we don't know what we're facing. Let's just wait a minute, get a drink, and then check outside. If it's gone, we can get back on the bus and go. If not..."

Mackenzie trailed off, unsure how to finish that sentence. What if it didn't leave? What if it simply retreated underground and waited for them to come out of the store? What if it decided it couldn't wait and wanted in? It could easily smash the store to bits, and yet it *had* waited. Something had made it stop. Mackenzie wanted to go, to get to Amy, to San Diego, to get Laurel to safety; yet he had a horrible feeling they were going to be stuck here a long time.

"Whatever," said James as he brushed past Mackenzie. "Come on, Vic, let's see if we can't find something stronger to drink than poxy water."

As James and Vic began to search through some boxes in a far corner, Mackenzie turned to Myles. "Try not to let him get you worked up like that. He's all mouth. He's just scared."

Myles offered a sheepish apology. "Sometimes I just snap, you know? Like I lose sight of what I'm doing." Myles looked at Laurel playing with Alyce. "You got kids?"

"One. Amy. She's in San Diego. Hopefully staying out of trouble. She's with…" Mackenzie never quite knew how to explain. He had raised Amy as his own, and he thought of her as his daughter. But biologically, he had had nothing to do with it. He didn't feel much like explaining the complications of his family with Myles, and settled for a simple response. "She's with her friend, John. He'll look after her."

Myles nodded. "You think it's gone?" He reached down and picked up a bottle of water. Breaking open the cap, he took a swig and offered Mackenzie the bottle. "What was that?"

Mackenzie hoped that James and Vic would find something stronger. It wasn't noon yet, but he could do with a cold beer to take the edge off. "I don't even know how to answer that. It was like nothing I've ever seen. You see how it came up out of the ground like that? How can something so big survive underground without us knowing about it? The tremors must be it moving through the earth."

"And the quakes," said Myles. "They've got to be linked, right?"

"It's like this isn't real, like we're living in a fantasy or a fairy tale. Giant beasts roaming the desert attacking people? I mean, am I dreaming? You'll be telling me the Brewers are going to win the series next."

Myles smiled. "You keep dreaming, Mac."

The building shuddered briefly, and everyone tensed up, waiting for impact. The building shook for two seconds, and then quietened down.

"It's still here, isn't it?" Myles didn't need an answer. They all knew the answer.

As the room remained silent, Mackenzie heard a faint sound. It was a high-pitched whining sound, almost like the mewing of a kitten. It was muffled, and at first he thought he must be imagining it. But the more he listened, the more certain he became that he was hearing it.

"Myles, you hear that? A sort of whining noise. What is it? Not that monster, surely?"

Myles frowned. "No way. It sounds like, well, it sounds like a dog. It must…oh, shit, Beers!"

"Myles, wait!"

As Myles bolted out of the room, Mackenzie ordered everyone else to stay put. Mr. Stepper and Akecheta wanted to follow, but they were of more use keeping an eye on James and Vic. Mackenzie ran after Myles and finally caught up with him in the store. Myles was standing by the door, his hand on the handle, and he was clearly about to go outside to get Beers. The problem was that the monster was still out there. It was standing over the bus, just doing nothing. It was as if it was waiting for them.

"Myles, hold on," said Mackenzie.

"I can't leave Beers out there. He's helpless."

Mackenzie could see the puppy, still tied up where Myles had left him.

"I can't believe I forgot him. Alyce would be devastated if anything happened to him. Look, that thing's not paying any attention to us. I can slip out quickly and get him. I'll be back inside before it even notices anything."

Mackenzie looked through the cracked window pane up at the thing's face. There were two sharp incisors poking out from its upper jaw, and a steady stream of saliva dripping from them. Its eyes were almost closed, and he couldn't tell if it was still looking at them or not. It felt like it was, but Myles had a point. Why hadn't it taken the dog, or even attacked the shop?

"Okay, you move slowly, and get Beers. I'll hold the door open for you. Just be careful, okay?" Mackenzie slowly opened the door, and felt warm air hit his face. "Slowly, Myles. We don't want to startle it. Get Beers, and get your ass back in here."

Myles slipped out and began to creep forward stealthily, as if he were a trained soldier sneaking up on an enemy. As he approached Beers, the puppy's whining got louder. When it finally saw Myles, the puppy began to get excited, and then began yapping again.

"Come on, Myles, hurry it up," said Mackenzie beneath his breath. He held the door ajar, half-watching Myles, and half-watching the monster. It still hadn't moved. Maybe it was resting, or maybe it just wasn't interested in them. Mackenzie didn't like it. It felt like Myles was taking an age to untie Beers. Every second they were out there and every time the dog opened its mouth, it felt to Mackenzie that they were going to alert the monster to their presence. "Come on," he hissed to Myles.

Myles nodded, and then freed Beers. As Myles tried to grab the puppy, it ran away from him. The second it was free, it made a mad dash toward the monster and took up a spot in front of the store where it began barking loudly.

The hairs on Mackenzie's neck stood up as the monster turned to look at the puppy. Beers continued barking at it, trying to defend its master, and Mackenzie knew just what Myles was going to do. The monster turned its head, and lowered its body so they could all now see its red eyes were wide open.

"Yakazar-yakazaaaar."

Mackenzie shuddered. When the creature uttered that noise, every bone in his body ached. There was something primordial about it, something unnatural. The monster drew back its head and then took a step forward. It was about to pounce. Mackenzie shouted to Myles.

"Get back here. Quickly, Myles!"

Mackenzie saw him turn toward the door, and then hesitate. Myles looked back at Beers. He was twenty feet away, far too close to the monster for Myles to reach safely. And yet, he didn't want to leave the dog to die.

"Don't, Myles, just…"

As the monster lifted its feet and reached a clawed hand out toward Beers, Myles ran. Mackenzie held the door open, not knowing if he should rush out there to help, or stay where he was. Beers was seconds away from becoming dog food, and as Myles ran across the dusty cracked road, Mackenzie knew there was little he could do but watch.

And pray.

CHAPTER 6

It was the glasses rattling in the display case that disturbed Sharyn. They started out just vibrating and clinking together, like jumping beans on a hot tin roof. She put down the dishcloth and watched them dance, before she suddenly realized the whole kitchen was shaking. There was a sort of humming noise too, like electricity was flying around her, making the air warm and fuzzy.

"Rusty? Rusty, you hear that?" she yelled. "The whole damn kitchen's shaking!"

The vibrations started to grow stronger, and she took hold of the back of a chair to steady her feet. She didn't know what to make of it. Earthquakes used to be pretty rare in Goodsprings, but lately they had been growing in number, and strength.

"Rusty, get your ass down here, right now!" Sharyn cursed silently and grabbed the dish that was threatening to throw itself off the table.

Ever since he'd been laid off last year, Rusty had spent more and more time in bed. Sadly for Sharyn, it only involved sleeping or occasionally eating Cheerios, much to her disgust.

As Sharyn felt the shaking start to calm down, she heard a thumping noise from above, and then the sound of feet running down the stairs. Rusty appeared wearing nothing but a pair of stained, Superman boxer shorts, holding a lamp shade above his head.

"What the hell was that?" he asked, his eyes wide and his dishevelled black hair sticking to his greasy forehead. Stubble ran from his nose to his chin, and flecks of dried cereal were stuck to his cheek.

"What the hell do you think? Another of those freaking quakes, that's what." Sharyn frowned when she saw her husband. "Is that my reading lamp? What the hell are you gonna do with that?"

"What?" Rusty lowered his arm and put the lamp carefully down, knowing better than to anger his wife when she was already in a foul mood.

"Look at the state of you. You're not going to find work looking like that."

Here we go again, thought Rusty.

"Never mind that, what's with these shakes? I thought the Goddamn house was falling down." Rusty walked over to Sharyn and planted a kiss on her cheek.

"You need to brush your teeth as well," she muttered as she returned to the dishes. There was a time she thought it was cute when he wandered around the house in nothing but his underwear. In fact, there used to be a time she was turned on by it. Now she was just sick of his laziness, both in appearance and attitude.

Rusty groaned and sat down, ruffling his hair as he poured out a bowl of Cheerios. He splashed milk on the table and began munching noisily.

"You're like a child, Rusty," said Sharyn. "Look at you. Never mind the damn quake; at least it got you out of bed. Are you gonna get dressed and get out there to find a job? Well?"

Rusty sighed. "You know, I don't feel so good today. I think the quake shook me up. Maybe I'd better take it easy today. I'll look tomorrow. My back's giving me shit, and..."

"Christ on a cross." Sharyn threw the dishcloth in the sink and scooped up her handbag from the sideboard. She marched over to the door and turned back to look at Rusty. He was staring out of the window, spooning piles of cereal into his mouth. A single Cheerio escaped his jaws and fell to the floor. She watched as he picked it up, blew on it, and then popped it back in his mouth.

"Rusty, so help me, you'd better clean your shit up before I get home. I've got to help Derek get the bar ready for the Sharp's anniversary dinner tonight. I'll be back later this afternoon."

Sharyn opened the front door and grabbed a yellow cardigan from a chair. Rusty was still staring through the window, paying her no attention. She sighed, and cursed. "Rusty, you hear me? You gonna clean up today?"

There was no answer.

"I'm not really going to Derek's, you know, I'm going on over to Randy Wyatt's place. He's going to screw me all morning in every position we can come up with. After he's through with me, I'm going to let his two boys have a crack. Young Pete, he's hung like a horse. Probably snap me in two, but what the hell, you only live once."

Rusty continued munching silently and staring out of the window, caught up in his own world. Sharyn slammed the door as she left the house they had shared for thirty years. "Asshole."

She walked in silence towards the road and paused. Did he really care that little? It was understandable he would be low on confidence since losing his job, but he paid her no attention and showed no interest in anything. Had he given up on everything? There used to be a time when he hated seeing her go off to work. There was a time when he would kiss her three times, once on each cheek and one on the lips, before he would let her leave the house. Now all he did was stare at nothing, or when he could be bothered, at the TV. She could walk around naked, and he probably wouldn't bat an eyelid. Maybe she should swing by Randy's farm and fuck him. Maybe that would wake Rusty up. She knew deep down that she would never do anything like that. As much as she wanted to get a reaction out of her husband, to see him stirred back into life into the vivacious man she had fallen in love with, she doubted she could ever bring herself to have an affair. She left that stuff for the celebrities, and Nancy Sharp.

"Morning, neighbor!" Nancy Sharp pulled her white Cadillac up to the kerb. It was immaculate and polished, and as usual, had the top down, just like Nancy.

"Morning," replied Sharyn, wishing she hadn't paused. Nancy Sharp was always sticking her nose in, desperate for gossip that she could spread around town. The only thing that spread faster around Goodsprings than Nancy's gossip were her legs. It was amazing that Mr. Sharp hadn't heard about it. Both of them were too self-absorbed to notice the real world. They had made a fortune out of the local mining industry, and now that the last of the mines had closed down, they seemed to enjoy flaunting their wealth as the town died. Half the population couldn't afford a car, certainly not a Cadillac.

"How's Rodney?" asked Sharyn politely, not giving a damn.

"Oh, he's just fine, fine. He's gone over to LA to check out an investment property."

Sharyn tried to forget the foreclosure notice the bank were threatening her with. Mortgage repayments were nigh on impossible with Rusty out of work, and here was her old 'friend' Nancy investing in rental properties.

"So he's out of town this week?" The sun was shining on the white car, and Sharyn had to shield her eyes as she looked at Nancy. At least the engine was still running, which meant the conversation would be a short one.

"Oh, he's back this afternoon. I wouldn't let him be late for our special anniversary tonight. Twenty five years and still going strong. You're going to Derek's place now to get set up, right? It's going to be a wonderful night. I've got a few errands to run before Rod gets back. I'm using the time to give myself a few treats, you know? I'm just off into town now for a manicure and a facial. I don't know if I could survive without my weekly treatments."

Sharyn knew that one of Nancy Sharp's weekly treatments was a visit to Randy Wyatt's farm. Rodney had the local businessmen's meeting on Tuesdays, and Nancy used the time to get herself checked up by Randy. Rumour had it that Pete was getting in on the action too. Looking at Nancy, it wasn't hard to see why. She still looked good for her age, and she didn't hide her body. She dressed in clothes that were meant for women half her age and clearly loved the attention it brought. There was a time Nancy had even made a play for Sharyn one drunken night a few years back. Nothing had happened, and nothing had been said of it since. Sharyn tried to keep Nancy at arm's length, which was difficult. Nancy made it her business to know everything and everyone in town. It was as if she and her husband owned the whole place. Nobody liked them, but the truth was that without their money, the town probably wouldn't last more than a year. There was no investment, no business, and more and more people gave up and left each year.

"You hear about Charlie Howitzer? Had a whole section of his farm go right out from under him yesterday. Said he thought a bomb had gone off. A sinkhole or something. Strange business. Poor Charlie's been struggling since Maryanne left him. Maybe I should check in on him, see how he's doing, you know?"

"You know, I really have to get going," said Sharyn. There was little doubt that Nancy would pay Charlie a visit and provide him with some much needed consolation. It didn't sound that odd if a sinkhole had appeared. What with the earthquakes, and the old coal mines and abandoned tunnels under the town, it happened. "I'll be seeing you, Nancy. Take care."

"You want a ride? You walk all the way in this heat, and you'll sweat all the way." Nancy pushed open the side door and sat up, revealing her ample cleavage.

"No, thanks, I enjoy the walk. The fresh air does me good."

Obviously disappointed, Nancy closed the door. "Okay, well make sure you clean Derek's place up for tonight. If there's anything wrong, I'll know who to come looking for."

Nancy winked, laughed and then the Cadillac roared off, showering Sharyn in a cloud of hot dust.

"Enjoy fucking Randy," said Sharyn as she waved Nancy off, ensuring her neighbour was out of earshot. "Maybe he and Charlie could tag team you?"

As the car turned a corner and disappeared, Sharyn began walking. She had to give Nancy credit, she sure had confidence. She could have almost any man she wanted, and usually did. Sharyn couldn't be like that. Derek's bar was a mile away, and it wasn't much of a walk, but that was about all the exercise she got these days. Rusty had lost his sex drive months ago, so they were lucky to get it on three times a year. It was almost as if Nancy knew too. She flaunted everything and made sure she got all the attention. People like Sharyn just sank into the background when she was around. There was no way Sharyn was about to accept a lift from Nancy. She would only have to endure more talk about how rich Nancy was, or even worse, fend off the woman's lecherous advances. The day was hot and the air thick, but Sharyn was used to it and it was quite pleasant walking through suburbia to get to work. She liked to look at the other houses, looking at how they'd been painted, how the gardens were, and imagine what was going on inside. She knew most of the people who lived in Goodsprings. There weren't many places to hide, and if there was any news, then Nancy always made sure everyone knew about it.

Goodsprings was a small, honest town, with a little under two hundred people left. Back when Sharyn was growing up, there had been more, but then the mines began to close and eventually people moved away. Her best friend when she had been growing up, Clare, had moved away when she was fourteen. Her parents had given up and moved to San Diego. The school had been threatened with closure for years, and one by one the stores began to close up. Now half of Main Street was just a series of boarded-up windows and dusty signs advertising stores that were no longer there. Derek's bar was the only place in town to get a drink and a good meal, and while there were people around, it kept going. Sharyn knew that in reality Goodsprings was a terminal case. There was no cure or remedy, and nobody seemed prepared to euthanize it quite yet. One day its end would come, and then everyone could wring their hands and wonder why nobody had done anything. Until that day came, it just kept slipping away, the cancer eating away at it, sucking the life out of it day by day, prolonging the agony.

Sharyn began to hum as she walked. It was no good dwelling on the negatives. She still had a job, a husband, and a roof over her head. At least for a little while longer, no matter what the bank said. Rusty might be lazy, but at least he was honest. He was always faithful, and treated her right, in as much as he had never lifted a finger in anger to her. He would come right eventually. He was just having a hard time adjusting. She shouldn't go on at him about finding a job. What was there to do? She was lucky that she still had her part-time job at Derek's. There were plenty of younger, hotter girls eager to work, and Derek had plenty of choices if he wanted to replace her. That was why she never complained, never bitched about the unsocial hours, and took any job he gave her. Most weekends it was just bar work, but occasionally they would host a function, like the Sharp's anniversary tonight.

Sharyn approached Main Street and sighed. There was Nancy's white Cadillac parked up outside the salon, and Pete Wyatt walking past it on his way to work. A dusty Ute was driving slowly down the street. It looked like Charlie was behind the wheel, but she couldn't be sure, so dirty was the window. The red paintwork was more of a deep ochre color, the Ute's body clouded by months of grime and inattention. Yep, that was Charlie all right. Sharyn smiled and raised her hand to say good morning to him, but as she did so, the telephone pole above her started to wobble. The wires that criss-crossed the street seemed to sway as if in the middle of a gale, yet there was no wind, just the incessant heat of the sun. A groaning sound erupted behind her, and then the ground began to shake and tremble.

"Jesus, not again." Sharyn stopped and waited for the shaking to stop. She was stood in front of the old sandwich store that had closed last month. In the window, a faded poster still claimed that they made the best subs in town. As the quake continued, the poster peeled away from the glass, and Sharyn watched as the building itself began to shake. She could barely stand upright and began to panic. This was stronger than earlier at home and way stronger than anything they had experienced in recent months. This was different. A huge roaring sound deafened her and the sandwich store began to crumble, its façade tumbling to the street, showering her in glass and masonry.

Screaming, Sharyn tried to run for the salon, hoping to find help there, hoping to find someone who knew what to do. Even if it was Nancy Sharp, it was better than dying out in the street. Sharyn tried to run, but the ground was jumping, and she immediately tripped, falling into the road. The concrete was tearing in half, splintering like old wood, and she lay flat on the ground, praying it wouldn't break beneath her. Sharyn was thrown around as she lay there, tossed from side to side as if she was on a waterbed. There was another tearing sound, and the telephone wires were ripped from their pins, falling down and landing on Charlie's red Ute that had stopped right in the center of the road. Sharyn tried to cover her ears and shut her eyes. The noise was terrifying. It was as if the earth itself was crying out in pain, bellowing in anger as it was torn asunder.

Please God, let me get home to Rusty, she thought. *Let there be a home to go to.*

Sharyn risked opening her eyes, and saw the roof of Derek's bar collapse. Huge plumes of dust were sent into the air, and then a fireball erupted. Even though it was the far end of the street, she could feel the warmth. Derek's bar was no longer there, obliterated as the ground continued shaking.

Suddenly, it stopped.

Sharyn unwrapped herself from the fetal position and slowly began to brush off the gray powder and residue that covered her from head to toe. The collapsed buildings around her had coated her in their remains, giving her an unwanted second skin made of glass and concrete. Some of the glass from the sandwich store had cut her, but as she rubbed her face, she realized it was only a few minor cuts. Her whole body was trembling, and she felt sick. All the noise and chaos had stopped only to be replaced by an eerie silence. There were no cries for help, no shouting or crying, just a blanket of silence that was even worse than the noise of the quake.

Pushing herself up with shaking hands, Sharyn slowly got to her feet. She was surrounded by rubble, and as she blinked the dust from her eyes, she heard a scraping noise from across the street.

"Hello? Nancy, that you?" Sharyn's eyes were watering, and now she was standing there was a stinging, pinching sensation in her leg. A droplet of warm blood rolled down her leg, and she figured she must have been cut. A jagged tear in her jeans told her exactly where, but as she ran her fingers down her leg and plucked out the tiny sliver of glass, she knew it wasn't serious. There were going to be people in far worse condition than her. Sharyn called out again, desperate to hear another voice, to know she wasn't alone. "Nancy?"

"Who is that?" The owner of the voice was hidden behind a white-gray cloud.

"Sharyn. It's Sharyn Barclay. Are you hurt?"

Stepping carefully, avoiding the large cracks in the road and the fallen masonry, Sharyn began to pick her way across the road to the scraping noise and the disembodied voice.

"I'm okay. You?" The scraping noise stopped, and then a figure emerged from the cloud. "Pete Wyatt," he said, holding out his hand and helping Sharyn across a large slab of concrete protruding from the road.

"Did you see anyone else, Pete?" asked Sharyn accepting Pete's hand. He was covered in a fine powder, and his thick curly hair appeared to have turned gray, but he appeared unhurt. "I thought I saw Charlie driving down, but I didn't see what happened. You think he's okay?"

"To be honest, ma'am, I don't think so. Last thing I saw before the world turned upside down was those poles coming down on his Ute. It's smashed up pretty badly." Pete wrinkled his nose and his soft, brown eyes bore into Sharyn's inquisitively. "I don't think we should hang around here too long. Can you smell that?"

Sharyn guessed what the sweet, invisible smell was enveloping them. "Gas?"

Pete nodded. "The quake must have ruptured the mainline. Probably what took out Derek's bar? We should try to get—"

Three sharp sounds interrupted him, but not from anything nearby, nor from anything natural. They sounded like an animal looking for something, calling out, and were loud; much louder than any dog could make, and they carried across the town like the gas filling the street. The sound echoed across Goodsprings like warnings, a message that something else was present now.

"What the hell kind of earthquake is this?" whispered Sharyn as she grabbed Pete's hand tighter. She had known Pete for years, watching him grow from a young boy into the man he was now. If there was anyone she trusted herself to be stuck with in an emergency, it was Pete. She felt a pang of guilt when she took Pete's hand, knowing that if Rusty saw her, he would have something to say about it.

The sounds came again, closer; short, staccato bursts, spat out rapidly, urgently, sounding almost like words.

"Yakazar-yakazar."

Sharyn gripped Pete's hand tighter. Rusty be damned, this wasn't right. "You know, I'm not so sure that..."

They were both abruptly thrown to the ground as the road beneath them jolted sharply. Sharyn landed painfully, a lump of jagged tarmac slicing through her skin from her elbow to her shoulder. She cursed and grabbed Pete's arm.

"Shit, Pete, what the hell is…?"

Panic enveloped her as she watched a shadow cover the both of them as they lay on the road. Something was emerging from the ruins of the main street; something that blocked out the sun and caused the very earth to vibrate with each lumbering step.

"Sharyn, is that you?"

Nancy stumbled from the salon, its door hanging on by a thread in the lopsided frame. Sharyn could see her pale face and the bruising around her eyes. There was blood running down her front, though Sharyn couldn't work out if it was hers or not. As Nancy emerged into the open, Sharyn gasped. The creature that had caused the shadow was stood right behind the salon now. Its hideous figure was emerging slowly through the dissipating cloud of dust.

"Nancy, don't move," hissed Sharyn. She stared up in disbelief as the huge monster stood surveying Goodsprings. Its head swivelled slowly from side to side, as if taking in everything. It had huge teeth poking out of its agape jaws and powerful muscles rippling its arms and legs. Had the earthquakes caused this thing to appear now? Had they brought this monster to life? Had it come up through the many sinkholes that had been appearing around the town of late?

Nancy saw Sharyn looking past her, over her shoulder, and she turned around. When she saw the thing behind her, she screamed and her knees buckled. Instantly, the creature's attention was brought down to her, and it happened so quickly Sharyn had no time to react. The monster took a giant step forward, and its two solid legs smashed the beauty salon to pieces, sending the building flying in all directions. Sharyn heard Nancy scream once more, and then she was scooped up into the thing's arms. Claws protruding from its hands dug into Nancy's body, holding her tightly. Sharyn watched as Nancy fought, pushing and punching at the thing's skin, but it had no effect. She doubted the monster even felt anything, so thick was its hide. Nancy was raised high into the air, and Sharyn watched as the monster shoved her into its mouth. Huge teeth ripped through Nancy's body, instantly tearing the upper half of her away. Sharyn heard the crunching sound of Nancy's bones being devoured and watched as red blood and saliva dripped from the monster's mouth. It ate the rest of Nancy quickly, and then let out a deafening bellowing sound, a triumphant roar as the final, twitching remains of Nancy slid down its throat.

Sharyn rolled onto her front and began to crawl through the rubble. She was living in a nightmare, in some parallel world. At that moment in time, she would've given anything to be back home arguing with Rusty, cleaning up his mess, but the sight of Pete made her realize this was really happening. He was frozen to the spot, horror etched across his young face as he stared up into those monstrous red eyes of the creature. A wet patch spread across his jeans and down his knees as the shadow spread over them again.

"Pete, come on, honey, take my hand." Sharyn held out her trembling hand to him, but he refused it.

As Sharyn reached for him, the ground shook, and a smell like burnt sausages enveloped her. The smell was foul, as if mixed with burning fat. It didn't seem right somehow, unnatural, and she knew it was right behind them. She looked at Pete, imploring him to take her hand, hoping he would think of something; yet as their eyes locked together, all she saw was hopelessness and fear. A huge claw like a spear appeared above Pete, and Sharyn watched as it was thrust downward, penetrating Pete's skull and tearing its way down through his body which convulsed as he was split in half.

Sharyn rolled onto her back and watched as Pete's lifeless carcass was thrown aside. The monster towering over her bellowed once again as an explosion from behind it sent shards of broken glass raining down on the both of them. Sharyn heard the crackle of gunfire in the distance, and the monster turned away from her, its attention drawn to the gunshots. The monster turned, and as it did so, its tail swung around behind it. It was short and stubby, but ended with a huge club, and it smashed through the rubble with ease. Sharyn sensed it coming, yet she knew she was also incapable of getting out of its path. The tail brushed aside the fallen masonry and wood, and Sharyn closed her eyes. As it scraped across the road, picking it up speed, the tail was whipped smartly behind the creature. The impact was like being hit by a truck at high speed. Sharyn screamed in pain and was sent flying across the street. Her body flew through the air as if she weighed no more than a rag doll, and finally, she smacked into the side of Nancy's white Cadillac, breaking her leg in the process. Sharyn saw the monster lumbering over the remains of Derek's burning bar, headed toward the center of town.

Goodsprings was no longer a quiet little town that nobody had heard of. Soon, it would be the most famous town in America. Sharyn looked at the piece of bone sticking through her jeans, just below her knee. At least she was alive. The monster bellowed again, and the blinding sun shone down on Sharyn. The sun faded like a shadow into her unconsciousness and she wondered if she would ever see Rusty again.

CHAPTER 7

Mackenzie knew it was still there. The sun was still shining brightly, and it sparkled off the upturned chassis of the bus, splintering its way through the air like a giant cobweb. The monster was out there, hiding beneath the surface of the Earth. It hadn't gone anywhere. The occasional rumble, the vibrations of it moving underground, shifting the soil like a giant worm told him that. It was waiting for them, waiting for a chance. He hated it. Mackenzie hated it more than anything he had hated in his life. It had killed innocent people, good people. What did it want with them? Why had it surfaced now?

"Thanks, Mac. Boy, that was close."

Myles lay on the store's cool floor, nestled between two overturned shelves surrounded by crushed boxes and spilt milk.

After scooping up Beers, Myles had changed direction sharply and narrowly avoided being crushed by the monster. Mac had ordered him to run and not look back. It was advice that Myles was only too happy to take. As he ran, he could feel the monster literally breathing down his back. Fire surged through him, and he ran straight for the door, not wanting to look back. If he had, he might've crumbled, succumbed to the terror and panic that drove him on. He had to get back to Michele, to Alyce, to the store where Mac waited for him.

From where Mackenzie was, with one foot outside and the other nestled against the door propping it open, he could see it all. The giant thing chasing Myles was all muscles and teeth. It was vicious, and its eyes suggested it was enjoying the hunt. It easily dwarfed Myles, and it could cover more ground in one step than

Myles could run in ten seconds. Mac was waiting for it to clasp its jaws around him, and it raised its head to snatch the man up into its mouth when it stopped. It gave Myles the extra second he needed, and he ran into the store with Beers tightly tucked up in his arms. Once they were inside, Mackenzie slammed the door shut and watched as the monster stopped again. It stood up on its haunches and called out. This time it was a soft sound, quieter than before. Was it calling to anything in particular, perhaps a mate or another of its kind?

"That was close," said Myles.

"Yeah, too close," replied Mackenzie as he peered out of the windows. After losing the chase for Myles and Beers, the monster had retreated to the hole from which it had first appeared. Mackenzie wasn't fooled though. It hadn't gone anywhere. It was just waiting, biding its time until someone else made the mistake of going outside.

"I need to see Michele," said Myles. He stroked Beer's fur, and the puppy nuzzled up against Myles. "I nearly crapped myself out there. It was the thought of not seeing her again, or not seeing our Alyce that…"

Myles bit his lip, afraid if he went on he would break down.

Mackenzie let out a sigh of relief and picked up a bottle of lemonade. He screwed the top off and took a drink. "Let's get back there, see how Chris is doing. I'm sure your family will be pleased to see you're still with us. Just do me a favor and don't pull any stunts like that again."

Myles nodded, and they quietly picked themselves up.

As they re-entered the store room, Beers bolted from Myles' hands and ran straight to Alyce. Beers excitedly jumped up and down as Alyce tried to cuddle him.

"You okay? We felt the ground shaking in here." Laurel took the lemonade from Mackenzie. "What happened?"

"That thing out there tried to make a snack out of Beers and Myles. Luck for them its aim was off."

Mackenzie saw Myles comforting Michele, both of them watching Alyce carefully. The young girl was happy to see her dog and seemed oblivious to the danger they were in. As Mackenzie looked around the room, he wondered if he wasn't missing something. That monster out there had great power, and yet it had stopped short of attacking yet again as it had gotten close to the store. He wasn't sure how long their luck would hold out. It had gone back underground for now, but how long?

"Chris seems to be doing a little better," said Laurel. "Maria's got him wrapped up, and the bleeding has stopped. She gave him something for the pain, just some Aspirin. She's nice. She has a good way about her. Akecheta says we can trust her. It must be hard having us all back here, but she's not about to kick us out. There's a small bathroom around the corner too, so we can stay put for as long as this takes. I assume it hasn't gone?"

"No, it hasn't. It's gone back underground, but I got the impression it has no intention of just disappearing."

"So, just what is it?" asked Maria as she approached them. "Are you going to tell me what the hell that thing is?"

The ground shivered, and they heard the sound of glass breaking as the windows of the bus outside gave way.

"It would appear that we have a giant man-eating dinosaur right outside our door."

Everyone turned to look at Chris. He was propped up on his elbows, nursing a bandaged leg, and looking pale.

"You should be resting," said Maria.

Chris nodded in agreement, but carried on anyway. "Quite what it wants and where it came from is hard to say. I could really only speculate. It is here though, and it seems to be here to stay."

"A dinosaur? Chris, how many of those pills did you take?" Maria put her hands on her hips. "Forget your leg, I think I need to take a look at your head."

"Look, it's not Bigfoot, it's not an alien, and it's sure as hell not some rabid coyote. Maybe this dinosaur thing makes sense." Mackenzie could hardly believe he was saying it out loud, and yet it did make sense. It looked like a dinosaur, though nothing specific, at least nothing he could think of. It was like a strange version of a dinosaur.

"I would say it's linked to the dinosaurs," said Chris, "but it's not any particular one. If it was, then over time it has certainly changed. It has adapted, learned to survive. I would say the reason we've never come across it before is simply that it remained underground. For some reason, it's never had any impulse or reason to come up."

"Until now." Myles slowly stroked Alyce's hair, who in turn was stroking Beers. "There was nothing in the brochure about dinosaurs living in the Mojave."

Akecheta smiled, but said nothing.

"Look, hold on, this is freaking ridiculous." James emerged from the shadows carrying a bottle of beer. Vic was behind him looking sheepish, half a bottle of beer in his hand at his side.

"We'll pay you back," Vic muttered as he cast a glance at Maria and noticed her disapproving stare.

"Dinosaurs don't exist. They just don't," said James with confidence. "I think you must've had a bang on the head, Chris. Last time I read a book, the dinosaurs were annihilated, wiped out hundreds of millions of years ago, right?"

Chris nodded. All eyes in the room were on him. They wanted answers, but he wasn't sure he had them all yet. "Look, we can't really predict what it will do as we don't really know what kind of creature it is. It's obviously nothing like anything we've seen before. Is it naturally nocturnal, does it burrow, or does it lay in wait for its prey? Does it use sight or smell to find its kill? There's a lot more of it I need to study before I can make a one hundred per cent accurate assessment of what we're dealing with. My best guess is—"

"Sorry, boss, but I'm not putting my life in the hands of someone who is *guessing* at what we're dealing with." James took a swig of the warm beer and grimaced. "It's probably escaped from a fucking zoo. Some rich yank probably has a whole farm of these things somewhere and makes a quick buck by turning them into burgers. It probably started out life as a cow and got so pumped full of drugs, it mutated into that monster we all saw earlier."

"Mutated? Hmm." Chris seemed to ignore the pointed sarcasm in James' voice and frowned. He was trying to join the dots, to figure out what was going on, but the thought kept escaping him before he could grab it.

"I don't buy it," said Mr. Stepper. He had been listening intently. He still wanted to get up on the roof and find a signal.

These people were in his care now, and ultimately he wanted to get each and every one of them back home safe and sound, including the two obnoxious Brits. Quite how he was going to do that he didn't know, but getting a call out to the emergency services seemed like a good place to start. What was he going to tell them, that a dinosaur was chasing them? "I mean, it can't be real. It just can't be. I need to believe in something else."

"I don't like it either," said Myles, "but we all saw it. Hell, it took a chunk out of Chris' leg. If that thing's not a dinosaur, I don't know what it is."

"What a bunch of crap." James finished the beer and threw the empty bottle to the side. "I've heard about the genetic tampering that goes on in secret in American army bases. It's just a rogue escapee from a laboratory or something. Dinosaurs? Pull the other one, mate."

Trying to ignore how rude James was being, and putting it down to stress and alcohol, Mackenzie tried to coax more information out of Chris. "Are you a professor or something?" he asked. "Chris? Can you tell us anything else? It might help if we knew what we were facing."

Chris looked at Mackenzie with concern. "Lecturer at UCLA. I came out here for work. Figured I could combine my research with a little vacation."

"Our very own Richard Owen," muttered Mr. Stepper.

"So you come across anything else in your research?" asked Laurel. "Any other dinosaurs out there we should know about?"

"None that are still alive. I thought when we first saw it that it had a remarkable resemblance to Coelophysis. But it's not right. There was a discovery in the Gobi Desert; the Saichania I think it's called. There's not a whole lot of information widely available about it, it's still being studied, but I wonder if we're dealing with some sort of long-lost cousin. Maybe a slightly different version of it."

"But dinosaurs don't live underground. I'm no expert, but I don't remember seeing or reading anything about that," said Mackenzie. "They roamed the Earth, remember? They didn't burrow underground and live in caves."

"Well the Troodon was a nocturnal creature, and we are finding more evidence that some of these beasts could survive underground. If our friend is an ancestor of one of those things, then it has had millions of years to learn to adapt. If it had food and water, then feasibly it could survive underneath the planet."

"This must be a joke," said James moodily. "First the phones crap out, now we have to listen to this rubbish? Maria, you got a TV back here? Maybe we can find out what's really going on instead of theorizing?"

Maria shook her head. "I ain't got need for a TV. I live with my sister in Baker. There's no time for watching it around here."

James turned to Vic. "Okay, so where are the cameras? Am I on MTV? Come on Vic, spill it. This is a big joke, right?"

"All right, James, just quieten down for a moment, and we'll see what we can figure out." Akecheta approached the center of the room. "It would be a very good idea to find out if others are aware of our situation. We have no phone coverage here, no internet, and no transport with that thing outside. We can't just wait and hope it goes away. Maybe we're not alone in this. Maybe somebody out there saw or heard something. For all we know, someone is on their way. Then again, they might not be. So what can we do?"

"You know, the radio might still work." Maria stared at the ceiling as if the answer to all their questions was written there. "Where did I put it? It's worth a try. I'll see if I can find it. I rarely use it, except when I'm back here doing a stock-take. I'm sure I left it on one of the shelves. Now that everything's a mess, it might take me a while."

"I'll help," said Laurel.

"Me too." Michele joined the two women as they began searching for the radio through the scattered contents of the storeroom.

"I need to keep occupied. I'm going to help look for the radio, and anything else that might help us," said Mr. Stepper.

Mackenzie noticed the driver looked tired. He looked scared too. He might have lived a long life, but nothing had prepared him to face something like this.

"Chris, why is it still here?" asked Akecheta. "If it is still out there, underground, then it can't see us right? So why hasn't it left?"

Chris pushed himself up off the ground, wincing as pain shot through his leg. He propped himself up on a box, leaning on it for support. "Well, essentially it is an animal, whether it's a dinosaur or not."

James snorted. "Vic, let's go see if we can't find another beer back there. Leave these poor dumb folk to their fantasies."

As James and Vic snuck off to a dark corner of the storeroom, Chris went on, pleased they had left. James was distracting him from the real issue. He needed to figure out what they were dealing with. "Something that large is probably quite used to getting its own way. It will have little else on its mind other than eating and sleeping. I gather it's not tired right now, given its attack. We can also safely assume it's a carnivore, given its nature and those large prominent incisors. Basically, we have all the hallmarks of an apex predator. It has its prey trapped, cornered, and if it can't reach us, it'll wait us out. I've seen it countless times."

Mackenzie knew what Chris was talking about. He had watched enough National Geographic documentaries to know when something was being hunted. "She knows we're here. I don't think it's going anywhere," he said with nervousness. "We're dinner."

"But it can't see us?" Akecheta sat down on a box next to Chris and rubbed his lips. He kept pushing thoughts of his family to the back of his mind. He was responsible for these people now, although he also assumed his family were far from danger. There was no reason to think anything else, and he had to focus on finding a way out of their perilous situation.

"I guess not," said Chris.

"So what's stopping us from running out there now, getting to the bus, and making a run for it?"

"Well, that would be a major risk." Chris exhaled and shook his head. "Some animals use vibration and scent to track their prey. They don't all rely on sight. If this thing out there is used to living underground, it may be possible that it actually has very poor eyesight. If it's used to hunting underground then it begs two questions. One, why is it now above ground? What has forced it to come up?"

"Lack of food," suggested Mackenzie. "Something that size must need to eat a lot."

Chris nodded. "Anything that disturbs its natural habitat will make an animal move. It could be forced to move for a number of reasons. Maybe we're just the unlucky ones who were in its path."

"And the second question?" asked Akecheta.

"*How* does it hunt?" Chris winced again as pain shot through his injured leg. He knew he was going to need more meds, more than Maria had. He hoped they wouldn't be stuck in the store too long as the danger of infection was all too real.

"I would've thought you got a good look at that, Chris," said Myles as he left Alyce to join the discussion. He looked back at his little girl who was gently stroking Beers. "How it hunts is pretty obvious, isn't it? Big teeth, sharp claws, and a thousand tons of weight behind it; I'd hardly call it subtle, but definitely effective."

"All very true, I *can* testify to that." Chris felt a sweat break out on his forehead. It felt like the temperature was dropping by the minute, yet he knew it had to be getting hotter. The day was still young, and the sun was still warming the store.

"I think what Chris is getting at is how exactly does it *find* its prey? Does it sniff them out, watch them, or listen for audible clues as to where we are?" Mackenzie tried to remember when it had attacked Beers and Myles how it had happened. Had it seen them? Had it heard Beers barking? Beers had been going at it for a long time before Myles had saved the puppy, so why hadn't it taken the dog long before they got there? It had all happened so fast, he hadn't really had time to process it. They had been lucky to get away, he knew that. "Does it really matter?"

"Oh, yes. If we have to get ourselves out of here, it could mean the difference between making it out or not." Chris didn't mean to sound so dramatic, but the words were out of his mouth before he knew it. He saw Myles glance across to his daughter. They all had their reasons for wanting to get out, to get home, and Alyce was the most vulnerable of them all. "Look, if we can figure out how that thing thinks, then we can work out how to get around it. The more I think about it, the more I believe it could be as simple as movement. It would be unheard of in a dinosaur, but I don't think we're dealing with your old fashioned T-rex here. This thing has adapted. Living underground will mean its senses are better attuned to hunting in the ground. Above the surface, it's weaker. It would have little use for good vision down there in the darkness, and that might just be its Achilles heel. Vibrations, sounds that travel through the ground, pressure waves: all those things will tell it where we are."

"Okay, well we could try to minimise our movements, maybe it'll find something else for dinner," said Mackenzie. "You think it can hear us talking?"

"I doubt it. From where we are, our voices wouldn't carry far through the ground. Walking around, running, sudden movements—they're the triggers."

Mackenzie thought back to when Myles had rescued Beers outside. Had the monster attacked before Myles had started running, or after? Was it Beers' barking that set it off, or Myles going after the dog?

Akecheta stood up. "Mr. Stepper wanted to get up to the roof to try to get a signal. Maybe we can figure out a way to—"

The room vibrated strongly, and then stopped almost as soon as it had started. Then they heard the shouting.

"Who's that?" asked Myles. He closed his eyes and tried to focus on the faint shouting coming from outside. "Mr. Stepper didn't go out there on his own, did he?"

"No, I'm still here," replied Mr. Stepper as he emerged from a gloomy corner with a torch in his hands. He looked anxiously at Akecheta. "I'm sure that whoever is out there, they are *not* part of our tour group."

Akecheta raised his index fingers to his lips. "Listen." The noise was distant, as if underwater, and it sounded like two voices, not just one. There was no doubt that the shouting was coming from outside. Yet the words were muffled, and it was impossible to understand what was being said.

"Shit," said Mackenzie, "this is bad. Whoever is shouting is going to get the attention of that thing pretty quickly. We need to warn them away. We need to get them to be quiet."

"Nobody is safe out there." Alyce looked up at Mackenzie with sad eyes. She had Beers by her side and had snuck up on them quietly, keen to listen in. "*Nobody.*"

"Don't look so down. The situation's not that grim," said Mackenzie to her. He didn't know how much of the conversation she had heard, but all of it was unsuitable for a child. "We're not finished yet."

"Alyce, get back with your mother," said Myles. He shooed his daughter back towards Michele.

The ground shook again, but this shake was longer than the first one. More items fell from the shelves, and Mackenzie grabbed a shelf. He watched Laurel stagger over to him, using the shelf to keep herself upright, and then she grabbed hold of his arm. They looked at each other in silence. The whole room was silent, everyone lost in their own thoughts. Mackenzie kept his eyes locked on his wife's. He tried to convey to her that he wouldn't let anything hurt her, that he would do whatever it took to get through this. Did she understand? Could she? When he tried to read her mind, to understand what her blue eyes were saying, he found himself lost in them. He loved her more with each year, and those deep blue eyes of hers gave nothing away. All he knew was that he needed to get her away from here, to Amy. Maybe that was what she was thinking. Maybe he could read her better than he thought.

Laurel waited for the shaking to subside before speaking. "We found the radio. Michele's working on it now, trying to pick up a station. Mac, what's going on?"

The shaking abruptly stopped, and then from outside they heard a grunting sound, a sort of snorting as if a bull were about to charge. The noise stopped, and the shouting voices stopped too. Then a lone voice broke the silence.

"It's coming," said Chris.

The shouting voices outside were louder now, more urgent, insistent, demanding attention.

"We have to do something," said Maria. "You two, come help me."

James and Vic looked at each other, puzzled.

"Yes, you two, hurry it up," said Maria angrily.

"But…"

Maria ignored James' attempt to avoid doing anything and ordered him to follow her. She marched over to a box, ripped it open, and pulled out a child's plastic baseball bat. Maria thrust the bat into his hands, and then held another out to Vic.

"Why us? What can we do?" James looked at the toy in his hands. Quite what he could achieve with it against a giant monster he didn't know. Nor did he want to. It clearly was far safer inside than out there. He had no responsibility to anyone but himself and had no intention of going outside swinging a toy around under the shade of that thing.

"James and Vic are coming with me. I suggest everyone else stays here with Chris. Myles, you've got Michele and Alyce to take care of. Mac, you and Laurel can help Michele get the radio working and find out what the hell is going on."

James felt anger rising within him. This woman was insane. Who did she think she was ordering him around? "I am *not* going out there. Vic and I are going to stay right here, so you can take this piece of crap and shove it." James dropped the bat on the floor.

Maria looked at James with disdain and picked up the bat. She pushed it against James. "We have a man with an injured leg, a woman with multiple lacerations and bruises, and a family with a small child and dog. What have you got, other than a bad attitude?"

"Come on, James," said Vic. "We can't just do nothing."

James glared at Vic, and took the bat from Maria.

"What do we do?" asked Vic ignoring James. The beer had given him a little courage. It might not be enough to fight off a dinosaur, but it was enough to stand up to James. He didn't feel much like being pushed around anymore. Things with James had been good to start with, but it hadn't taken long before James had shown his true color. Once they got back to England, it was goodbye James. Vic had let himself be pushed around for too long.

"We're going to give them a chance," said Maria. "Follow me outside, holler all you can, and swing those bats around. I think we can confuse it, even if only for a few seconds. I'll get whoever is out there over here. I don't think we'll have to go more than a few feet from the store."

"I'm coming with you," announced Mr. Stepper. He smacked the torch he held against the palm of his hand. It was not much of a weapon, but it was solid and better than a plastic toy. "You can't do it all, Maria. I'm not much use in here, and I can be of more use to you out there. I'll get whoever is out there back inside."

Maria nodded. "Fair enough. We'll do what we can. I'm not taking any chances though. If I say it's off, we all get back here immediately. You know, there's a ladder around back. When this is over, you can get up there and try for a signal. We need to get some *real* help out here."

Leaving the back store room, Maria led Mr. Stepper, Vic and a reluctant James to the front. She opened the front door and a gust of wind blew her 'Open' sign to 'Back Soon.' She held the door open for the two young men, and Vic tentatively went outside. James remained in the doorway.

"I'm not going any further," James said. "This is a waste of time. Look around. It's not even here. There's nobody here."

Maria scanned the forecourt, but James was right. The bus was still where they had left it, and the hole in the ground appeared to be deserted. There was no one shouting, no one at all. Maria shielded her eyes from the sun, but she saw nothing.

"I don't see it," said Vic. "I don't see anything."

"We didn't imagine those voices. Someone might be hurt." Maria lifted her gaze to the Kelso Depot but saw nothing. The grand building stood motionless, empty, and yet something wasn't right. Maria could sense it, like a pressure point building in her head. It felt like they were at that moment before a thunderstorm hits; when the air thickens and comes alive, and the very atoms squeeze and pinch each other in anticipation. As much as she wanted to believe James that there was nothing out here, she didn't believe it. She knew it was close by.

And so were whoever those voices belonged to.

"Too bad," said James as he hurled his baseball bat into the yard. "I'm going back inside. This is ridiculous."

Mr. Stepper shook his head disapprovingly. "You can't just quit when—"

It sounded like a bomb going off. One minute the bus was there, the next it was flying through the air. The monster appeared from behind it, roaring and charging through the desert toward the store. With every step of its heavy, powerful legs, the ground shook, and Maria almost felt pleased to see it. She wasn't about to let it destroy her place, not after all the time and effort she had put into it.

The bus smashed back down to the ground, the windows all exploding outward and showering Vic with glass. A dust cloud blew out from the now destroyed bus, and James shouted for Vic to get back inside. A huge plume of dirt had been thrown into the air, and for a moment, Maria lost sight of the creature. She coughed as the hot air was filled with grit and grime.

"Mr. Stepper, you okay?" Maria felt suddenly alone. She could hardly see more than a few feet in front of her.

"Maria, get back here."

She heard the order, but was disorientated. Someone ran past her, close enough to touch, but all she saw was a shadow in the air.

"Vic?"

"Maria, where are you?"

The dust cloud drifted through the air, and then the monster appeared. Maria wiped her eyes, watching as the giant materialized close by, silently, its head emerging first, then its red eyes glaring at her. Soon, its shoulders and arms followed, and then its giant body. It towered over her, casting the store into shadow as the bus settled and the dirt dissipated. The monster let out a bellow that made her bones shiver with fear. It was letting them know who was boss, letting out a roar that was to tell anyone in the vicinity that their days on this planet were over. It was time for something else to go to the top of the food chain. Maria's hairs stood on end and her arms shivered despite the heat. This animal meant to kill every last one of them.

A male voice in the distance called out. "Hilfe! Bitte!"

Maria stepped forward, but couldn't see anyone. The words were foreign, but the meaning was clear. Somebody was in trouble. She began waving her baseball bat around, to see if she had the monster's attention. Was it looking at her anymore, or had it heard the voice? It was just standing there, as if waiting for a challenge.

Vic, encouraged by Maria and with the beer coursing through his veins, began copying her and waving the pathetic bat around. Standing alongside Maria, he started slamming it into the ground and shouting.

"Get the fuck back in here, Vic." James remained in the doorway of the store, petrified. The thing standing out there was unnatural, and looked big enough to fight an army. Was it a dinosaur? It certainly looked like it would fit right in with those creatures. It undoubtedly lived to kill. This was no herbivore, but a real meat-eater, one that relished eating as much as it did killing. It seemed hesitant though, as if torn between stamping on the store, or wiping out Vic and Maria.

Mr. Stepper startled James from his revelry. He thrust the end of the torch into James' chest and pushed him back into the store. "If you're not going to do anything, then get back inside and help the others. Tell them what's going on. Tell them to take shelter and hope to God this thing doesn't come for us." With that, Mr. Stepper rushed out to Maria's side.

Glancing at Maria, Mr. Stepper took a tentative step forward and stared up at the monster. It was huge, more terrifying than anything he'd ever seen. It was hard to believe it was real, but the stench coming off its body, the sound of it, the sheer size of it, the thick scaly skin covering its legs that were themselves the size of a house, meant he had no choice but to accept it was real.

"What now?" Mr. Stepper tore his eyes away from the beast, and looked at Maria. "What the hell do we do now?"

Maria could sense it was about to move. She wasn't about to let anything tear her life apart again. Tony being taken from her had almost destroyed her. This animal could threaten her, her friends, even her livelihood, but she wasn't about to give into any kind of bully, no matter how much bigger than her it might be. She looked across at Mr. Stepper.

"Let's send this thing a fucking message."

She said a quiet prayer, and looked up into the monster's eyes. "Come on then, you bitch. Come get some fresh meat."

CHAPTER 8

Cold spread across Mackenzie, though it wasn't just the dark corner of the store room. Fear gripped him, and he kept imagining the creature crashing through the walls, killing and destroying everyone and everything in its path. What was going on out there? Would Maria really be able to do anything to stop it? They had all heard the roaring, felt the ground shaking, and been waiting for the impact. When it didn't come, Mackenzie suggested they go and check out what was going on.

"No way, Mac, you stay here with me." Laurel had a firm grip on his arm. "We need you here. We need to stay put. You're no good out there."

"I'll go," said Myles. He gently stroked Alyce's head, and kissed Michele on the cheek who was still trying to find a radio station. "I can't sit back here waiting and wondering."

Akecheta was tending to Chris, who was looking worse and worse by the minute. Sweat was pouring from his pale face, and he was mumbling incoherently. Mackenzie knew he needed a doctor, but how they were going to get him one he had no idea. They were trapped.

"No," said Mackenzie. He pushed Laurel away, ignoring the hurt and fear in her eyes. "I'm not helping in here. I need to know what's going—"

"It's here. It's fucking right outside." James burst into the back room and stumbled to the floor. He reached out for the nearest beer and began to gulp it down.

Mackenzie frowned. "Where are the others? What do you mean it's here?"

James was panting, his breaths coming quick and short. He pointed to the doorway. "That fucking monster is right outside. They're dead. They're all fucking dead."

Mackenzie waited for more, for an explanation, but James just began drinking again. Exasperated, Mackenzie snatched the bottle from James' hands and threw it away. He grabbed him by the shirt collar, and hauled him to his feet.

"Mac, don't," pleaded Laurel. She could sense her husband's frustration, but punching James' teeth out wasn't going to help anyone.

"What are you going to do?" James sneered. "What, you a tough guy? You tough enough to take on Chris' dinosaur?"

Mackenzie looked at his wife. She was sat on the cold ground beside Michele, her back propped up against some shelving. She was now holding onto Michele, her eyes scared, her body trembling. Mackenzie looked around the room. All eyes were on him, all with the same question. What was he going to do? Myles was all too ready to join the fight. Mackenzie could tell he was angry with James, and Akecheta wasn't far behind. Chris appeared to be out cold, and Mackenzie was ready to lay into James. Then he looked at Alyce. The little girl was cradled in her mother's lap, holding onto her puppy. Her eyes weren't full of fear, they were sad. She seemed resigned to her situation, as if sadness was all she had now. Even Beers was quiet.

Mackenzie pushed James away. "Stay here. Myles, keep an eye on him. I don't trust him." Mackenzie looked around for something to take out with him. He needed to have something in his hands, to just feel some weight so he didn't feel like he was going out there empty handed. There was a rack of sunglasses in a corner, and Mackenzie grabbed it. He twisted the top of the central pole around, and lifted off the top. Brushing aside the glasses, he withdrew the shaft and held the makeshift spear in his hands. It was barely four feet long, but it was better than nothing.

"Mac, let me—"

"No, Myles, you need to stay here with your family." Mackenzie needed to know there was someone back here he could rely on to protect Laurel. "Please. Just take care of everyone for me."

"I'm going back out there," announced James. "I need to make sure Vic's okay."

"So now you grow a conscience? Why bother?" asked Mackenzie. "Why not just stay back here where it's safer."

"I'm going. I don't care what you think. Would you rather I stay here and keep Laurel company?"

The smirk on James' face told Mackenzie all he needed to know. Maybe it was better that James did go with him.

"Fine. Move your ass. But you do anything to endanger me or my family, and I'll take your damn head off."

James had found another bottle of beer, and took it with him as he left the back room.

As the store began to shake again, and more items fell off the shelves, Mackenzie turned his back on Laurel. He couldn't face her now. He had to do this. He would be able to do more to protect her by going out there, than staying back and doing nothing. More than that, he didn't want to say goodbye. He didn't want to acknowledge that this might be the last time her would see her. If he accepted that, then he may as well give in to his fear like James had. Clutching the metal pole in his hands, Mackenzie crossed through the doorway and headed for the front of the store.

Without turning back, he headed for the gargantuan monster outside that was threatening to destroy his world, vowing that one way or another, this was going to end.

* * *

Maria watched in horror as the huge beast stopped dead in its tracks just short of the store.

"What's it doing? Why did it stop?" Vic looked alarmed, and motioned for James to come over. Though he had disappeared for a short time, James was back now, staring at him from within the store. Vic watched as James shook his head and took a step backward, away from danger. He raised a bottle to his lips, and smiled.

Maria watched as the monster just seemed to stand in the road, its head cocked to one side. Its fangs dripped bloody saliva onto the ground and its head swayed slightly, from left to right. Was it watching them, weighing the situation up, or waiting for something?

"Do you hear that?" Vic closed his eyes in concentration. "There, you hear it? It sounds like someone calling for help."

"Yeah, but I don't know where it's coming from," said Maria. "I've not seen a soul all morning and there's no one else out here. I just don't..." Then she saw them. "Oh no."

A young couple were standing in front of the Kelso Depot, beneath a tall Date Palm. Both carried large rucksacks on their backs and wore scuffed walking boots. The woman was wearing a red singlet and had long blonde hair tied back in a bunch whilst the man with her wore a khaki colored shirt and shorts. He was waving his hands above his head and shouting something.

"Oh my God, we have to stop them before they get themselves killed. They must have been hiking and gone into the building earlier." Maria looked at the monster and the two young people behind it near the Depot. There was no way of getting to them and no way for them to get to the store. The towering beast stood in their path, and she had no idea what to do. All she could think was that they had to distract the monster for long enough to get them inside. She waved the bat around again, trying to keep the monster's eyes on her.

"Maria, this is useless," said Mr. Stepper. "It knows we're here and it's not coming. Maybe it's leaving. Maybe it hasn't noticed them."

"It has now," said Vic. "Look."

They watched in horror as the creature turned around and faced the two teenagers. The man in khaki stopped waving as the thing faced them. Maria could see the fear on his face and heard him calling out for help.

"Was ist das? Hilf uns. Ich bitte Site, etwas zu tun. Hilfe!"

The young girl too, fear aging her, screamed as the monster approached.

"Ich möchte niche heute sterben. Lassen Sie es nicht nehmen Sie mich. Ich will nur nach Hause gehen. Oh Gott. Hilfe! Oh Gott, ich..."

The monster exploded into action, racing across the open ground to them, charging with thunderous footsteps that rattled the teeth in Maria's head. Its footsteps sent reverberations throughout the store, and within seconds, Mackenzie was at James' side in the doorway.

"Jesus, what… " Mackenzie felt rapidly drained of energy as he saw the beast charging across the open desert toward the other building. He heard the backpackers shouting, but his eyes were drawn up to the beast that was bearing down on them.

"Hey, over here. Over here! Leave them alone!" Maria began running after it, waving her bat around frantically, not thinking about anything but saving the two young tourists.

Mackenzie pushed past James who was blocking the doorway like a statue, his feet stuck to the ground with apparent fear.

"Mackenzie, get back here!" Mr. Stepper reached for his arm as he ran past, but he was too slow and Mackenzie ran after Maria, after the beast, after death. Vic began to retreat to the store, and Mr. Stepper found himself caught in a sort of no-man's land, unable to determine whether it was best to fight or flee.

They were all far slower than the giant creature.

The two young backpackers abruptly turned and ran for their lives. The girl turned her back on the monster and ran for the side of the Kelso Depot as the young man with her sprinted toward the store. He tried to weave from side to side as he ran, weaving an erratic path across the street, as if dodging a hail of bullets instead of the outstretched arms of a resurrected dinosaur. It was close enough now to grab them, but it seemed momentarily confused as to which one of the tourists to go after.

"This way!" shouted Mackenzie as he beckoned the young man over. "This way!"

Maria screamed as the beast picked its target. "No!"

"Sagen, mein Vater, dass ich—"

The girl never finished her plea. She almost made it back inside the Depot before the thing got her. It practically jumped on her, placing a foot on her legs, crushing them instantly, and piercing her back with a claw that shattered her spine in a second. The girl's screams echoed across the desert, and her wails were reminiscent of a dying animal. The monster repeatedly dug its claw into her as she lay on the floor, plunging it in and out of her, penetrating her soft body, ripping apart the tissue and muscles as she helplessly lay there clutching at the dirt uselessly. The beast then lifted her up into the air, scattering the woman's blood over the ground. In a mad frenzy, it quickly thrust her back to the ground with a sickening thud, slamming her body against the desert floor three times in quick succession. Finally, the screaming stopped.

The girl's lifeless body lay prostrate on the ground as the monster retracted its claw. It lowered its head, devoured the body, and then turned to concentrate on its next meal.

"Run," pleaded Mackenzie. He just couldn't give up on the man although he sensed the monster had already decided the backpacker's fate.

"Come on." Vic waved his bat around aimlessly wishing it was a RPG or something he could actually use. "Fucking move it!"

The young male backpacker had stopped to look back at his girlfriend and was still several yards away from Mackenzie. Clearly torn between going back and standing his ground, the young man had succumbed to a sort of desperate numbness. His legs were dead weight, and the shock and awe of seeing his girlfriend killed had turned him into a zombie. He slowly turned back and faced Mackenzie. The expression on his face was quizzical, as if he couldn't understand what was happening. It was as if he had wandered onto a film set and found himself surrounded by aliens instead of enjoying a rest break on the way to LA. The young man hadn't seen everything of what had happened to his girlfriend, but he knew what it meant. He didn't need to see it all to know she was gone.

Mackenzie saw terror in the man's eyes as well, and sweat poured from his shaven head down his face, dripping from the end of his nose. It was an expression that Mackenzie was getting to see in too many people.

Maria forced a smile upon her face. "This way. To me," she said quietly. She held out a hand, a token gesture that she hoped the stranger would understand. She wanted him to know she was there for him. She didn't recognize the words that he spoke, but the meaning was clear. He wasn't going anywhere.

"Warum hast du nicht etwas tun?"

The monster powered forward and crashed down on top of the man, obliterating the backpacker's body under the full weight of one leg. One moment he was there looking at Maria and the next he was simply gone, disappeared underneath the scaly feet of the beast. Slowly, the monster raised its foot up to reveal the flattened backpacker. His bones had been crushed and his flesh was splayed out over the road. His mangled, twitching body lay strewn across the road, foul innards oozing into the sand.

A wave of nausea passed over Maria as she sank to her knees. "No, no, no."

"Dear God." Mackenzie began retreating, walking backwards while keeping his eyes on the monster. He quietly ordered Vic to go back inside. Then he grabbed Maria, and hauled her back toward the store. "We have to go, now. It's too late."

Maria stared at the giant beast as it lowered its head to the squashed body of the young man and began to devour it. It sunk its jaws into the man and Maria turned away to throw up. Her vomit spilt over the sand like the young man's blood and she stumbled to her knees. Maria let Mackenzie pull her back and she dropped the plastic bat as he pulled her away. He left her there in the doorway and took a look back. The dinosaur, or whatever it was, had finished eating the two backpackers and stretched up its head, high into the air. It let out a short grunt, and then snapped its head back down. Mackenzie saw its red eyes look at him, and then drift away. For a moment, he thought he understood the beast. When their eyes locked, he could feel it, sense what it wanted. There was no compassion or consciousness in those eyes, just a hunger to kill: it wanted to feed.

Mackenzie followed the monster's head as it slowly turned. The red eyes came to rest in the direction of the upturned bus that was now a smoking wreck. Only then did Mackenzie actually see what it was the monster wanted, what it was looking at.

"Mr. Stepper," hissed Mackenzie. "Get your ass over here, *now*."

The driver's once crisp, light blue shirt was now coated in dust, and patches of it were a dark navy. Sweat made it cling to his body. He took a single step toward the store, suddenly aware that he was very exposed. His boot kicked a small stone, and the monster honed in on the sound. It raised a leg and then brought it down sending waves through the ground that spread out like ripples in a pond.

Mackenzie struggled to stand upright as the monster did it again, sending an even larger shockwave through the ground.

"Mac? What are you...?" Laurel was in the doorway to the store now with an arm around Maria. She was pulling her inside to safety. Mackenzie saw James and Vic at the window, watching intently to see what would happen. Neither of them were helping.

It's like a car accident, thought Mackenzie. It's like they want to see the aftermath of the accident, the broken bodies and the blood.

The thing that loomed over them all suddenly burst into life. It charged toward Mr. Stepper, breathing loudly as it ran. Its snout was covered with blood, and slime and blood dripped from its jaws.

"Mr. Stepper, go for the bus!" Mackenzie knew the old man would never make it back to the store. The monster had a head start on him and the driver's only chance was to hide in the wreckage of the bus.

"Close the door," ordered Mackenzie, and he pointed at Laurel. "Now!"

With concern spreading across her face, she did as he asked, pushing the door closed. Mackenzie had no time to think through what he was doing, but he had no desire to see a third person devoured by the beast. He thought as he ran, hoping he had remembered it right. Taking off toward the store, Mackenzie began to shout, urging the monster to follow him. It had been distracted once before when faced with the two backpackers, and all he needed to do was buy Mr. Stepper a few seconds so that he could find a hiding place.

Mackenzie sprinted around the east wall of the store, side-stepping a refrigerator that had been left out to display a variety of ice-creams and drinks. He could feel the ground shaking, so he knew the monster was still on the move. Was it still going for Mr. Stepper though, or had it changed direction? Was it at his back now, about to smash through the store? Were its jaws hovering above him, ready to take his head off? Mackenzie dare not even glance back. He knew he had little time, only seconds really, and so he kept shouting and running. He had to make it to the rear of the store where the ladder was. If he could just get to the roof, maybe he could find a way out of this mess. He still had his cell in his pocket. Maybe he could reach someone, get a call out that they needed help, *urgent* help.

"Yakazar-yakazaaaar…"

Mackenzie heard the dinosaur's tell-tale calling and knew immediately from the volume that the monster wasn't with him. Mackenzie stumbled as he rounded the corner of the store and slipped over in the dust. He picked himself up, rubbing his dry hands together as his eyes scanned over a pile of rubbish. The whitewashed walls of the store were blinding in the sun, and Mackenzie was trying to locate the ladder which would get him up to the roof. There were flattened cardboard boxes tied up neatly in a pile and another refrigerator that was rusty and broken, its lid on the ground beside it. A Whiptail lizard darted across the discarded lid and scuttled under an empty metal cage, a basic box on wheels that housed a crate of milk cartons and pomegranate juice, turning warm and sour in the sun. On the ground under several layers of dirt, Mackenzie finally spotted the ladder. He raced to pick it up, embracing the warm wood in his hands as he pushed it up against the wall.

"Yakazar-yakazar."

The monster called out again, and the ground stopped shaking. Had Mr. Stepper escaped? Had he found refuge in the remains of his bus? Mackenzie cautiously climbed the old ladder, every step he took causing it to groan and creak like an old house. When he reached the lip of the roof, Mackenzie hauled himself up and over, and he slipped onto the concrete roof with ease. He could see the Kelso Depot building over the other side of the road, its arches and walls still standing, as if nothing unusual had happened, as if it was just waiting patiently for another round of tourists to show off its history to.

Mackenzie crouched low and scuttled over to the far wall. He had to tread carefully, navigating a path around the solar panels that were laid out in a grid formation, leaving little room to maneuver. The sun was shining and shimmering, and as he made his way over to the front of the store, Mackenzie found his eyes watering, so bright was the reflection in the panels. There was heat in them too, and he kept a cautious distance.

Finally, Mackenzie put his hands on a section of wall somewhere near to the front of the store, above the doorway, and he pulled himself up. His pulse was racing and Mackenzie licked his lips. They were dry and cracked, and his head was throbbing with a dull pain. He had no time to think about anything else but how they were going to get rid of the monster. He had to know if Mr. Stepper was safe. He had to know that it wasn't coming for the store where Laurel was sheltering. Mackenzie poked his head up, feeling like a soldier guarding a castle, as if sticking his neck above the parapet might draw flying arrows from an advancing army.

The monster hadn't followed him at all. It had clearly followed Mr. Stepper, and now the thing stood over the bus. Mackenzie watched on as the gargantuan behemoth kicked it, drawing its sharp claws against the bus' metal, and snorting in frustration. There was no sign of Mr. Stepper anywhere. Perhaps he had made it back to the store after all?

With a roar, the creature bent down and picked the bus up in its arms. It lifted it high into the air with ease, as if picking up a child's toy. The monster shook the bus back and forth, sending shards of metal raining down on the ground. A tyre spun off and hit the ground, wheeling away until it came to a stop near the Depot. The bus door blew open and swung violently as the bus was torn apart.

Then Mackenzie saw him.

Hanging on to the driver's wheel was Mr. Stepper. He must have crawled inside the wreckage before the monster had time to get to him. Mackenzie stood up. He intended to shout and stamp his feet and make as much noise as he could to draw the monster away. But what would that achieve? Even if the thing did put the bus down, and Mr. Stepper managed to get away, what then? The monster would be drawn to the store, and there were nine people inside who were all facing a horrible death if the monster didn't stop.

The bus was raised higher in the air as the monster lifted it to eye level. It seemed to be looking into the heart of the bus, searching for its prey. It didn't take long to find it. Mackenzie saw Mr. Stepper try to run to the back of the bus, away from those inquisitive red eyes of the beast, but it was a futile attempt to escape. Mackenzie knew it now. There was no way to evade this thing, no way to escape being hunted down and killed; it was just a fluke it hadn't attacked the store yet, and when it did they were all going to go the same way as the backpackers. Mackenzie felt for the phone in his pocket. He had to at least try to get help. Quite what the emergency responder would say when he told them a giant dinosaur was attacking them in the Mojave Desert would be was debatable. If he had gotten a call like that, he would put it down to kids making a crank call. Still, he had to try.

Punching 911 into his phone, he waited for it to connect and watched as the monster ended Mr. Stepper's life. The bus was thrown down to the ground with such force that the impact left a hole in the ground and sent shockwaves through Mackenzie's body. The bus was almost flattened, and as the monster pummelled it into the ground, the gas tank exploded sending a huge ball of flame up into the creature's face. It reared back, bellowing out in pain, its face scorched and blackened, and though he knew it meant certain death for Mr. Stepper, Mackenzie couldn't help but smile. Finally something had hurt it. Finally, no matter how small a victory it was, Mackenzie felt a sense of hope. It could be hurt. It was still flesh and blood after all. The monster wasn't invincible.

Realizing that his call wasn't connecting, Mackenzie looked at his phone. There was no signal.

"Damn it." Mackenzie climbed up onto the lip of the roof, above the guttering, and stuck his arm up as high as it would go, hoping he might find some reception. The store's roof was trembling, but he ignored it. The burning bus was of no significance now. The most important thing he could do was to find help, and alert the whole world that they had a new terrorist in the country; one with big fucking teeth. He stared at the phone's screen intently, and then he saw it. One bar appeared, indicating he had got something.

"Fuck, yeah." Mackenzie slowly lowered his phone, dialled again, and then put his arm back up to where he had found the signal. The shaking continued, stronger than before, but

Mackenzie ignored it. The monster was probably burrowing back underground, waiting for the next fool who wanted to run outside into its territory. Mackenzie was watching the phone, making sure he didn't lose the signal. Once the call connected, he could shout, make himself heard, and demand help for them. He felt better now that he was doing something. He felt sorry for those who had died, but there didn't have to be any more deaths. He could...

A shadow fell over him, enveloping his very soul. The shaking increased, and he stumbled back off the lip of the roof, aware that the shadow had brought with it cold, stinking air that reeked of malevolence. He lowered his arm and looked straight up into the eyes of the monster. Huge gobbets of thick saliva dripped from the creature's jaws, viscid blood oozing from the blackened sores on its face where boils wept yellow pus. Mackenzie noticed one of its eyelids had been seared off in the explosion. The moment of satisfaction at its obvious pain was quickly replaced by panic. The monster took a step forward and was above him then, towering over the store.

Mackenzie stumbled backward. Where could he go? Where could he run? There was nowhere to go. He was trapped and he knew it. If he tried to run for the ladder, he would get no more than two feet before the monster scooped him up and ate him alive. His skin broke out in a cold sweat, and Mackenzie looked at the phone in his hand. The single bar was still there on the screen. The call had gone through! Mackenzie brought the phone slowly to his ear, watching as the monster came closer. It leered over him, and Mackenzie felt like the thing was smiling. It was as if a salacious grin had spread across the monster's features as it prepared to devour him.

Mackenzie took a step backward and tripped over a solar panel. He fell painfully, slicing open his left hand on one of the panels and banging his head as he landed on the roof. As the monster peered down at him, its deadly teeth coming closer and closer, Mackenzie brought the phone to his ear once more.

"Hello?"

CHAPTER 9

Inside the front of the store, Maria slumped to the floor crestfallen and Laurel collapsed beside her. The adrenalin was still pumping through Maria's body. The store was hot, but not as hot as it was outside where the harsh sun was drying the blood and vomit quickly. The air tasted warm as Maria took it in. She was sweating profusely. Her shirt was soaked through with perspiration and she felt embarrassed that she had thrown up. What had happened out there was horrific. She had never seen or experienced anything like it. Everything was out of control, and her head felt dizzy. It was too much. She needed a minute's contemplation to gather her thoughts, to get just a moment of peace so that she could reconcile what she had just seen with what she believed the world was.

"Did you hear it, Vic? It was like a cat eating a bird. You could hear the bones crunching." James was well back from the windows, but had watched what had occurred outside with a beer in his hand and a glint in his eye. It was better than any TV show.

Now that it was almost over, he still couldn't take his eyes off the grisly sight. Mackenzie had run around back, and Mr. Stepper had taken refuge inside the bus. Quite how he thought he was going to escape the monster he didn't know, but James was fascinated to see how it played out. When the monster had devoured the female tourist, its powerful jaws had easily crunched and smashed the bones as if they were made of rice paper. James had been reminded of the Craps table back in Vegas where he had flirted briefly with lady luck and lost. It sounded like dice rattling in a tumbler when the monster ate. James was only glad the girl had died quickly. Her family would probably never know what happened to her, and there was nothing left to bury. The man she had been with too was nothing more than a bloody smear in the dirt. It wasn't that James wanted people to die, but there was really nothing he could do about it. Plus, he thought, better them than him.

Maria got up and walked over to James before slapping him sharply. James, caught by surprise, gasped as the sting in his cheek grew. He took a step back from Maria, the red anger in her face matching the sting of embarrassment in James'.

"Come on, Maria, there's no need for that," said Vic as he put himself in between them, eager for things to not develop any further. "James, you're okay. You're okay, right?"

Maria's hand was trembling. She couldn't even remember the last time she had hit anyone. It wasn't something she enjoyed, but he had deserved it, of that she was sure. "One more word out of him and I'll feed him to that Goddamn thing myself. That poor girl out there deserves better. We all do. You need to teach your friend some manners, Vic."

"Maria, leave it, he's not worth it," said Laurel.

Maria wiped the corners of her mouth. The taste of bitter bile soured her throat and it was not something she had tasted in many years. She lowered her head and went back to Laurel. "Sorry, I just…I just couldn't ignore it. *Like a cat*? What does he think, that this is a game?"

Laurel said nothing. She was worried about Mackenzie and what he thought he was doing out there. The monster was still outside, stomping around in the dirt, looking for them. It was as tall as a skyscraper and probably weighed a thousand tons. It didn't feel like they could do much against it at all. It was like an ant taking on an elephant. She put a hand on Maria's shoulder. "It'll be okay. It'll be fine." She sucked in a deep breath and let it out slowly. "It has to be."

James coughed. "When we get out of here, I'm reporting you for assault. You fucking Americans think you run the world." James had been shocked by the slap, but now that Maria wasn't in his face, he had calmed down. He had been able to think things through coolly. The others were outside, or in the back, and now with him and Vic it was just Maria and Laurel. The odds had evened. He grinned and went back to the window, watching as the beast made its way toward the bus. "Maria, what is your problem? Not getting any? Your husband not up to the job anymore?"

Laurel had no patience for James either and could see that James was trying to rile Maria up again. They were more concerned with what was going on outside, yet all James wanted to do was cause an argument. Lives were in danger, Chris was seriously hurt, and she didn't know how they were going to get out of this. Two people had just died and Mackenzie was still out there. Yet James was trying to bait Maria back into a fight. She looked at Maria who told her with a mere nod of the head that it wasn't worth getting into it with him. "James, just shut your mouth. How many times do you have to be told?" Laurel winked at Maria. They weren't going to get sucked into childish games. "Just sit down or make yourself useful and go help my husband."

"Or what? Who the fuck are you to tell me what to do? I don't know you."

"James, you did kind of ask for it," said Vic defensively. "I mean, sometimes you just don't know when to shut your mouth. We've talked about your temper. Remember what happened last time? Just remember the breathing exercises that we—"

"Fuck the breathing exercises, Vic. I'm sick of it. I'm sick of you. I thought we…look, just leave me alone. Nice to know whose side you're on." James pointed at Maria and Laurel. "You two just made my list." He thought of forcing them outside, letting the dinosaur do his work for him, but he wasn't sure if Vic would help or hinder him. This whole situation had turned into a right shit storm. "I'm going to the bathroom. Then I'm going to see if they got that radio working. Okay, Maria, fine, we'll do it your way. I can wait this out all day long." James rubbed his cheek for effect, even though the pain had long gone. "And when the police show up, you're leaving here in handcuffs."

James left and ordered Vic to come with him. Following meekly, Vic mumbled an apology to Maria for James' behaviour, and then the two women were alone.

"I can't stand this," said Maria as she approached the door. The monster was astride the bus now, sniffing it, trying to figure it out. "Where are they? Where did they go? What are we going to do?"

Laurel bit her lip before answering quietly. "I don't know. I know Mac will do what he can, but..." She joined Maria at the glass door, watching as the monster began kicking the bus.

"I've a gun under the counter," said Maria suddenly. "I didn't want anyone to know in case things got out of hand. I guess we're past that point, huh? It's just a Crosman Semi-Auto. Nothing much, but I thought I should have one, just in case, you know? I read too many stories of serial killers hitch-hiking their way across the state, picking off lonely women." Maria managed a small laugh. "I'm quite sure they go for younger women than me. Anyway, I've only a couple of rounds of ammo. Never thought I'd really need it to be honest with you."

"You think it's going to work against that?" asked Laurel. She couldn't imagine it penetrating the dinosaur's thick skin, let alone hurting it. "It's not going to do much damage to that monster outside."

"It's not the monsters outside I'm so worried about." Maria turned to face Laurel. "We need to watch out for each other."

"Well, I've never even held a gun, so I think we should keep it just between us for now. You can handle it, right?" asked Laurel. "And when did you go around hitting people? Not that I'm saying James didn't deserve it."

"I'm sorry. I just snapped. I suppose I should apologize to him, but I'm fairly confident he would just dismiss it. I worked ER for a few years, met a lot of odd people, a lot of hurt people, and a fair few dangerous ones too. That boy is messed up. One who slipped through the cracks. There's something about him I don't like."

"Fair enough." Laurel looked around the shop. The counter was full of boxes of chocolate bars and snacks. There was one row of shelving left intact at the center of the shop which was lined with a variety of books and maps. The cooler in the corner near the corner was stocked full of cans and bottles of assorted sodas. She looked at the dining area and the upturned tables. The store must have looked good when it was running normally. Now, after all the fighting, the tremors and the monster outside rattling it constantly, it was a mess. "You know we can't stay here long." Laurel thought about her daughter, about how Amy was coping. She didn't know if the monster was isolated to the desert, if it was the only one that had appeared. Morbid thoughts swam around her head of what might be happening elsewhere, dark thoughts that she couldn't allow to gather momentum. She just hoped San Diego was unaffected.

There were echoing noises above her head, clattering sounds that were like footsteps, and she glanced up.

"I bet that's Mac," said Maria. "He got up on the roof." She whirled around to look at the bus, hoping to find Mr. Stepper running back to the store. Instead, she saw the monster had picked up the bus and was in the process of destroying it.

"Holy shit. I think Mr. Stepper's in there," said Laurel. "Should we—?"

The bus smashed down into the ground, and then the monster set about tearing it apart.

"We need to get back. It's not safe here." Maria took Laurel's hand. "If Mac's up there, he'll be okay. We can—"

The bus exploded, engulfing the monster in a fireball. The warm blast shattered the store's front windows, and Maria and Laurel fell to the floor, covered in tiny shards of glass. They screamed as they scrambled to get up and away from the open windows.

Laurel shook the glass from her hair and stared outside at the black smoke rising up into the blue sky from the remains of the bus. "Mac? Mac, are you there?"

Maria began dragging Laurel away, pulling on her arm, shouting at her to get to the back store room. Laurel tried to refuse. She had to know that Mackenzie was all right. "Mac, answer me!"

Laurel watched, terrified, as the monster began lumbering toward the store, leaving the smashed smoldering remains of the bus behind. She lost sight of the giant creature's head, and then its upper body disappeared as it got closer. All she saw were its thick strong legs getting larger and larger, filling in the now empty windows, blocking out the sun like an eclipse.

"Laurel, move it!" Maria finally got Laurel moving, but only an inch at a time. With the rate at which they were moving, the monster would be upon both them and the store long before they had moved into the relative safety of the store room. Maria didn't want to give the thing any excuse to get into the store. They had to be quiet and hide. "Mac will be okay. We can help him another way. There's another way up to the roof. Just come with me, please?"

Laurel nodded and let Maria lead her back, away from the advancing monster.

* * *

"Akecheta," hissed Maria. "We need to get Mackenzie back inside, quickly. I need your help." Maria told Laurel to wait and ran her hands through her short hair. "In the corner over there is an access shaft. I haven't used it in years and the only ladder I have is outside. You think you can help me get up there?"

"Hold on, what the hell is going on? What was that explosion?" asked James. He was sat on an upturned bucket drinking a beer. "If that monster is right outside, I hardly think exposing ourselves by opening up a hatch right above our heads is a good move."

Maria didn't have time to argue with him, much less debate the merits of whether they should rescue Mackenzie or not. She already knew what James wanted: self-preservation. All he was interested in was riding this out and saving his own neck.

"Akecheta, Myles, can you help me? We'll see if we can get the roof access open, get Mac down from there before that thing sees him."

Myles cast James a dirty look, and then asked Michele to stay with Alyce. Michele had finally got the radio working and set it up on a small table by the door. Myles wanted to fill the rest in on what they had heard, but it was clear from the urgency in Maria's voice that any updates would have to wait.

"Be careful," pleaded Michele before letting her husband go.

Akecheta started pulling boxes out of the way. "Mr. Stepper. Is he…?"

Maria nodded. She tried not to think about it, but she knew he was gone. There was no way he survived the destruction of the bus.

"Damn it," muttered Myles. He helped Akecheta move some boxes out of the way, trying to ignore the fact that James and Vic were doing nothing to help. He knew there was no point in asking the two men. Any conversation with them seemed to end in an argument. He looked at Akecheta and, ensuring he was out of earshot of his daughter, asked if anyone would miss them if the bus didn't return or check-in at a certain time.

"We're not due back to Baker until six this evening. Nobody's going to figure out we're missing for a long time. Right now our focus is just staying alive. I'm not even thinking beyond surviving the next five minutes."

As they threw boxes aside, the store continued to shake. It was evident that the monster was close.

"You knew Mr. Stepper well?" asked Myles.

Akecheta closed his eyes briefly, and then looked intently at Myles. "I worked with him for years. He was a good man. He served his country more than once and was good to everyone we took around the area. Never had a single complaint about him; only compliments. He was a man of few words, but I shall miss him. I don't want to have to mourn anyone else today, so let's get this done."

Myles helped Akecheta drag one of the shelves over to the roof's access hatch. There was little room to maneuver, and they had to negotiate their way around piles of boxes that seemed to clutter up every spare inch of floor space. There were no windows and only one fluorescent strip light above to see by, and despite the cold gloom, both of them were sweating.

As they dragged the shelf over the floor, with Maria and Laurel trying to move things out of their way, Myles noticed for the first time the various refrigerators that lined one wall of the room. The center of the room had one tall shelf still standing, stacked full of items for the shop: boxes of canned food, emergency first-aid kits, camping equipment, postcards, pens and a variety of souvenirs.

"Hold it steady," said Akecheta, snapping Myles' attention back to the job in hand. "I'll go."

The ground rumbled and rolled, as if constantly moving and shifting. Myles and Maria held the metal shelving firmly, and Akecheta quickly climbed it, as if he were no more than a nimble boy scout climbing a tree. He banged three times on the hatch above him.

"Mac? Mr. Brown, you there?" Akecheta paused, and looked down at Maria. They waited for what seemed years for an answer. Surely he had felt the vibrations? Had he not heard the shouting outside?

Laurel saw concern in Akecheta's eyes and she couldn't help but to call out. "Mac, come on, open up. Please, Mac, just come down."

"Laurel, why don't you go check on Chris," said Maria. She knew that although Chris was unconscious, Laurel needed distracting. It was clear that Mac might be in trouble.

"No, I'm waiting here. I'm not going anywhere without Mac."

"Mac, open up," said Akecheta again as he banged with his fist on the roof. The metal shelving shook, but he kept his balance, and Maria and Myles did their best to keep it upright.

"You think he's okay?" whispered Laurel.

"He'll be fine," said Maria as she gripped the cold metal shelves tighter. She lowered her voice and looked at Laurel with steely determination. "He'll be fine. It'll all be fine. It *has* to be."

"What about Mr. Stepper and those two kids? What about the bus? What's going to happen to...?"

"I don't know, Laurel, okay? Just hold this thing steady, and stop asking me questions that you know I can't possibly answer."

Laurel looked away furtively, and Maria instantly regretted snapping at her. The woman was just worried about her husband. It had been so long since Tony had passed that she had forgotten what it was like to care about someone so deeply.

"Look, I'm sorry, I didn't mean..." A deep rumble from underground turned into a wave that rippled across the store's floor, and threatened to upset the shelves entirely. A huge roar from above sent jitters down Maria's body and she had to hold onto the shelving with all her strength as the vibrations threatened to topple it over.

"You got it?" asked Akecheta as he braced himself between the upper shelf and the roof.

Myles nodded. "We're good."

"Hurry up, Akecheta. This thing is bucking wilder than a horny bull in rodeo season."

Maria tried to catch Laurel's eyes, but she was avoiding her, looking across the room at Alyce and Michele. Maria knew she had spoken out of order, but apologies could come later. For the moment, it was all they could do to keep the shelving upright, and she was worried about what was going on up on the roof. Maria was genuinely afraid that the dinosaur, the monster, or whatever it was, was about to come crashing through the store's roof and kill them all. When she looked at the worry on Laurel's face, and the concern in Akecheta's brown eyes, there was nothing there to reassure her that her fears were misplaced. It was what she couldn't see that scared her the most. It was what was outside causing the ground to shake that really bit into her and made terror run through her blood.

Daylight flooded into the room, the square access hole above Akecheta's head opening up suddenly. The hatch was lifted up into the air, and sunlight burst into the room, penetrating the gloom. Maria was momentarily blinded as the bright sunlight punctuated her vision and she had to look away to allow her eyes to adjust. When she looked back, Akecheta was gone, already up through the hatch and onto the roof.

A shadow slowly spread across the hole in the roof, bringing back the desolation and gloom. Maria and Myles looked at each other as they began to hear scuffling noises from above.

"Laurel, hold this," said Myles. Without waiting for her to grab hold of the shelving, he began to climb up.

"Myles, get down here, now." Maria's arms and muscles ached. Her grip was weakening as the shelving tried to wrench itself free from her grasp as the building shook. She watched Laurel replace Myles, and too quickly, Myles was gone up through the small opening onto the roof, exposed to the monster.

Suddenly, the vibrations stopped, the building settled, and there was nothing but the sound of her own quick breath and the radio in the background. Maria's ears rang loudly with the silence, and she lowered her arms, her muscles and tendons grateful for the release, however short.

A thud, followed by a hollow banging noise, and then the silence was replaced by the familiar yet unsettling bellowing of their dinosaur. Maria looked at Laurel as suddenly a spray of red mist came down through the square hatchway, showering them both in fine warm droplets of blood. It splattered their faces, entered their open, shocked mouths, and dribbled through their hair like a strawberry shampoo. The coppery smell of the blood invaded Maria's senses, and the taste made her gag.

Laurel looked up at the hatch. "Mac!" she screamed. "Mac?"

CHAPTER 10

"Hey, honey, what's going down?" John spotted Amy through the throng of passengers exiting San Diego's Lindbergh Field airport, and began to walk toward her, the bunch of yellow roses tucked under his arm.

Amy smiled and gave him a hug. "John, come on, that's lame. I'm not a kid anymore." They had developed a ritual over the years that her father still clung to, despite the growing distance between them. He would ask her what's going down, she would ask him what's up, and then he would pull a face that she would inevitably laugh at.

John hugged his daughter close, relishing her warmth and smell. It had been too long since they had seen each other. "You'll always be a kid to me."

As they parted, Amy took the roses and looked at him. He was tired. He looked older than her last visit. Though that was literally true, it looked as if he had aged in the last few months. There was excitement in his eyes, and she knew he was pleased to see her. But she detected a hint of sadness too, and all of a sudden she wanted to keep the ritual going.

"Anyway, what's up?" Amy grinned as her father's eyes lit up.

"Nothing. Everything's sideways." John furrowed his brow, stuck out his tongue and pulled his ears out.

Amy genuinely giggled. It wasn't so much the face that made her laugh, but the fact that he still tried; he was still there for her, still trying to show her how much he loved her.

"All right, weirdo, let's get out of here." Amy reached for her trolley case, but John beat her to it.

"I've got it. Car's out front."

As they left the airport, Amy looked at him. Had he lost weight too? He still wore his uniform from the zoo, and it hung off him as if it was a size too big.

John caught her looking at him. "I know, the uniform, right? Sorry, but I had to come here straight from work."

Amy just nodded and said nothing. They had a strange relationship, but they made it work. She knew he was technically her father, but she always thought of Mackenzie as her dad. He had brought her up and was the only father she had known. John was more like an uncle, or a friend. She was pleased they knew each other. So many of her friends' parents were divorced, and it felt like so many of them were torn between choosing sides. Amy knew she didn't have the most conventional family, but who did these days? They made it work, and everything was cordial. It wasn't like her biological parents had ended their relationship terribly, it just wasn't meant to be. Amy had come along when they were still young, and they'd been honest with her from the start.

"Here we go," said John. He opened the trunk and put Amy's bags inside.

"What happened to the Ferrari?" asked Amy as she climbed into the passenger seat. The thought of John driving a Ferrari was amusing to both of them, and they chuckled together. John lurched from one old car to the next, only changing when they completely died. He didn't have the money for a new car, and Amy knew that even if he did, he probably wouldn't buy one. He would rather save the money for her trips to see him. She smirked when she saw the mess on the back seat. It was littered with pizza boxes, old books and dirty boots.

"The Ferrari?" John slipped behind the wheel and turned the key to start his battered old Toyota. The engine whined, and then gently wheezed into life as John revved it up. "Swapped it for this old baby," he said, slapping the dash. "Thought I'd upgrade." John winked at Amy, and then pulled out slowly, taking them away from the airport and into the city.

"Shame you couldn't get a clean one," said Amy as she glanced again at the back seat where she had placed the roses.

"Yeah, I was going to clean it up, but I just haven't had time this week. I pulled a double-shift all week. A couple of guys took leave, so I thought I may as well. The extra will come in handy."

Amy stared out of the window at the blazing sunshine and snapped her sunglasses on. She wound down the window to feel the breeze on her face. "You know, we don't have to do a million things when I come. Sometimes it's nice to just chill out and hang with you. I don't want you blowing all your money on me."

"On you?" John pulled the car onto the freeway. "Oh, the extra's not for you. I was going to spend it all on hookers."

Amy burst out laughing. "Gross! John, don't say things like that."

John wished he could get Amy laughing on tape. It was the most beautiful sound ever. He had long ago given up on getting her to call him dad. Mackenzie was her father and John was more like an outsider now. There was no way to change the past, and so he took what he could. As he drove, he stole quick glances at her. She was growing up and not the kid anymore that he liked to think of her as. Her blonde hair was long now, flowing over her shoulders, and she was undeniably pretty. In a couple of years, the boys were going to be all over her, if they weren't already.

"So, you seeing anyone?" he asked.

"Shit, John, why don't you just ask me straight? Stop being so subtle."

"And why don't you stop avoiding answering the question. I'll take that as a yes, then?"

Amy sighed. "Well…" She wound down the window some more. The traffic was thick, slowing them down, and she wished she had taken an earlier flight in. "Not really."

"So what's his name?"

"John, it's nothing serious. Honestly."

"Fair enough, I won't interrogate you anymore." John knew Amy didn't want to talk about boys with him. Heck, she probably didn't want to talk about boys to anyone but her friends. Still, he couldn't help but be concerned. "Just tell me one thing. Is he a good guy?"

Amy pulled on her safety belt, trying to pull it away from her chest. She was getting hot and sweaty, and the belt was chafing her shoulder. "Yes, John, he's a good guy. Don't worry, I'm not about to ruin my life and get pregnant before I turn eighteen."

"Okay then."

As the car was suddenly filled with silence, Amy realized she had just said completely the wrong thing. Getting pregnant and ruining her life was just what her mother had done, and John had played his part in that. "Shit, sorry, I didn't mean—"

"Music?" John flicked on the radio. Immediately, a country song began belting out at full volume, and he turned the volume down. "Oops."

"Country, huh?" Amy could feel her cheeks blushing, and felt awkward. Time to change the subject.

"I don't usually have passengers, so I tend to sing along while I'm driving. Sorry, it's just an old radio. If you want to play anything on your iPhone thingy, you'll have to wait until we get home."

"Yeah, you finally get rid of your old record player?"

"Are you kidding? Why would I get rid of it? No, I just meant I really like this song."

John began humming along, and Amy knew he would never change. It was like he was living in the past. He refused to upgrade his old record collection, refused to get cable, and ate too many takeaways and TV dinners. She knew he still thought of her as a child too. The truth was, she was scared of what was coming. Next year, she would have to decide about where to go to college. That might mean fewer visits to see him, and it wasn't something she wanted to talk about. This trip she could still be his little girl, instead of the seventeen year old thinking about boys and her future.

"How's Laurel doing? Mac still looking after her?"

"Yeah, they're good. The business did really well this last year."

"That's great. Maybe that means you'll get more vacations over here."

"Yeah, maybe." Amy could tell what was coming. She had only just arrived, but already John was fishing for when she would next visit. She really had no idea what the future held, and decided to change the subject.

"Can we go to the zoo?"

"Now?" John looked at her with his eyebrows raised. "I thought we'd swing by mine so I can get changed and we can hit the town."

"Well, you're still in your uniform anyway, so why not now? We've got all week to go out."

John sighed. "Amy, I've only just left work, I didn't really want to be going back so soon, you know? It's like I live there these days."

Amy shrugged. "Fine, I guess we can go another day."

John detected true disappointment in her voice, and knew he couldn't say no to her. "No, you're right. Let's go now. Like you said, I'm still in my gear, so why not. You know, they're expanding the enclosure for the lions. You want to see? It's not open to the public for a few weeks yet, but I've still got my magic keys. Can open any door I want."

Amy smiled, happy to be going to the zoo, and relieved she had taken his mind off when she would be able to visit next. "Step on it, John, you're driving like an old woman. Those lions haven't got all day."

Laughing, John quickly changed direction and took them to the zoo. He was a senior janitor, but it was still an important job, and he enjoyed his work. In the summer months, it was busy, and he reasoned they had enough time during the week for what he had planned. He was going to take Amy shopping, out to restaurants, and spoil her every second he could. He didn't get enough time with her, though he couldn't complain about it. That was just the way it was. But now that she was here, he didn't want to take his eyes off her for one second.

When they arrived at the zoo, it was already nearly full, and John took them in the staff entrance. There were queues formed outside the front entrance, and Amy was pleased they were able to bypass the hordes trying to get in. John organized a visitor's pass for her, and then they were in. John took her to the staffroom first, so he could grab a cold drink. The room was large, but empty and quiet. Framed photographs of the animals adorned the walls, and there was a hum of noise from beyond, indicating the masses just outside.

"You want a Coke?" John asked as he fed small coins into the vending machine.

"Diet, please."

After John had paid the ransom and freed the cans of drink from their prison, he handed one to Amy. "Right, you want to start with anything in particular? Pandas? Crocs? I remember when you were about ten, and it was all I could do to get you away from the chimps. That was all you wanted to see."

Amy smiled at the memory. "You know, I think I'd like to see the lions and this new enclosure. I want to—"

The vending machine began to vibrate, and suddenly the whole room joined it. Amy grabbed onto John's arm as, for a few seconds, everything shook. The white plastic tables and chairs, the picture frames and the cutlery; Amy felt herself going weak at the knees and looked at John for answers.

"It's passed," he said, as the shaking stopped. He put an arm around his daughter. "Don't worry. We've had a few tremors lately. It's nothing to worry about. See? It's stopped."

Amy could tell the room had stopped shaking, but she hadn't. She clung onto John as they left the room.

"That happen a lot?"

"Not usually, but like I say, these past few weeks we've had a few. I'm sure it's nothing." John swiped his pass through a lock and opened a gray steel door. They emerged from a clinical white corridor into glorious sunshine. The park was heaving, and Amy saw families and children everywhere. There were tourists too, and nobody seemed bothered by the tremor. Although it had unnerved her, she trusted John. If he wasn't bothered, and nobody else was, then she was just going to have to forget it and enjoy the day.

"Right then, where are these lions?"

"This way, my lady." John kept his arm around Amy as they walked through the park. He could see she was still worried, and he left his arm draped over her shoulder more for reassurance than protection. He liked the park when it was busy like this. It was much better than when it was closed. There was a certain vibrancy to the place when it was open. The people here were all happy, fascinated by the animals. He had to admit it. Even though he didn't earn as much money as he would like, he had no idea what else he would do.

They passed a cart selling hot dogs, and a queue of small children all wearing identical yellow hats. Amy watched as they lined up in pairs, holding hands, and their teachers instructed them to wait patiently. She liked people watching as much as visiting the animals. Seeing the wonder on the children's faces, and hearing their chatter, she soon forgot the tremor.

They approached the lion enclosure. Three lions were sitting idly in the shade of a large tree. They looked content, peaceful; a large fence had been erected at the back of the enclosure, painted green to blend in with the environment, and John told her how they were expanding, making it twice as big so the lions had more room. He took them through a side door with his magic keys, around the back and past where the lions slept, into the enclosure behind the fence. There was a small shed where the workmen kept their tools, and John pointed out the new viewing platform that was being built.

"Are we safe here? They can't get in, can they?"

"No chance. There is literally no way through. Not yet. When it's ready, they'll pull that fence down, but until then it's strictly off limits." They walked into the center of the enclosure on freshly laid grass, to where a series of boulders and rocks had been arranged. The uppermost rock had been flattened out, providing a natural place for the lions to be lazy and would be clearly seen.

"It's good, huh?" asked John as he picked up a discarded hammer. "You know, I'm always on at those guys to pick their shit up."

Amy walked across to the temporary fencing and placed a hand on it. It was solid, and stretched the length of the enclosure. On the other side, she could hear the crowds of children gawking at the lions, who themselves were quiet. She knew it was too hot in the afternoon for them to be active. Turning back to John, she caught him looking at her. "When's it going to be open?"

"Couple of months. Grand opening is scheduled for August I think. You should come. They're going to have a whole day of events planned, the real red carpet treatment. I'm sure I can get you in."

Amy sipped her drink. "We'll see. I'm pretty busy at school."

John smiled, although Amy could see it was a poor attempt to hide his disappointment. She put her hand back on the fence, and it seemed to pulsate beneath her fingers. What started out as a gentle throb suddenly developed into a rocking motion that spread from the fence to the ground she was standing on.

"John, why is…?"

She turned around, and then it was as if the very ground beneath them had turned to mud. She saw John try to run toward her, but he was thrown off balance and sent crashing to the earth. The huge mountain of boulders close to him began to move, and smaller ones from the top started falling down around him.

"John!" Amy screamed. She needed to warn him of the rocks that threatened to collapse on top of him, and yet she was unable to say anything more than call his name. As soon as she tried to walk, her feet were taken away from her. The earth bucked and rolled underneath her, and she fell down painfully. A terrible wrenching sound filled her ears, and she scrambled onto her knees, listening as the solid fence behind her was pulled out from its foundations and ripped away like it was nothing but flimsy paper.

Amy was bounced up and down on the ground, and she wished John would come to her. She couldn't see him anymore, and it was hard to maintain her balance as the earth churned beneath her. She fell again, and again, only to pick herself up as she tried to crawl over to John. The awful sound of the fence being ripped open stopped and was followed by a deep mournful wailing sound that echoed all around her, as if it came from something under the ground. The rolling motion began to subside, and Amy caught her breath. She hadn't even realized it, but she had been holding her breath the whole time. Now that whatever was happening seemed to be coming to an end, she drew in deep lungful's of oxygen, her brain demanding her body get more and more. Her arms and legs were shaking, her lips trembling as she fought back the urge to panic and run. She had to make sure John was okay. The once aesthetic pile of boulders had been reduced to rubble, and the beautiful manicured grass was now churned up into a muddy field that looked more suitable for playing football.

Between the gentle tears that ran from her eyes, she slowly crawled over to the place where she had last seen him. "John, are you there? Are you okay?" The ground was soft, and she had to dig her fingernails in to get purchase. She climbed over a huge boulder now covered with loose dirt, and then she saw him.

"Amy?"

He pulled himself to his feet, brushed himself down, and then John reached out a hand. Amy took it and they held each other saying nothing. There were screams in the background, desperate cries for help coming from within the park and beyond. Sirens were already present in the distance, and there was a muffled booming sound of something exploding.

"Amy, are you all right?" John looked her up and down. His girl was okay.

"I'm fine. Look at your head. What happened?" Amy ran her fingers gently across John's forehead.

"It's nothing. One of those flying rocks caught me, but I managed to avoid getting squashed completely."

"Shit, you were lucky. I just... What was that? Another tremor?"

John frowned, relieved that Amy was okay. "That was more than just a tremor. Must've been a big one. I've never felt an earthquake like that. Listen, we need to get out of here, out of the park. It must..." John suddenly noticed the fence behind Amy.

"What is it?" asked Amy, seeing the terror spread across John's face.

"Fuck."

John pulled Amy around behind him, stepping in front of her as the first lion advanced upon them. "Stay close," he whispered.

Amy peered over John's shoulder and saw a lioness moving slowly towards them, staring at them intently. Another slightly smaller lioness was behind it looking on curiously, and the third lion, a male, was watching intently from the side. Amy could see the cracked glass where the children had been so eagerly looking at the magnificent animals. Thankfully, it still held in place.

"John, what do we do?" Amy didn't know if she should run, or stay still. Wasn't there something about playing dead? Amy had to admit she knew little about these sorts of animals. Lions were behind cages or on the TV screens, not walking across an open field with their eyes locked on you.

"Just walk backward very slowly," said John, not taking his eyes off the lioness. "The exit's about twenty feet behind us."

A plume of dirt suddenly erupted to the side of the enclosure nearest the broken glass, and the ground began shaking violently. It was like standing atop an exploding volcano as the earth flew up into the air, and John took his eyes off the advancing lioness as he saw something emerge from the ground, something far more terrifying than the lions.

Amy screamed, and John realized the lioness was caught in two minds: attack or run. It's once glossy coat was now covered in dirt, and it turned to see what John was looking at.

It could only be described as a monster. It was like nothing John had ever seen; certainly like nothing they had at the zoo. It clambered from beneath the ground and stood over them all, easily over fifty feet high. Its huge body dwarfed the oak tree, and John barely had time to take in its glory, its powerful legs and arms, before he reached the thing's head. It was monstrous, as big as a car, with sharp teeth that seemed to go on forever.

The lioness ran. John knew it was protecting itself, its own territory. He also knew it stood no chance. The lioness managed to grab onto one of the thing's legs, and it sunk its teeth in as it clawed at the skin. There was a ferocity about it that John hadn't seen before. The animals had always been placid and were well trained to stay in their enclosure. The lioness was large, and if it had decided to attack John like that, he had no doubt he would've been dead in seconds. Yet this towering creature hardly seemed to notice. With a deft flick of its legs, it sent the lioness flying through the air. The poor animal crashed into the solid trunk of the oak tree where it fell to the ground and remained motionless, either dead or unconscious.

Amy pulled on John's arm. "What the fuck is this? What the fuck is going on?"

John whirled around and pointed to the exit. "Run, Amy. Run and don't stop. I'll be right behind you."

As Amy ran, more terrified than she had ever been in her life, she heard the growling of the lions, and the ground trembling once more as the giant moved. No other thought ran through her mind other than escape. She had to get out of the zoo, away from whatever this thing was.

John still held the hammer in his hands and knew he couldn't let the animals be massacred like that. The other two had converged on one point, in between him and the monster. They were poised, ready to strike, and the monster appeared not to care. As the male lion rushed at it, the abomination lifted a foot and then slammed it down on the advancing cat. The lion was killed instantly, its strong frame smashed like precious china. John saw the blood splatter as the monster retracted its foot, and the lion was gone, now just a lifeless husk, shattered bones and blood indicating where it had made its final stand.

"No, leave them alone!" John ran, waving the hammer above his head. He was more scared than he wanted to let on, but with Amy at the exit, he had to try something. If he could at least distract the thing, maybe the third lion would retreat. Surely, it would see it was no match for this thing? John had no intention of putting himself in harms' way. He figured he was too small for this thing to worry about, but he might be able to at least give the lion a chance.

A giant claw suddenly reached down from the sky and scooped up the lion. It fought back, scratching and biting, struggling and tearing its way through the monster's claws. Yet the thing took no notice and dropped the lion into its mouth. With one gulp, it was gone.

John stopped running. He had failed. What kind of animal could swallow a lion whole? It had all been over so quickly. The lions, one of the most fearsome predators that walked the Earth, had been dismissed as if they were nothing but common house-flies. What was this thing? He hated to admit it, but it almost resembled a dinosaur. Had he gone insane? Was this all a hallucination? Amy's scream pierced the air, and he knew this was no dream.

"Amy, get out. Get out, now!"

John felt the ground move, and then the lumbering creature above him turned. Had it heard Amy's scream? There was so much noise coming from the park that John had hoped the strange dinosaur would move on, or perhaps be scared and forced back underground. The expression on the monster's face told him it was anything but scared. In fact, it looked...hungry.

As the monster turned, it dropped its head slightly, opened its bloody jaws, and let out an almighty roar. The noise that emerged from the thing's throat was so loud and deep that it felt real enough to touch. John felt his whole body vibrate, and he dropped the hammer. What was he thinking? He should've made sure Amy was safe before he tried to help the animals. Now the thing knew they were here, and it didn't sound like it wanted to do anything but make sure they were as dead as the lions.

Amy screamed again, and John turned to her. He dropped the hammer and began to run. She stood by the exit door. Her face, though still beautiful, was suddenly old. She wasn't a girl anymore, but a young woman. She was scared too, terrified. John looked at her as she receded from view. He kept kicking his legs, trying to run to her, but he was kicking at thin air. It was so quick that he didn't even have time to register what was happening. It was only as Amy began to get smaller that his brain accepted he was being lifted up into the air. It was odd seeing Amy from above, as if he were flying. She was his beautiful girl, always the little girl chuckling at his bad jokes and funny faces. He tried to shout to her, to tell her to run away, but he found nothing came out of his mouth. There was too much pressure on his throat. It was as if he was in a vice and it was crushing his body, squeezing all the oxygen out of his lungs. He saw Amy open her mouth, her face full of terror, but he didn't hear anything. There was just silence.

John heard nothing but the sound of his own pulse throbbing in his head. It was odd, but he didn't really feel frightened. It was almost inevitable, and his brain had no choice but to accept it: he was going to die.

The sky abruptly turned dark, and John felt the creature's grip around him loosen. Blood dripped over John's face and he understood then that it wasn't the sky turning dark, but that he was upside down and looking now at the creature. Its head was glorious, and its eyes deep red. John took it in, amazed at what he was looking at so closely. He could hear Amy's screaming but was mesmerized by the fantastic creature. Suddenly, he was falling. He fell only a few feet, but the landing was surprisingly soft. He was in its mouth now, on its tongue. A smell of fetid death threatened to overpower him, but John grabbed onto a tooth to steady himself. He wrapped both hands around a front incisor and tried to pull himself away from the creature's throat. There was a glimmer of sky above, but it was disappearing quickly as the monster closed its jaws. It was like a steel door shutting on him, and John lost his grip on the tooth, falling backward onto the tongue, his feet slipping in a mixture of blood and saliva.

As his heart quickened, John tasted blood in his mouth. It was thick, like syrup trickling down his esophagus. He started to gag as the warm liquid filled his throat and he coughed up great globules of sticky phlegm and blood. With his throat partially cleared, he tried shouting again, but the creature's jaws tightened around his midriff and he felt incisors tearing into his flesh, scything through his intestines and guts like a knife through butter.

The monster had gotten him good. There was no escaping this. He could take the pain. He could accept he wasn't going to make it. He just wished he could see Amy one more time. The jaws opened briefly, and his body had been twisted around so he was now facing the thing that was eating him. He could see right into its eyes. Did it want him to know he was dying? Was this a game, a chance to prove it had won? Did it even know what it was doing? John reached out a hand and pulled a fragment of bone from between two teeth. It was nestled there beside a stringy piece of his own flesh that dangled like a fish on a hook. John wondered if the bone belonged to the lion it had eaten, and then jammed it back into the gap between the tooth and the gum. The monster's eyes flickered, and John knew he had hurt it. He was pleased. Why should this thing have everything its own way? Suddenly, the world began to turn black as he was turned around in the creature's mouth, and pointed down toward its throat.

Searing pain blinded him and he lost feeling in his lower body as his legs were ripped off, the hips pulled from their sockets. Frantically, he pushed his arms upwards and felt nothing but the inside of the creature's mouth. His hands slipped across the roof of its mouth as he was pulled downward, the muscles contracting and sucking him towards its throat where he would be pulled down into its stomach to be digested.

John saw a flash of blue, a tiny crack of light appearing between the monster's closing teeth, and he knew that would be the last he saw of the world. He felt faint now. He tried to pull himself upward but there was nothing to get hold of, and he had no strength. Half of his body had been torn away, and the rest was nothing but a mangled mess.

Slowly, he fell backward, sliding down the monster's leathery tongue, and the throat closed around him, crushing what was left of his pulverized body. His eyes popped out of his skull, and he tried to imagine Amy's beautiful face as he died. All he could think of though was how horrible it was to be eaten alive. John died, with Amy's scream the last thing he heard.

"Dad!"

Amy staggered backward. John was gone. He was dead, torn apart in front of her. The cacophony of sounds suddenly filled her ears: the sirens, the screaming and shouting, the crying.

"Dad?" Amy sank to her knees as goose bumps rippled down her arms. The monster was standing before her, its belly satiated by the two things it had just devoured. Amy watched it take a step toward her, and a trickle of pee ran down her leg.

"I'm sorry, Dad. I love you." Amy sank to the earth, and let her tears fall. There was no running from this thing, nowhere to go where it couldn't find her. She wished this nightmare would end soon, and thought of what her mother and Mackenzie would think when they found out she was dead. She had always thought she would die peacefully, perhaps in her sleep years from now. Eaten by a monster had not been part of her plan, and Amy tried to find comfort in her tears before she died.

CHAPTER 11

Akecheta crawled up onto the roof and found Mac standing at the front of the store. The bus was burning far away in the distance and black smoke palled into the blue sky. The store's roof was covered from end to end in solar panels. With the sun overhead, they sparkled like an ocean, and Mac was nothing but a vague shadow in their midst, a ship surrounded by glassy waves of pure, warm light. The heat radiating from the panels made him gasp for air. It was like being submerged in a hot bath, so encompassing was the heat on the rooftop.

"Mac? Over here." There was no way Akecheta was going back down without him, but it appeared that Mac hadn't heard him. He was holding his cellphone high in the air, trying to make a call. As Akecheta spoke, he watched as the black smoke parted and the monster emerged, a giant and monstrous sight that sent shivers down his spine. It was like a mirage, a vision of Hell wrought real. The beast approached with a lumbering gait, each leg planted on the ground heavily, as if the gravity was too much for the sheer weight of the monster. Although it was slow, it could be quick too. It seemed to take only seconds to reach the store. All the time that it was approaching, Akecheta had also been creeping forward, ready to drag Mackenzie to safety back down the hatch.

Akecheta knew they only had seconds. The monster was advancing on them now, bringing with it only one certainty: death. Mackenzie didn't see it until the last moment, and he fell back as the monster prepared to take a swipe at him. Akecheta saw Mackenzie fall and cut his hand on one of the panels.

"Mac," hissed Akecheta in barely more than a whisper. Should he make a run for it and try to grab Mac? Should he risk calling out and alerting the monster to his presence? Mackenzie brought the phone to his ear and said something. Akecheta then heard a noise behind him and saw Myles appear through the hatch.

"Get back," said Akecheta. "Get away from here."

Myles ignored Akecheta and climbed up onto the roof. His face was full of wonder when he saw the creature above Mackenzie. From a distance, it almost didn't seem real. Up close like this, only a few feet away, it became all too real. The smell, the scaly skin, the deep red eyes and the monster's rasping breaths all sent shivers down his neck. Myles took two steps forward and saw Mackenzie lying on the roof. Instinctively, Myles began to jump across the solar panels, shouting for him to get clear.

"Myles, no, stop." Akecheta stood up, and what he saw made him suddenly regret ever getting on the bus that morning. The monster had been looking down at Mackenzie, but now its head was raised, and its fiery red eyes locked first onto Akecheta's, and then Myles'.

"Run!" screamed Akecheta as the monster came forward.

Straddling the store, it snaked an arm across the rooftop with its claws extended, each one the length of a man. Two thick claws like saw blades raked across the roof, gouging out a deep line in the roof and destroying some of the solar panels, narrowly avoiding cutting Mackenzie in half. Myles wasn't as lucky.

Mid-step, Myles was scythed into two distinct pieces, severed at the waist, the monster's claws cutting him in half like he was no more than a gingerbread man being snapped in half by a child's greedy fingers. His legs continued to run for three steps before tripping and falling beside Mackenzie. The upper half of his body was thrown over the edge of the store, and Akecheta caught sight of the shock on Myles' face before he plummeted over the side. So quick was the attack that Myles had no time to shout for help, to scream in pain, or to say anything that suggested he knew his death was imminent. One moment he was there, the next he was simply gone. When Myles was cut in half, huge plumes of blood cascaded over the roof, showering out from his dismembered torso and exposed arteries. Much of it cascaded over Akecheta and the hatchway behind him. Myles' life was reduced to opulent amounts of red liquid, bestowed upon Akecheta like some cruel wicked gift, one that he wished he could refuse, but found wiping from his chin and face.

With Myles dead and gone, the monster reared up and bellowed, the somber sound echoing across the hot desert. Was it a call of victory, or something else? Akecheta watched as the monster looked down at him and their eyes locked together. Slowly, it backed away from the store, each step of its powerful legs shaking the store to its foundations. The monster was leaving. Akecheta felt momentarily confused. Was it actually leaving? It could so easily take him and Mackenzie out as well, yet it was backing off. Seizing his chance, Akecheta wiped the blood from his face and jumped over the broken line of panels to Mackenzie.

"Take my hand." Akecheta reached down and hauled Mackenzie to his feet.

"Wait. The phone," said Mackenzie urgently as he got to his feet. "I dropped it when—"

"No time," said Akecheta, worrying that their carnivorous friend might rethink its retreat and attack them again. He risked a glance up at the monster, and noticed it had stopped. It seemed to be looking at them with what passed as curiosity. Akecheta couldn't figure out what had stopped it, but he wasn't going to let the opportunity pass. If they could get out of sight, and keep quiet, they stood a chance. Perhaps it wouldn't just back off, but leave altogether; burrow itself back underground and find someone else to haunt. "Leave it."

Mackenzie knew Akecheta was right. Hanging around on the roof was akin to writing a suicide note. He ushered Akecheta back toward the hatch and they began the journey across the roof, monitoring the beast that still cloaked the building and could attack again at a moment's notice. Mackenzie's left hand was bleeding, but now that he was up on his feet, he felt a throbbing in his leg that overtook the pain in his hand. He noticed a rip in his jeans, the outer frayed edges sodden with blood, and he realized he had cut his leg as well on one of the broken solar panels. A sliver of one of the panels had gouged a deep line in his shin, tearing through his slacks and skin almost down to the bone. Despite the pain, he couldn't help but feel guilty. Myles had suffered more than a few cuts and wouldn't be coming back down with them. The lower half of Myles' body was still there on the roof, the splayed legs cooking on the remaining intact solar panels. Such was the intense heat that Mackenzie wondered if they actually would burn. There was a faint smell in the air like burnt charcoal, as if someone had left a grill on too long and burnt hamburger meat. The smell permeated the hot thick air and tickled his nostrils. The monster's odorous stench still lingered over them too, an exquisite stench of rotting seared meat. As they passed Myles' remains, waves of fetid air swept up in the heat and made Mackenzie feel dizzy. He felt like he was standing on the precipice of a cliff with an unseen presence threatening to push him over.

How was he going to explain to the others what had happened? How could he tell Alyce and Michele that Myles had been horribly killed?

"We're coming down." Akecheta began to climb down into the store and Mackenzie followed, his hands trembling as he gripped the lip of the roof. He closed the hatch as he descended, casting the store room into gloominess again. A sense of relief hit Mackenzie as he closed the hatch. Somehow having a physical barrier between him and the beast provided some comfort, no matter how flimsy it was. Still, the relief was tinged with grief and guilt. Whenever they tried something, it was one step forward, two back. Myles was dead. Mr. Stepper was dead. Mackenzie couldn't help but wonder who was next.

There was a lot of chatter and whispering in the room as Akecheta helped him down. When his feet finally hit the floor, he found Laurel hugging him tight.

"What happened up there?" She kissed him all over his bloodied face. "I thought I'd lost you. What were you thinking?"

Mackenzie noticed Laurel was covered in blood too. "What about you? Are you hurt?" he asked her in a panic. "God, Laurel, it's all over you."

"It's not mine. From the roof. I thought—"

A single scream silenced the room. It quickly faded into a muffled sobbing, and the whispering in the room stopped instantly. Mackenzie looked over Laurel's shoulder to see Michele in

Akecheta's arms. Alyce was tugging at her mother's waist, a look of desperation in her eyes. There was a reluctance to accept the truth, but he knew Alyce could understand what was going on. Her father hadn't returned from the roof. The hatch was closed. The beast had claimed another victim.

Beers seemed to understand too that his master was not coming back. The puppy whined and nuzzled up against Alyce. Michele was sobbing into Akecheta's arms, and Mackenzie watched as Alyce dropped her arms and sat back down on the floor. She hugged Beers and stared at the floor with glassy eyes. Mackenzie wanted to say something, to explain how it had all happened so quickly that there was nothing either of them could do. He wanted to help to comfort Alyce and Michele, but he knew there was nothing he could do or say to help them. A part of him was relieved that Akecheta had already taken responsibility and spoken to Michele. He had to admit the prospect of telling Michele what had happened scared him. He wasn't anyone special, just a man from Milwaukee with a garage full of cars to sell. He fulfilled a certain role in life and being a hero wasn't one of them. He had a slightly paunched belly, a receding hairline, and a stepdaughter who he loved as much as humanly possible. He didn't have the words or the experience to deal with this situation, and though he felt miserable and ashamed, he knew it was best to let Akecheta deal with it.

"Let me take a look at you," said Maria as she pulled Mackenzie away from his wife. "I need to dress that cut on your leg before you get an infection. Was it the thing, the...dinosaur?"

The whispering died down, and Mackenzie sat down on an upturned case of bottles of sun screen as Laurel fussed over him. Maria began to examine his leg.

"No, I fell and cut it on those panels you've got up there."

"I only had them installed a week ago. Something tells me they're not in pristine working order anymore?"

"You could say that," said Mackenzie trying not to let the pain show as Maria continued to work on his leg.

"Mac, we need to elevate your leg and stop this bleeding. Laurel, grab me something to rest his leg on will you?"

Laurel dragged a huge box full of Cheetos over and Mackenzie raised his injured leg.

Maria looked at the leg with concern. It was a mess. The cut was just below the knee and scythed all the way down the shin to the top of the ankle. Some of the skin had peeled back exposing tender muscle and tissue. Blood was dripping everywhere and she knew she had to wrap it up quickly or Mackenzie could go into shock.

"Laurel, there's some first-aid kits up there on the second from top shelf. Grab a couple for me, please. Then find me an emergency blanket - you know the silver ones? There should be some close by to the first-aid kits. I need to clean this up. There are some bottles of mineral water over in the fridge at the back there."

Vic approached them as Laurel retrieved the items Maria needed. "Can I do anything?" Mackenzie looked pale, and Vic hadn't needed to hear the conversation between Akecheta and Michele to know things had turned sour up there.

"I'm fine," replied Mackenzie. "Although that cold beer you've got looks mighty good right now."

Vic handed the beer over, and Mackenzie drank swiftly. "Don't suppose you've got a cigarette as well?"

"No, he hasn't," said Laurel as she dropped the first-aid kits and a blanket at Maria's feet. "Really, Mac, do you think that's a good choice? How many times—?"

"All right, all right, I know. Don't start on me now." Mackenzie regretted snapping at Laurel, but once she got started on her anti-smoking crusade, she was likely to get a bee in her bonnet all day. And that would be the end of any chance he might get to sneak a cigarette.

Vic took the empty beer bottle from Mackenzie, intending to replenish it. He tried not to look at Mackenzie's injuries too closely. The beer had helped take the edge off his fear, but still, he didn't want to get too involved. "You want another? There's a whole case back there."

"Vic, can you go out front with James and give us some space? Keep an eye on that thing. We need to keep everyone calm and quiet as best we can, and for that thing to stay outside, well away from here." Maria turned back to her patient. She really just wanted Vic out of the way. She felt like he was watching in the same way as people watch a car crash. He couldn't do anything to help her, but she could find another use for him and get him out of her hair at the same time. "It's important that we know where it is, Vic. If it comes back at us, we need as much warning as possible."

"God Almighty, what happened?" asked James as he approached with a bottle of beer swinging in one hand. "You get in the ring with that thing? Bad idea, bro'."

"Mac's hurt, but he'll be fine. Mr. Stepper and Myles..." Maria didn't need to finish her sentence.

"Shoot." James shrugged and looked around the dim room. Michele was gently crying, her head low, her shoulders slumped, and Akecheta unable to console her. Chris was still laid out unconscious, and the little girl and her dog were picking at a packet of chips. "This is pretty fucked up."

"You got that right," said Vic as he hesitated, reluctant to head out front on his own.

"Thanks for that enlightening piece of information, James." Maria sighed and rifled through one of the first-aid kits looking for something to suture Mackenzie's cut with. Once she was done with the leg, she still had to look at his hand. "Look, just go with Vic and check on our visitor."

"What's the deal? I'm just trying to show a little compassion. I thought Mac might need a little support. I mean, there's not much we can do for the driver or Myles. They're history. Six feet under. Worm food." James shrugged. "So what do we do now? You stitch up Mac and we make a break for it? Did you get through to anyone, Mac?"

"For the love of...look, James, just leave it will you? Just go with Vic and keep watch out front." Maria took a deep breath. "I really need to concentrate on what I'm doing."

"James, I think it best you go," said Mackenzie. Whilst Vic had shown some empathy, James' sympathy evidently only extended as far as it helped in saving his own neck. His inquisitiveness was insensitive and unwelcome, and Mackenzie could see that Laurel was uncomfortable around him. "I'd appreciate it if you didn't start talking about Myles like that already. His little girl is right over there. You understand? If you want to help find a way out of this mess, do as Maria asks and check what that thing is doing. The bus is gone, our driver is gone, and we're going to need to find another way out of here. Surely you want to help with that?"

James smiled. "So, I guess running around out there waving those kid's toys didn't help much then?" James rolled his eyes and slapped Vic on the back. "Vic, you nearly got yourself killed and for what, some senile old man? Mr. Stepper got gobbled up by the monster anyway. I guess he was dessert after those two backpackers. This is ridiculous. Anyone who is stupid enough to go out there deserves what happens to them if you ask me. It's Mr. Stepper's fault we're in this mess, so if he's fucked himself up, he's got no one to blame but himself."

"You know, I've just about had as much as I can take from you," said Maria, getting up.

"Bring it on, old woman." James smirked as Maria attempted to stare him down. He still had the knife in his pocket and wasn't afraid of an old nurse. "Let's see what you got."

Mackenzie saw fear spread across Laurel's face. He couldn't afford to let things get out of control again. Everyone was tense and afraid, and nothing was getting solved by fighting. "Sit down, Maria. Save it. Please."

Maria shook her head and knew what she had to do. She got back on her knees and resumed attending to Mackenzie's leg. As much as she had been tempted to try and teach James some respect, she knew that Mackenzie was right. James got on her nerves and refusing to let him wind her up was the best thing she could do.

"Listen," said Mackenzie, "we don't know what we're dealing with here, but we sure don't need to give that thing any more reason to come over here again in a hurry, do we? So, James, for *everyone's* sake, including your own, let's all keep the noise down. I think if we try not to antagonize it, or draw it in, we might just stand a chance of getting out of this alive. I'm quite sure you want to get home as much as I do. Arguing amongst ourselves won't help, so while Maria patches me up, we need to start thinking this through and figure out what the hell we do next. Like it or not the bus is gone. We need all the help we can get, James."

Mackenzie hoped that appealing to James, asking him for help, might soften his mood and make him see sense. Obviously, he didn't like being told what to do, and trying to coax anything positive out of him was mission impossible. Not even Tom Cruise could get James to say a good word about anyone.

"Right. Nice one, Mac. I'm pleased to hear that you're starting to see some sense. I was beginning to think I was on my own." James cast a sideways look at Vic which only Mackenzie noticed. It was not a look of love, or friendship, or even indifference. It seemed to border on loathing, and Mackenzie began to think there was more to this relationship than they were letting on. Trouble in paradise, perhaps?

"May I offer something to the conversation?"

With the exception of Maria, all eyes turned in surprise toward the far side of the room. Lying on the floor between a stack of hardbound guide books on the formation of the Mojave Desert and two slightly crushed boxes of peanut butter snack bars was Chris, his eyes fully open, and his hands behind his head.

"Thought I should join the party," he said smiling weakly.

"Chris, welcome back." Akecheta was closest and leant across to rest a hand on his arm. "How are you feeling?"

"Better, actually. I don't think I'm going to be running anywhere anytime soon, but...better."

"Now we're cooking on gas," said James as he popped the top off another bottle of beer. "A full house. Now we can really kick on."

Mackenzie was pleased to see that Chris was conscious again. He had been out a while, and it looked like he was on the road to recovery. Mackenzie had to admit that he wasn't convinced that Chris was going to make it. The monster had cut him badly, but now that he was awake, things seemed better. All of a sudden, the future wasn't quite so gloomy. James was right. They could kick on now and figure out what they could do to get out of their prison.

"Let's start with what we know," said Chris, "which is not really very much. It's pretty evident that these earthquakes we've been experiencing were as a result of the dinosaur. What damage it has done to the rest of the state we don't know. We don't know for sure if it's been picked up on elsewhere, but my guess is that someone *is* looking for the source of the quakes. It's knocked out cellphones and landlines, which suggests the problem isn't just localized to here. The larger the area affected, the more chance we have of being discovered. On the other hand, the larger the area affected, the more stretched the authorities are. One way or another, communication is out for now."

"Maybe the big chief can send out a smoke signal," muttered James looking at Akecheta. Vic punched his partner on the arm and told him to quieten down.

"It would help if we knew what we were dealing with. I don't even know what to call it," said Laurel. "Is it really a dinosaur, Chris?"

"Probably. Some sort of mutation at least. Unless we study it, it's impossible to say for sure. There could feasibly be gargantuan beasts that live underground. It's not like man has truly explored every last inch of the planet. The oceans are constantly revealing new creatures that we thought were extinct, or that we didn't even know existed. The more our technology advances allowing us to explore these places, the more we learn. In the Himalayas, we're still discovering new creatures that we didn't even know existed. Just recently, we found out there's a fish that can walk on land, so who knows what this is."

"A fish that walks on land? Chris, I think you need to lie back down," said Akecheta.

"I'm serious." Chris rubbed the top of his right arm. "I might not be in the best of health, but I wouldn't lie about this stuff. I've still got all my marbles."

"There is another explanation," said Akecheta. He looked at Michele, concerned that the conversation might be too much for her. If she was taking any of it in, she showed no sign. Her face was calm, her eyes red and watery, and she gave the appearance of a wax dummy. Her eyes occasionally flitted to Alyce, but otherwise she was not there. Physically, she was right next to him, but mentally she was somewhere else. Her mind was getting used to the prospect of not seeing Myles again, and for that, he was grateful. She had to be able to move on, to look after Alyce. Terrible thought it was, he had kept telling her to focus on Alyce.

Evidently, she wasn't paying much attention to their discussion now, and he felt he could no longer hold it in.

"My grandfather used to tell us stories about the Moerkhanee. I think he used to enjoy scaring us when we were little. My brother and I would listen to him for hours. I only remembered when I was up there on the roof. It was the eyes that reminded me; those big, red eyes. Just like the monsters he used to tell me about."

"Moerkhanee? I don't think I know it," said Chris. "What period is that from?"

"No period from your history books, professor." Akecheta remembered looking at his grandfather when he had told them the story. It had seemed so real that he was unsure if it had been just a story to frighten young children at bedtime, or if it was a part of their history. His brother was slightly older and told him that their grandfather didn't lie. All the stories he heard were based on a truth. Over time, things got changed and warped, distorted to fit the modern world. Yet there was something deeply real and unsettling about the Moerkhanee, something that still made Akecheta afraid to this day.

"The Moerkhanee isn't an *it*. The Moerkhanee is what we call *them*: a race of huge creatures that live beneath the surface of the planet. They swim through the dirt as easily as an eagle flies through the sky. They are solo creatures, all birthed from one mother, who can reproduce but once a year in spring. The Moerkhanee exist only beneath the world we know, stirring up the land and causing it to shudder and quake with fear. They are afraid of nothing, except each other. My people never saw them. They didn't need to. These monsters churned up the earth and could cause whole continents to tremble, such was their power. Nothing could match their awesome power, and so we learned to live with them under our feet, respecting their privacy as they respected ours."

"So what changed all that?" asked James. "Huge monsters that live underground and suddenly decided to come topside? You sure you haven't been smoking something funky, Akecheta? I've heard about you lot and what goes in that peace pipe of yours."

"Oh my," said Maria. She had finished up with Mackenzie's leg and was now bandaging his hand. "Can you just let him finish?

Akecheta knows a hell of a lot more about the Mojave than you do, James. Not everyone is as full of shit as you are."

James shrugged and laughed. "Look, I don't know if that thing outside is a dinosaur, or a mythical creature come to life, but I can tell you one thing. It's real. It's here. And it's hungry."

"We finally agree on something," said Mackenzie.

"I've been thinking about something else," said Chris. "Unless we study it, we'll never know exactly what that thing is. But if it *was* living underground, then it's not a coincidence that it surfaced around here."

"What do you mean? Why here?" asked Laurel.

Chris rubbed his right shoulder again. The pain had started up again and spread down his arm. It was like pins and needles stretching from his neck to his fingertips, and he was trying to get the circulation going. He should probably walk around, but he wasn't entirely sure that if he stood up he wouldn't just fall on his ass.

"We're in California, but only just. The Mojave Desert stretches into Nevada, and it seems just too much of a coincidence that this thing has appeared now, not just in this area but at this point in time. Something has to have drawn it out, or forced it up."

"You're talking about the test sites aren't you? Yucca Flats?" Akecheta stood up and began pacing up and down. "Of course. You could be onto something there, Chris."

"Care to share?" asked Laurel. "What are the Yucca Flats?"

"Jesus," whispered Maria. "Chris is right. *We* did this."

"Sixty years ago, the US started testing atomic bombs at a location in the Yucca Flats. They stopped in the early nineties. Around ninety-two I think." Chris looked up at Akecheta. "When did they start again? Last year? A few months ago?"

"So what?" asked Mackenzie. "We're nowhere near there, right?"

"Right," said Chris. "But we're close to the San Andreas Fault, and the bombs were tested *underground*. If the creature was disturbed, affected maybe by the radiation, then—"

"So that abomination outside the store is a mutated, radioactive, fucked-up dinosaur? That's what you're suggesting, right?"

Akecheta screwed his eyes up and blinked them open rapidly. "This is fairy-tale stuff."

"Oh, but your Moerkhanee theory is more realistic?" scoffed James. "I reckon you've all been out in the sun too long."

Ignoring them both, Chris went on. "What I mean is, from what I can tell, this thing is descended from the dinosaurs. It has a lot of qualities that are reminiscent of Dromaeosaurus, even Saichania like I mentioned before. At first, I thought we were looking at something from the Triassic period, but it's more like a Troodon, and probably not fully matured. The species is clearly subterranean in nature, perhaps even nocturnal, and its habitat has been disturbed. This thing could well be exactly what your ancestors talked of, Akecheta. The Moerkhanee and this dinosaur could well be one and the same thing. Why not? Only it has been affected by the recent atomic testing, affecting it on a cellular level, even so much as re-writing its DNA. I'd have to extrapolate some blood or plasma to really know what it is and how it survived."

"Chris, you want to slow things down a bit? You're losing me," said Mackenzie. "Dinosaurs are dead, Chris, dead. They've been extinct a long time and are about as likely to make a comeback as JFK's political career. You want to try again? I find it hard to believe that thing is a dinosaur."

"That's what I'm trying to say. It *was* a dinosaur. It's not beyond the realms of possibility that a creature can stay undetected from man for a long time. Species that we once thought were dead can reappear suddenly. There are animals out there we haven't even discovered yet, living at the bottom of the ocean or deep within the rainforests. We're not exactly far from the NTS, and despite what the authorities are telling us, or *not* telling us, I think they've unleashed something out of their control."

"NTS?" asked Mackenzie.

"Nevada Test Site," replied Akecheta. "It's where the army blows up shit."

"So, this is some sort of monster cooked up by military scientists, now?" asked James. "A weapon?"

"Oh no, not really," said Chris. The cut on his leg was irritating him, and he resisted the temptation to scratch it. It felt like something was eating away at him, making his blood want to leap from his body. He figured he would have to get used to the pain until they could figure a way past the monster and went on. "I don't think that they intended this at all. I would suggest that this creature lived peacefully, well away from man, in underground tunnels and caves. There are a plethora of them beneath us, particularly under the desert. There are plenty of abandoned coal mines it could use without us even knowing if it wanted a quick look topside. Back in the fifties, the US army tested a load of atomic bombs just north of here at the Yucca Flats. It left the area decimated and irradiated. They began testing again just recently, testing smaller bombs, but with a *lot* more energy and power. Some were exploded underground, and I believe this is the result. That monster out there was a dinosaur, the Moerkhanee perhaps, and the radiation has accelerated its growth, distorted it beyond what it once was into a new kind of creature, something we can't possibly comprehend. This is not a creature by design, but by accident."

"But why didn't the bombs kill it? Why didn't the radiation kill it?" asked Laurel.

Chris shrugged. A wave of nausea swam up his throat and he swallowed it down. Others around him had died and he refused to buckle. Besides, he found the conversation stimulating and it kept his mind off the pain. "I would say it was far enough away from the blast to survive, deep in the bowels of the Earth where it was protected. It's possible that the radiation didn't directly affect it, but entered the underground rivers and caves and tunnels. It was absorbed into its home, its food, air and water; it's likely that the creatures first exposed to the radiation did indeed die. But what about the offspring? What if the original dino had young, still growing? Without knowing what these things are, we couldn't say for sure how it would be affected. Those bombs may have accelerated the young's growth, shaped its DNA, its emotions; turned it into the thing that's outside this store waiting to eat us."

"Awesome," said James. "So we have a giant radioactive dinosaur on our backs. What a vacation this is turning out to be."

"If it wasn't for the tests, we may never have encountered it. It probably would never have surfaced, and we could live for another millennia never crossing paths. This thing could have been dormant, until our angry bombs gave it a wake-up call that it has well and truly answered in style," said Chris.

"Style?" Mackenzie looked at him, amazed that Chris could be so matter-of-fact about it all. "You seem impressed by this thing. Don't forget, it's already killed two of us, and is waiting to finish the rest of us off. My wife is terrified, and frankly, so am I. What should—?"

Without warning, blood spurted from Chris' mouth and splattered the store room's cold floor. He gasped for air, clutching at his throat as he collapsed.

"Chris?" Maria darted across the room as Chris' eyes rolled back in his head. She caught him as he fell, and felt his body convulse as more blood erupted from his mouth. His jaw was locked rigid, and his whole body was shaking as it tried to fight off the infection. His heart began to beat fast, too fast, and his nervous system began shutting down.

"Help me," shouted Maria as the store began shaking, and Chris began dying. The walls of the room trembled just as Chris went still. His theories and explanations evaporated as quickly as the life in his lungs. "Help me," Maria said again, wishing her Tony was at her side. As she watched Chris die, she couldn't help but think that she would also soon be joining her husband.

CHAPTER 12

Chris' body was covered over with one of the rescue blankets. Everyone was in shock. Even James had retreated into his shell. They had tried to help Chris, and Maria had spent several minutes attempting to resuscitate him, but in the end, there was nothing they could do. Maria explained it was likely the infection from the monster that had done it. He was weak from loss of blood, and Chris' body just didn't have the necessary antibodies required to fight the foreign infection that was in his body. She thought he would pull through, but ultimately he was doomed as soon as he was cut.

The shaking had continued for a few minutes as Chris died, but soon stopped. Akecheta had taken Vic out to the front of the store to check if the monster was attacking again, but they had seen nothing except for its hind legs disappearing as it burrowed underground. They were tempted to go out and look at the massive hole it left in the ground, to see if it had gone far, but something told them it was still there. If it had continued to bury its way further away from them, the shaking would surely have continued for some time. Suspecting it was just waiting for them, they returned to the rear room with nothing to offer other than the news that it was still out there somewhere. They had time, but nothing else. Another dead body, and nowhere to turn; it was another reminder that they were constantly in danger of losing their grasp on life whilst under the shadow of the beast.

"I can't just sit here doing nothing," said Mackenzie to Laurel. "Sitting in this room with Chris over there is like hanging out in a morgue."

"I know," she replied quietly. "It's like we're just waiting to die. I can't stand it. I almost want to go walk out there and get it over with. It's only the thought of Amy that makes me believe I can keep fighting."

Mackenzie hoped Amy was safe and sound, but he was troubled. Chris and Akecheta had indicated that the monsters that roamed underground, living their secret lives away from man, had been awoken recently, perhaps from the army's recent nuclear testing. If that was the case, then their subterranean tunnels might not be confined to the Mojave Desert. What if they were connected further afield? What if they ran all the way to the coast, to LA or to San Diego? He agreed with his wife that Amy was very much at the forefront of his thoughts. He had to know if there was anything left to go to if they got out of here.

"The radio." Mackenzie squeezed Laurel's hand. "It was working, right? Before? We need to know. We need to do something. I'm not going to sit around here waiting for rescue that isn't coming, waiting to die."

Together, Mackenzie and Laurel approached the radio that had been knocked off its little table by Michele. Every step made Mackenzie wince with pain, but his leg was tightly bandaged up and it was only a few short steps across the room. He picked up the radio, and then set it down on the table carefully, turning it back on. To begin with, there was nothing but static and hissing.

"Michele, can you get it working again?" Laurel bent down and brushed the hair from Michele's sad eyes.

Michele looked at Alyce who was softly brushing Beer's coat, and then at Laurel. "It's cold. I'm cold. Aren't you?"

"Yes, it's cold, Michele." Laurel and Mackenzie looked at each other. There wasn't much they could do to help Michele, and Laurel could feel that the woman wasn't all that cold. Her hands were warm. "We can go outside soon and warm up, but first we need to get the radio working. Someone might know what's going on. Someone might be coming for us. You want that don't you? You want Alyce to get home, don't you?"

Michele blinked rapidly and Laurel thought she was about to swoon. "Yes. Help. For Alyce." Michele looked at the radio plainly, as if it were of no more significance than a fly on the wall.

"Ninety three. About ninety three," she said. Michele dropped an arm and began to stroke Alyce's hair. "For Alyce. Help for Alyce."

"Thank you." Laurel turned back to her husband.

"You got it?"

Mackenzie began tuning it in and sure enough, just above ninety three on FM, he found a station. The voice was faint, and still crackled with static, but by turning the volume up to its maximum level, the voice was clear enough to hear.

"Will it go any louder?" asked Maria. "I want to know if Baker is okay." She prayed it had escaped attention from the dinosaur outside. What Akecheta had said scared her. What if there was more than one? What if there were two, or three, or more? Maria shivered. She looked sadly at the blanket that hid Chris' body. Another victim, another friend to bury; her thoughts were turning to home now, to Baker, of what might lie beyond her store should she ever get out. She began to accept that perhaps there were giant monsters marauding through her home town. Unlikely though it was, she wanted to know.

As the voice on the radio became clearer, more of the others joined Mackenzie around the little radio. Soon, he had a gathering around him, as if he were leading a prayer circle. He doubted their prayers would be much use.

"The sound isn't great, but it's a special news report. I think they're reporting from a chopper," Mackenzie told them. "I think someone is over San Francisco. Listen up."

"...that I can see is unbelievable. Damage on this scale has not been seen before in the once beautiful city of San Francisco. Below me is what was once the beautiful Union Square. The city of course was full of tourists as well as locals. On a typical summer's day, there would be thousands and thousands of people out here. The scene I see now is utter carnage and devastation. The streets are full of collapsed buildings and there is little movement below. The plaza is gone, literally hidden beneath a mountain of rubble. Theatres, shops, hotels, all destroyed in a matter of seconds. The Westfield center is unrecognizable. Macys, Bloomingdales, Gap, Prada, souvenir shops, cafes, offices: all gone. Quite how the city can ever recover from this is unthinkable right now. How many *people down there must be injured or killed? What we are seeing is something we hoped would never happen, Trent."*

"Stacey, any estimate on how many injured or killed yet?"

"None so far, Trent. The mayor's office is liaising with the sheriff's and the state police, but to be honest many, many officers are feared dead. Co-ordinating any kind of search and rescue is going to take some time. It is believed the mayor, David O'Clare, and his staff were in the mayor's chambers at the time of the earthquake. That building is now nothing more than a burning pile of rubble. I spoke to a contact at the White House who said, unofficially, that they estimate the number of dead at around two to three hundred thousand. It's not unrealistic to say at this point that close to half a million could have lost their lives this morning. I've heard reports that those numbers are way over the top whereas someone in the police department at LA I spoke to think it is only the tip of the iceberg. Remember that the epicenter of the earthquake, now believed to be a 9.1, was in Redwood City, just south of San Francisco, so the effects were felt a long way. Los Angeles reported minor tremors and a few injuries so far, but of course the worst situation is in San Francisco where I am now. We can expect aftershocks and tremors for some time, some of which may be quite heavy. Many experts are predicting this quake has followed the San Andreas Fault line, where of course so many Americans live."

"Stacey, have you heard any reports of, um, large creatures roaming the area? Anything unusual at all?"

"Say again, Trent, I don't think I heard you right. It can be a little difficult up here in the air."

"We've had some reports of wild creatures cropping up. A couple of school children in Fresno told me they'd seen, and I quote, 'a big freaking dinosaur,' walking down the street before it disappeared underneath a tower block that subsequently collapsed."

"Trent, I did hear a couple of stories, but officially the word is that there is nothing out there. A lot of people get scared by these events, it stirs up a lot of emotions and traumatized people can often see things that aren't there. I wouldn't put too much stock in those reports."

"*Stacey, I'm going to have to cut you off, but we'll come back to this developing story with you shortly. I'm getting updates all the time and pieces of paper shoved under my nose so fast that it's hard to know where to focus this special news report, but I wanted to cross now to one of our reporters in San Diego. Karl Whitelaw has been with us for several years and is someone for whom I have the utmost respect, which is why this report is just so shocking. He sent us this recording just a few minutes ago, and we're going to relay it to you just as he sent it to us. Please note there is some strong language in this report.*"

"*Trent, this is Karl Whitelaw here in downtown San Diego. The quake that woke us all up this morning was nothing to what I have just witnessed. Let me put this into some context for you. The residents of this city have been sent into complete turmoil. I've seen tears of sadness, of frustration, of anger, and right now I...I don't know how to describe to you what is going on. A short while ago, I was covering the quake in the downtown area, getting interviews from a variety of people, when there was another quake. This one was short-lived, but notable for one thing. It wasn't a quake. I repeat, Trent, this was* not *a quake. Not in the sense that we recognize them at least. When the ground started shaking, I took shelter in a coffee shop. People were scared. People are genuinely terrified for their lives, Trent. The tension in the air is palpable. What has transpired here can only be described as fantastical. When I left the refuge of the coffee shop, I became aware of people running from the zoo, masses of them all streaming* away *from the zoo. There were screams and people crying. I tried to ask a young man what they were all running from. I feared there must have been some sort of explosion or perhaps a building had collapsed. The man I spoke to said there was a giant, a sort of goliath that had come up from the ground. Before I could press him, he left, and joined the throng of people all heading away from the zoo. I began to pick up on more of the same. I asked a cross-section of people and they all reported the same thing. A huge beast had crawled from the ground and began to devour people. Let me repeat that, Trent. A beast, a monster of unknown origins, had crawled up from the ground and begun to devour people. There was a...hold on, I'm getting...wait.*"

A loud booming sound blocked out what was being said, an explosion that interrupted the reporter's commentary, until the noise subsided and they could hear him again.

"...incredible, just incredible. Trent, a huge explosion just rocked the whole area. I think a major gas line went up. There are people all around me, and we just don't know what's going on. A woman..."

A female voice cut across the reporter's.

"Did you see it? Did you see it? Oh God, oh God, what is it?"

The voice faded away to be replaced by heavy breathing and crackling. Just when Mackenzie thought the signal had been lost, the reporter's voice came back.

"Trent, Trent, if you can hear me, I'm running, I'm running away from it. I see it now. I can see it. Oh my God, it's so fucking big. It's dwarfing all the buildings and must be nearly a hundred feet high. It's hard for me to tell you what I'm seeing. This is nothing like I've ever seen before. This is certainly no animal from the zoo. It came up from the ground, right up from underneath us. Trent, it has massive claws that can rip through anything. When it emerged from underneath us, it immediately began attacking people. I saw it, oh my God, I... It just grabbed two, three people and ate them. It's so large it just tossed them straight down its throat. Trent, I..."

A horn blared out, drowning out what the reporter was saying and was followed by breaking glass. Occasionally, shouts and screams could be heard in the background and the quick frantic breathing of the reporter. Eventually, there was a muffled booming sound, and then the report continued.

"...picked up a courier van and tossed it aside like you and I would toss a paper cup. I have to get out of the street. I'm trying to corral people down this alley here. There are a few of us trying to find shelter, but how do you hide from a goliath like this? It's killed so many, Trent, so many. There's blood everywhere. It's pouring down the sidewalk, splashed across the buildings, dripping from the monster's jaws. All this blood, this Goliath, I don't think I'm... It's charging through downtown now. It's so close, that...quiet. Jesus. Fuck. Just be..."

Voices intermingled with the reporter's then. So many of them spoke all at once that it was impossible to understand what was being said. Mackenzie picked up only one thing: fear. Finally, the reporter came back through.

"...and it...oh no, Trent, you've got to...it's right on top of us now. It just walked through that building as if it wasn't even there. This thing has deep red eyes, so dark and malevolent that it's as if it comes from another world, another time. This is not natural, Trent, it's evil, an abomination, a magnificent bloody Goliath. Oh Jesus. Oh fuck, it's...it's..."

A short sharp crack interrupted the reporter, and then they heard screaming. It was undoubtedly the reporter's voice. He pleaded to be saved, for someone from the station to get him, and then the report stopped.

"Oh God," said Mackenzie quietly. He saw tears fall from Maria's eyes, and Laurel was shaking.

"As I say, that was Karl Whitelaw, a colleague who we can only hope, and pray, is still safe out there on the streets of San Diego. Quite what he was allegedly seeing is still unknown. We have tried to get confirmation of what is happening downtown, but so far the authorities have been completely silent on the matter. The police have refused any media access, and we understand a cordon has been erected around the city so getting any kind of detail is difficult."

Akecheta asked Mackenzie to turn the volume down. "What a surprise. The government won't do a thing until they're forced to. Maybe when a hundred-foot dinosaur bites the President in the ass, then they'll believe us."

"Unbelievable," said Vic. "San Francisco, San Diego...the whole area is under attack. Don't you see? This isn't just us. This is larger than what we thought. They said it would come one day. God's wrath, the second coming, Armageddon or whatever you want to call it. I thought it was crap—we all did, right? This is unbelievable."

"I've got friends in San Francisco," said Maria. "God, I hope they're okay. What are we going to do? We need to tell someone we're here. If we wait this out, there's only going to be one outcome."

"What are we going to say?" Mackenzie put an arm around Laurel. "Forget San Francisco, forget San Diego, and just get the military down to the Kelso Depot? *Nobody's* going to be interested in us now. They've got thousands of people to look after. You think anyone is going to take notice of a handful of tourists? Even if we did manage to contact someone, nobody is going to listen."

"Mac, what if Amy…?"

Mackenzie knew exactly what his wife was thinking, but he couldn't allow her to go there. Not yet. Amy had to be safe. John would've taken her home, looked after her. He might not have been around to raise his daughter early on, but since then he had stepped up. There was nothing more important to him, and Mackenzie didn't doubt he would ensure she was safe.

"She'll be okay. I'm sure of it." Mackenzie cupped Laurel's face and looked into her blue eyes. "Amy will be fine. We're going to find a way out of here, get her, and go home. Just you see. This time tomorrow, we'll be back in Milwaukee, all of us wondering just what the hell we were worried about."

Laurel smiled but said nothing. She feared that if she opened her mouth it would be like opening Pandora's Box, releasing a torrent of fear and horror and panic that she could never stop. So Laurel smiled and turned her attention back to the radio. She needed to learn all she could about what was going on out there.

They all listened to the radio some more, about how they should stay indoors, keep people inside where it was safer, and not venture out into the streets. The official advice was to remain in their homes. The news announcer kept repeating it like a mantra, but his words were hollow. It was as if the radio announcer was being ordered to read from an autocue.

"Stay indoors? No shit. They think we want to go out there?" James had popped open another beer and was pacing up and down. He was agitated, frustrated; everyone felt the same, yet all they could do was stay put and listen to the radio, hoping for some useful information. "I'm going to the bathroom." James marched out of the room, and Mackenzie turned the volume back up.

"Okay, okay, we've managed to get a link back to Stacy in the news chopper. Stacey, can you hear me?"

"Yes, Trent, I've got you now. What I've seen since you last spoke to me is nothing short of a miracle. The Hilton San Francisco was a 27-storey building, and like so many other buildings in the city, has been devastated by today's events. We have had word that a small contingent of army personnel have made it into the city and started looking for survivors. The Hilton collapsed leaving nothing but a pile of rubble, and it was assumed everyone inside was dead. However, a small child has been pulled out of the wreckage alive. No official word yet on the name of the child, but it is believed the child was found alone so one can only assume the worst for his or her parents. We are trying to get closer to the city center, but you can imagine the difficulty we are having in getting access right now. The city is soon to be taken over by the military, and we understand martial law may be imposed soon."

"Stacey, are we aware of any other survivors at this stage?"

"None. None at all, Trent. As I said, rescue teams at this point in time are very thin on the ground. The local police and fire service are not operating and the state is very much relying on the US Army and National Guard for assistance. The President has committed all available troops to the search and rescue effort now being arranged, and the US Missouri is being recalled from training in the Pacific to help. This ship has over two thousand personnel on board and is expected to reach us sometime around 2100 tonight.

"Trent, I don't know if you are really able to understand the scope of the devastation wrought upon this once beautiful city. It is almost incomprehensible. We've been up in the air for a couple of hours now, and it is horrendous. For miles and miles, there is hardly a standing building. We've been over the city center and some of the outlying suburbs too. We weren't allowed to fly over Redwood, but the CAA has just given us approval so we are heading over there now and hope to bring you information soon. I can't...yes...um, Trent, I just received word that the President is going to be making an announcement soon, so stay tuned."

James strolled into the room wiping his hands on his jeans. "Any mention of dinosaurs terrorizing the nation yet?"

"Nothing," said Vic.

The news report continued and they heard various reports of buildings that had collapsed, schools buried under tons of rubble and hospitals that were now morgues. They heard Stacey report from over the Golden Gate Bridge, deserted save for a few abandoned cars. Some of the rivets and cables had come loose, but the structure was still intact and could be repaired. They listened to a variety of talking heads, all with their own suppositions and ideas about why this had happened and now. They heard from meteorological experts, geological experts, and scientists: all hypothesizing, but none with any real factual, useful information. They didn't hear any more reports of wild creatures, or giant beasts.

As they listened to Stacey fly closer to Redwood City giving an impassioned speech about helping one another, a can of lemonade fell off a back shelf and rolled out of sight into a dark corner. Another did the same, and then more of the items still on the shelves began to jump about. The floor and the walls of the store began to roll and shake, sending fear rippling through the tour group cowering in the back of Maria's store.

"Is everyone okay?" asked Akecheta as the trembling stopped.

Mutterings and exclamations followed as everyone breathed a sigh of relief. Other than some churning stomachs and shot nerves, nobody had been injured.

"We can probably expect a few of those," said Akecheta.

"You think? That fucker's right outside our front door, probably figuring out how best to pick us off one by one. I'd say it's just having a stretch before it takes our damn heads off." James sighed and ordered Vic to find them something to eat. "Listen to this shit. This is some jumped up media spokeswoman for the US Army who apparently knows better than any of us."

"*The exact test sites are under military control, and we have rigorous procedures in place to ensure that their location is safe and secure. No harm can come to anyone from our testing which is done under the strictest supervision and controlled conditions. Allegations that the army are responsible for what happened at Goodsprings, or the loss of life of any civilian as a result of our officially sanctioned tests are entirely unfounded, unwarranted,*" *and will be defended in court. We deny fully any culpability for the death of a single American civilian.*

"We are also aware of the rumors of sinkholes appearing in the Mojave and have sent specialists to investigate. It would be normal given the magnitude of the earthquakes today for such phenomena to occur at this time. In the meantime, we would encourage everyone to stay calm, and let us do our job. We are working in coordination with the local authorities to ensure the safety of everyone in the area. Whilst we would not normally comment on gossip, you have asked us about the appearance of the monster that reportedly destroyed Goodsprings and killed all its inhabitants. It is disrespectful to the good people of that poor town to suggest anything other than the truth that led to their deaths. Due to the unchecked tunnels and disused coal mines beneath the town, it was dragged down into a sinkhole. The resulting fires and damaged buildings meant nobody could survive. You will be let in to view the area in due course.

"As for the rumors of a dinosaur, or other such animals, I can assure the people of this fine nation that no such creature exists. This so called monster is nothing more than a fictional story created by the media desperate to fill air-time. It is no more real than Chupacabra or the Loch Ness monster. The army will not enter into any further discussion on this ridiculous matter."

"We're fucked," said Vic. "Everyone knows Loch Ness is real."

"Jesus, what a shitstorm," said James. "This is bullshit. They're denying everything."

"All right, James. What did you expect?" Mackenzie looked at James with something approaching pity. If he wasn't so annoying, James just might be worthy of some sympathy. "The army are hardly going to front up and admit they created a monster are they? Look, sooner or later, they'll have to admit it." Mackenzie tried to placate James, but he knew it wouldn't be an easy task. "Someone out there is going to find us, find evidence that this thing is real, and then we'll be okay. There's no way that giant can stay hidden for long."

"You heard them, man, they're going to cover this up. Goodsprings is just the start of it." James began pacing back and forth. "How many people died there? A hundred? A thousand? I bet you your last dollar that the military are there right now declaring it an accident, telling everyone that it was a natural sinkhole that swallowed up the town. They won't let cameras in to see what a mess they created. Once they find out it's here, we're as dead as those people who lived in Goodsprings. Nobody is coming for us." James grabbed a chocolate bar from Vic and shoved it into his mouth. "We're *so* screwed."

"Yeah, okay, James, just keep a lid on those thoughts can you?" Mackenzie nodded at Alyce. "For her?"

James shrugged and continued shoving the chocolate bar into his mouth.

"You doing all right, princess?" Michele hugged Alyce close, fighting back the tears. Her little girl seemed fine, but the weight of responsibility was growing. How was she going to get her daughter safely out of here? Where were they even going to go? It sounded like their home was probably gone, so where could they turn now?

"Can we go home now? I want to go. I miss Daddy." Alyce yawned and looked up at her mother with sad tired eyes. "I just want to go home."

"You'll be okay. We'll find a way to get home soon, pumpkin."

Laurel crouched down beside Alyce and patted Beers. She looked up at Michele. "We'll figure it out. Just hang tight."

Seeing James and Vic tear into a box of chocolate bars reminded Maria that the others might be hungry too. It had been hours since they had first arrived, and despite all that had happened, despite the wonder and fear and death, some of the others might want to eat too. Maria announced that if anyone had the stomach to eat, she was going to serve up some food. She still had some cold sandwiches and fruit, which she had prepared for a tour group that was due in later in the day. It was packed up behind the counter in the front and retrieving it shouldn't be too hard while the monster was still under the ground.

"I could eat something," said Laurel, "but can you bring it back here? I can't go out front. Not with…you know."

"Of course. I'll be quick, but I want to see what it's up to. Apart from the shaking, it's gone remarkably quiet, don't you think?"

Maria. "No point in attracting any unwanted attention, so I'll be quick and quiet."

"Not on your own. It's too risky. I'll come with you," said Akecheta. Together, they ventured in silence to the front of the store.

James and Vic took a seat as Mackenzie tried to make the radio signal clearer. Laurel was busy trying to keep Alyce entertained, and he didn't want to miss anything. With San Diego in trouble, he needed to know what exactly was going on and what was being done about it. As much as he didn't want to admit it, Amy might need help. There was currently an 'expert' discussing the manifestation of people's fears and how terrorism had changed the way people thought and acted under duress. He said a traumatic event could skew one's perception of reality which may explain the rise in reports of large dinosaur-like creatures emerging from the rubble of the earthquakes. Once the idea took hold then mass panic was liable to set in, and so they had to look at it logically. The expert said there was no way anything could have lived underground undetected for so long; that it just wasn't rational.

"Rationalize my ass." Mackenzie wondered what it was going to take before they actually accepted what was happening. He didn't doubt for one moment that they weren't alone in this. Other creatures had appeared, by all accounts all over California. They were isolated by geography, but united in their cause. Everyone wanted answers, but as far as he could tell from listening to the idiots on the radio, nobody was asking the right questions. After the interview was over, they started to advise on where local shelters were being set up, complete with supplies and medical facilities. He tried to listen out for anything nearby, but he didn't recognize any of the names that were mentioned, and there was no more information forthcoming about San Diego.

Maria and Akecheta returned armed with two bags of food which they handed out to everyone.

"What's it looking like?" asked Mackenzie as he took an over-ripe banana and meatball sub from Akecheta. "Any sign of it?"

Akecheta sat down wearily. "Nothing. It's there all right. You can feel it. It's not gone anywhere. Maybe the heat of the day made it go back underground. I don't know. It's not a nice feeling being out front. The windows are all smashed in, and you can hear it breathing. Plus there's..." Akecheta glanced at the corner of the room where Chris lay. "Plus there's, you know, blood on the road. Mr. Stepper didn't stand a chance."

"Did you work with him long?"

"He was a tough old bastard." Akecheta smiled wistfully. "Ex-military. He left them about ten years ago and a few years back started up this tour business. He was born and raised in San Bernardino, but he always loved this area. He was a great help to us."

"How did you get involved with him? You do this for a living?"

"No, no, no," said Akecheta. "I only help out at the weekends in summer, or school vacation. I teach at Fort Mojave full-time. My family live on the Fort with me. Two boys," he said smiling. "You know, I enjoy this. It gives me a chance to teach you guys about the desert and the area I love. Well, usually. My family have been here for generations. Mr. Stepper didn't have to take me on, but he appreciates that I'm honest about life out here, and I have a lot of knowledge that I like to pass on. The Mojave is a beautiful place to live. I can't imagine raising my boys anywhere else."

"Don't suppose you know anything about giant dinosaurs, or how to get rid of them?"

Akecheta thought how to answer as Maria came around with bottles of water or soda. He took two waters, one for himself and the other he handed to Mackenzie. Maria sat down beside them, wanting to gather any ideas the group might have in how to escape the store and avoid the monster.

Akecheta wasn't sure he had any real answers. The longer they had to sit around pondering their fate, the more the memories of the stories of the Moerkhanee came to mind. Maybe his grandfather had encountered these things. Maybe there was something in those stories he could use against it. If only he could recall more. It had been thirty years since he had spoken about them, and even back then, they were dismissed as nonsense, just children's bedtime stories based on myths and legends.

"Well, there's really not much that would take on anything of that size. What did that reporter call it—a goliath? I can't imagine it has any concerns. Humans are probably their biggest enemy. But unless the Incredible Hulk turns up, I guess that's out. I've been trying to remember more of the tales my grandfather used to tell me, to see if I couldn't come up with something useful. It's difficult. My father wasn't around a lot, so my grandfather had a lot to do with my upbringing. He used to tell me and my brother stories. You know the usual collection of boogeymen, monsters and how I was going to be a star quarterback for the Chargers?"

"I'm sure he meant the Packers, but go on," said Mackenzie slyly.

Akecheta merely raised an eyebrow and continued. "Well, the Moerkhanee was different. He seemed apprehensive when he spoke of them, as if he was scared almost to mention their name. It was as if even talking of them would anger them. I used to think he was doing it for effect, but now that I've seen it with my own eyes, I'm inclined to think he wasn't just making it up. There were different stories he told us, and there were different creatures too. The Moerkhanee was the collective name for them, but there were three types of monsters: those that live under the ground, those that live in the oceans, and those that dwell only in the sky."

Mackenzie rubbed his injured leg. "Akecheta, don't jinx us. One giant animal is all we need thank you."

"Supersized monsters," said Maria. "Akecheta, you really believe this Moerkhanee stuff?"

Akecheta smiled. "Maybe."

Mackenzie watched as Laurel helped Alyce to sort through some colored pens. They were leaning over a black and white book, yet to be colored in. There was almost a smile on Laurel's face. Alyce was a good distraction. They were good for each other. Mackenzie glanced at Michele. She looked terrible, as if tiredness had a grip on her and was forcing her eyes shut. She hadn't touched the sandwich that Maria had left for her.

"You know, I think Chris was onto something," said Mackenzie. "He said this thing was a relic, a relative of the dinosaurs. Before he died, he was telling us about the Yucca Flats, remember? The radiation? I think what we have on our hands is a good, old-fashioned fuck up. Whatever it once was, a lizard, an alligator that someone flushed down the toilet, or maybe some long lost dinosaur, it was affected just like Chris said. All those bombs, all that radioactive waste and pollution and fallout —it all stayed underground, mutating and twisting that thing and its family until they finally got so pissed off that they decided to come for us. Hell, I don't know."

"How did the stories end, Akecheta?" asked Maria. "What happened in the end?"

Akecheta looked down uncomfortably. "My grandfather said the tales foretold of a new race that would one day walk the Earth: the Moerkhanee. The Moerkhanee were Gods taking the form of giant creatures that were larger and deadlier than anything that had walked the Earth before, bigger and more fearsome than even the dinosaurs. He told me they would take many forms; some would have long tails with teeth, some would have a hundred eyes, and some with senses so acute they could smell a man a hundred miles away. Yet they would all have one common trait; a hunger for man. He said they would wipe out all existing life on Earth, and then the natural Gods of the land, the ocean and the sky would live forever."

"I'm not sure who I would prefer was right," said Maria. "Mac with his radioactive dinosaurs, or you, Akecheta, with your Gods here to reclaim the planet."

"It doesn't mean anything." Akecheta sighed loudly. "For all I know, my grandfather made the stories up. Perhaps he just remembered them from his childhood."

"Hey," said Vic loudly. "You're going to want to hear this."

Mackenzie noticed that Vic and James were sat by the radio, a beer in each hand. "What do they want now?" he muttered.

"The radio. They're finally saying that these creatures are real." Vic almost seemed happy at the news. He held the radio up and put a finger to his lips, indicating that they should all listen to what was being said.

"There's more of them," announced James solemnly. "Just listen. Jesus, we are so fucked."

CHAPTER 13

"America will not only survive this, but grow stronger from it. Nothing can destroy us; not our cities, not our resolve, and certainly not our spirit. These Goliaths have but temporarily stopped our tracks of progress. I am with you in this time of need. Have no doubt that we are all in this together, and we will pull through. God Bless America."

"So there you have it, Trent. As usual, the President's speech is full of rhetoric and soundbites, but has little in the way of concrete information about these attacks. We now know the official line is that they are calling them Goliaths. Quite what type of creature they are is still unclear. The official stance is that we are looking at a new breed of carnivore, one we have not encountered before. The term 'Goliath' seems to have taken off as more and more sightings come in; however, the government is refusing to categorize them until, I quote, 'further research and analysis can take place.' Trent, surely we've all heard the…"

"Turn it off," said Mackenzie. He was disillusioned, hoping that the President's speech might have provided them with some hope. Instead, he felt more scared than ever. Reports of the monsters were coming in more frequently. The media had come up with a name for them, simple yet accurate: Goliaths.

"Try to rest, Mac." Laurel had laid herself down and was resting her head on his lap. "Close your eyes and ignore it. There's nothing we can do right now, so save your energy."

"I'd be able to rest better if the radio was off. Listening to it isn't getting us anywhere."

"It stays on," said James firmly. "I want to hear more." He had gone through at least half a dozen bottles of beer, and Mackenzie was only too aware that an argument was no more than a split second away. "There's some wanker on now trying to say these things aren't even real. Listen to this moron."

"...only we're not, are we? We're talking about subterranean creatures, abominations rising from under the ground, surfacing right now, and taking us on as if they hadn't a care in the world.

"Trent, this is preposterous. Next, you'll be telling me that sea monsters are swimming around the Pacific and, and, and... the whole thing is farcical, simply farcical. Some bored teenagers create a video of a grainy-looking image that they tell us is a dinosaur, put it on the internet, and you're all sucked in. Listen to me, this is insane. There are no monsters. There are no dinosaurs. Mythical creatures are exactly that—mythical."

"Doctor Allenby, what would you say to those who claim to have seen these monsters? I mean, we're not talking about an isolated sighting. This isn't one of those times when a whacko spots Elvis working in Walmart. We're getting numerous reports now—"

"Trent, if I may. Your Goliaths are about as real as the tooth fairy. Earthquakes are both scary and deadly, and deserve to be treated with the healthy importance that we usually reserve for them. Let's not degrade them by suggesting they are anything more than a natural scientific occurrence."

"I'm just going to bring in Professor Justine Keystone here, Doctor Allenby. She is a zoologist at Washington State, and has analyzed the latest pictures of these Goliaths."

"Thank you, Trent. I think it is extremely important to recognize what we are dealing with here, and not sweep it under a rug like Doctor Allenby would have us do. These things are very similar in nature to other animals I have studied. Take your typical spider, for example, which will catch a fly to drain it of its blood. These Goliaths that we are witnessing rampaging across America are after blood too. But they are so much more aggressive than any kind of spider I have ever studied. Their size and agility is astounding. I have been discussing the situation at length with my colleagues and the supposition at this point in time is that these *are mutants, some sort of long lost cousins to the dinosaurs. It is quite feasible that they have surfaced now after living underground or in a deep network of unexplored caves somewhere, perhaps beneath the Mojave or Yellowstone. Perhaps they were already here and have really only just awoken. There are vast areas of the ocean unexplored, so who's to say that there isn't something buried beneath the ground that we haven't come across before? I was one of many who signed the petition against resuming nuclear weapon testing, and it is clear to me that what we are seeing is the fruit of—"*

"Justine, you almost sound like you envy these things, that you admire them? You do realize that you sound more like an obsessed fan than a professor."

"So you will at least admit they are real then?"

"Look, we don't know anywhere near enough about these animals, let alone if they even exist or not, without you going and classifying them on your own just so the whole of the scientific community can kiss your ass. Even if these things supposedly did exist, then how do you suppose they have remained undetected for so long? This isn't a fly or a fish we've potentially uncovered, this is a huge animal. Something like that can't live beside us on this planet, not in peace anyway."

"Doctor, I'll agree with you on one thing. We don't know enough about these things. We don't know their lifestyles, mating habits, reproduction ability, lifespan—we need a thorough analysis in a laboratory where the country's best minds can work on this. Doctor, I assume you are familiar with the Goliath Tarantula that dwells in the rainforests of Southern America? Its fangs are one inch long, its body a foot long. These are ancient predators we are talking about. Out of human reach, they grew much larger than their domestic cousins. There's no reason why something else couldn't have grown to the size we see today. If these things developed and lived underground, or at least out of range of mankind's touch, then with no natural predators they may have reproduced very quickly. How, we are not sure yet. With an abundant food supply, their population would be able to spread rapidly."

"Justine Keystone, you haven't changed one bit. Come on. That food supply you talk about is human beings. *How can you be so blasé about the death of so many and come on here to extort your bizarre theories without any substance or facts to back them up? Trent, can we move this conversation onto something more serious? I mean, really? Really? The only footage we have is poor, and I am very sceptical about the validity of where it has come from. Show me a dinosaur in downtown San Diego, and I'll show you a big fat liar. As for Justine and her crackpot theories, frankly, she is pissing in the wind and you know it."*

"Doctor, you've always been jealous of me. Why don't you...?"

The discussion turned into an argument and Mackenzie gave up. It was impossible to listen to any coherent debate about what was going on out there. The so-called experts were arguing amongst themselves whilst people died.

"The Moerkhanee won't be brushed aside so easily. They are as strong as the Gods and as lethal as the most poisonous substance known to man." Akecheta stood up, stretched his arms up into the air and then down to his toes, before finally crossing them. He yawned. "And sadly, as real as my back pain."

"This is bullshit," said James. "The Moerkhanee are just kids' stories. You're not buying this, are you?" His eyes wandered around the room and nobody met his gaze except Mackenzie. They locked eyes for a moment, neither of them wanting to back down. It was Vic who spoke that made James look away.

"I've seen this movie," said Vic. "You know, the one where everyone bands together and holes up in some shopping mall?"

"Yeah and it usually doesn't end well for everyone," said Maria. "The old woman *never* makes it out."

Mackenzie cleared his throat. "So let's change the script." He knew what everyone was thinking. If they stayed in the store then finally they would get caught; that somehow the Goliath would get in. "Let's get out of here. We wait too long and eventually we will run out of food and water. Or perhaps we wait long enough and that thing out there will find a way in. Either way, we all die. Sitting around waiting for help that may never come, it just seems...pointless. We need to be proactive about this and find a solution instead of waiting for one to fall into our lap."

James clapped Mackenzie and stood up excitedly. "Now *that's* more like it. A man of action, I like it. So there are some smart people in this room. Let's figure it out, figure out how to get past that thing, right?"

Akecheta looked at James disapprovingly. "Just don't get your hopes built up, James. It's one thing to talk about getting out of here and quite another to actually go through with it. Don't forget some of us already tried and lost that fight."

"Yeah, well they were unprepared. We're going to be ready for it next time. Right, Mac?"

Mackenzie nodded slowly. He had no idea what they were going to do, but he was at least prepared to discuss it and see if they couldn't come up with something. The radio hadn't told them anything of use. The phones still didn't work, and the only time they had found a signal was up on the roof. It would be suicide trying to retrieve the phone, so for now they had to be masters of their own destiny.

"Mac, I'm going out front," announced Akecheta. "Anyone care to join me? I want to keep a watch. We need to know when, or *if* it resurfaces. There's always a slim chance that someone else might pass through. We'd hate it if some transport came through and we missed it. Those two backpackers came from somewhere, right? So as long as we're quiet, there's no reason why we shouldn't be able to keep a watch going in the front of the store. I mean, if you're okay with that?"

"I think it's a good idea," said Maria. "I'll come with you. There's also always the chance it will just leave. Slim I know, but we wouldn't want to be sitting here on our asses for no good reason."

"I'll leave you to hammer out the plan," said Akecheta as he scooped up two water bottles from beside Mackenzie. "You come up with anything, you let me know."

"Say, James, do me a favor, please?" asked Maria. "Keep listening to the radio for me. They might have news about this area. Just listen out for Baker, see if they mention it at all. My sister's there and...well I'd just like to know if she's okay. Times like this, family comes first, no matter what."

"Sure thing. Baker. Got it." James had no intention of listening out for any such thing. He wanted out, that was all. With Maria and Akecheta out of the way, he could try to convince Mackenzie that they had to do something. He seemed to be the only one with any kind of belief that they didn't have to accept their fate. Vic was a pushover and would do whatever James told him to. James knew if he could get Mackenzie on side, he would start to get the whole group on his side. Picking up another bottle of beer, he brushed against the knife inside his jacket. Soon, he told himself. Just be patient.

"Be careful." Mackenzie watched as Maria and Akecheta left the room. He was worried that going out there might draw its attention, but it already knew they were there. It could attack any time it wanted, so they may as well keep a look out and try to be prepared for when it returned. Mackenzie was under no illusion that at some point it would return. Its return was a case of when, not if. He stroked Laurel's hair. She was tired. Behind the tiredness in her voice, though, was worry. They were both worried about Amy too. Getting out of Maria's cramped store was becoming more and more urgent with every passing minute. There were more of those things out there, and he had to know Amy was safe. Quite how they were going to get back to civilization he didn't know. Getting to San Diego felt impossible. He couldn't even figure out how they could get more than six feet from the store. There was still something puzzling him. On the roof it could have picked them all off. Why had it left him and Akecheta? Why had the Goliath backed off at the last second?

Mackenzie felt a tugging at his sleeve, and he turned to find Alyce gently pulling his arm. He looked over at Michele, but she was asleep. At least her eyes were closed. Given what had happened to Myles, it was probably for the best.

"What's up, Alyce?" Mackenzie attempted a smile. The girl hadn't said much, but she was old enough to understand what was going on.

"I finished my book." Alyce pointed to a large book on the floor by her mother. "Snow White is my favorite. I love the evil queen too. You should read it. It's a very good book. I think it's the best book ever, actually."

Mackenzie felt his heart beating and wished he could bring Myles back for her. Alyce was a precious girl, innocent and honest. He had no doubt that she thought Snow White was truly the best book ever written.

"You know what, Alyce, you remind me of Snow White. I think one day you'll meet a prince and get married, and maybe even be a Queen yourself one day."

"Don't be silly, I'm not going to get married. I told David Frobisher the same thing. He's in my English class. He said we should get married, but I told him I'm not ready." Alyce sighed and looked down at her shoes. "I'm just not ready for that kind of commitment."

Stifling a laugh, Mackenzie thought how much Alyce reminded him of Amy when she was younger. She had an old head on her shoulders. "You know, Alyce, it's okay to be scared. We're safe in here. The monster outside is sleeping now. The monster is really like the evil queen. It'll never be able to get you, not while we're all here to look out for you."

Alyce nervously bit her lip. "I wanted to ask you something, Mr. Mackenzie. It's just that mom is asleep."

"Sure, what is it?" Mackenzie let Alyce lean in closer, so close that he could still smell the sweet kiwi and pomegranate shampoo she had washed her long pigtails with that morning. "If you want another book to read, I'm sure that we can find something else for you in here. I think I saw some books over in a box over there. You want to get—?"

"No, sir, I...I need the bathroom. I don't want to go on my own. I wanted to ask Daddy, but..."

"Oh, right, the bathroom." Mackenzie's heart strings were pulled close to breaking point. She wanted her daddy and had thought that Mac would be the next best thing. It was good she didn't know the full truth of how Myles had died.

"I'll take you," said Laurel as she pushed herself up off Mackenzie.

"I thought you were sleeping?" Mackenzie saw Alyce's face brighten as Laurel slipped her hand around the girl's.

Laurel shook her head and then winked at Alyce. "I was just pretending so Mr. Mackenzie didn't try to tell me one of his long boring stories. He didn't try to tell you one, did he?"

Alyce giggled. "No, he didn't."

"Good. Believe me they are *really* boring."

Alyce giggled.

"Come on, Alyce, let's go. I need a bathroom break, and the truth is I didn't want to go on my own. Will you come with me? Please?" asked Laurel as she winked at Mackenzie.

Alyce glanced at her mother, but Michele was out of it, her eyes closed. She definitely wasn't pretending to sleep.

"Okay, I'll look after you. Come on then, we don't have all day."

* * *

"What is it?" asked Akecheta.

"What is it? Everything, Akecheta—everything." Maria rubbed her eyes and sighed. They spoke in whispers. "I'm worried about my sister, about how Michele is coping, about how we're going to explain what happened to Mr. Stepper, about…about fucking everything. Mackenzie's cuts were deep, especially the laceration to his leg, and I did what I could. He really needs proper medical attention. As far as our situation goes," Maria said, wandering over to the front of the store, "well, it's pretty fucked up."

"Can you see it?" asked Akecheta. He stood by the counter, waiting for a reply.

Maria shook her head. The dusty ground in front of her store was still. An achingly blue sky seemed to pulse with life above the smoldering remains of the tour bus. It was late afternoon, and the heat had yet to leave them. Experience told her it would take a while, but when the dark crept up on them, they would get cold quickly. She really didn't want to spend an entire night in the store. As she looked around for any sign of the monster, she noticed in the distance that the blue sky was turned to gray. Dark clouds blotted the picture perfect sky that looked like lumps of clay ready to be molded and sculpted into anything she could imagine. All she could picture was that poor man, the backpacker whose life had been so cruelly wiped out. Although the Goliath had eaten his remains, a dark bloody splodge on the ground outside marked the spot where he had died.

"No, I don't see it," said Maria quietly. "It's still underground. I can see the hole it made in the road where it can sit and wait us out. It's out there, waiting for us. Waiting for us to make a move, to make a mistake, and then..."

Was it waiting for them? Maria shivered in the sunlight that was beaming in through the store front. A breeze blew some fine sand in under the front door. "The country's gone to hell, Akecheta."

"Maria, don't think like that. We'll get through this. We've got to get these people home. We're... *I'm* responsible for them. I'm not staying here waiting for it to come get us. I need to get to my family, you've got your sister to think about; we've all got our reasons to get out of this mess."

"I don't see that we have any choice but to wait for help. For some reason, that thing out there *isn't* attacking us right now, but you step outside and it'll go for you, same as it did Mr. Stepper. I don't understand what it is, or what it's doing here. Maybe it's licking its wounds. The bus exploding must have hurt it, at least."

"This isn't fair, Maria, this just isn't fair. My family..." Akecheta ran his hands through his thick hair. "I need to know my family are all right. Even if I don't make it, I need to know they'll be okay, looked after. Maria, please, if anything happens to me..."

Maria returned to the counter. "Akecheta Locklear, I've never heard you talk like that in all the years I've known you. Stop this nonsense. Things are pretty bleak right now, yes, but we'll get through it together. Right?"

Akecheta looked at Maria, and she looked back at him with fire in her eyes.

"*Right?*"

Akecheta looked outside, at the large hole in the road where the Goliath hid. He knew he had to relax. It was as if he expected the monster to jump up out of the hole any second and charge at them. He kept seeing it, remembering how it had been on the roof; how it had cut Myles in half and almost killed him and Mackenzie. "Together. We stick together. We'll make it, Maria."

Maria began to rummage around beneath the counter. "The others are listening to the radio out back, so they'll keep us up to date with any developments. I'm sure this will be taken care of soon. I still have faith that someone is looking out for us."

"I just want that thing to leave." Akecheta looked beyond the monster's lair at the burning bus. Without transport, how were they going to get away from it? It was too far to go anywhere on foot. There had to be an alternative to hiding in Maria's store all night. Akecheta looked at the darkening sky, recognizing the developing storm clouds. It would probably pass over, or not even fully realize itself. They often blew themselves out.

"Maria—the Kelso Depot building across the street—would we be better off over there?" Akecheta asked. "The glass front of your shop worries me. All that broken glass is dangerous, especially if the storm comes up and starts blowing things around. We're quite exposed in here. We could do with some better protection. The Kelso Depot is a lot bigger than your store."

Maria weighed it up. "Yes and no. It's bigger and stronger, true. But other than the visitor center, it's deserted now. The café closed down; there are no toilets, no facilities, nothing. At least here we have plenty of food and water. There's a bathroom out back which might be basic, but it's better than nothing. I suppose we might get across to the Depot in my car, but I don't see much point in going. We certainly wouldn't make it on foot."

"You have a car? When were you going to tell us this?" James appeared in the doorway, an empty beer bottle in his hand and his eyes wide. "A fucking car? What the hell are we doing here?"

"James, how long have you—"

"Give me the keys, Maria." James slammed the empty bottle down on the counter.

"I don't have them on me. I don't need to lock my car out here. We trust each other round here, James."

"Trust?" James laughed and his eyes looked from Akecheta to Maria. "We could've been out of here hours ago, and yet for some reason we're still here debating what to do when we have a car right outside. I don't get it. I vote we get the hell out of here. I can drive if you're not comfortable. I'll take Vic and whoever else wants to come. If you want to stay here, fine, but it's time to leave. What are we waiting for?"

"I vote you shut the hell up," said Maria. "You're not taking that car anywhere, we may need it. Besides you can't go out there, you saw what happened to those two kids earlier. That monster took them down in seconds. And you saw what it did to the tour bus. You think it's going to ignore you and the car? You think it'll—"

James laughed. "Don't worry about me. I've got an idea."

As he turned and left, Maria looked at Akecheta. For a moment, she wondered if she was going to have to get the gun out from under the counter. James really pressed her buttons. "What is that guy's problem?"

"I wish I knew. He's been nothing but trouble since he got on the bus this morning. Maybe I'll have to have another word with him."

Maria sighed and looked outside. There didn't appear to be any movement from the monster. It seemed so peaceful and quiet. She knew that moments like this could be fleeting, especially given how the morning had been. The silence was like a glimpse into her old life, when all she had to worry about was when the next tour bus arrived or what time the delivery guy was arriving with more ice. That was before a giant dinosaur had wrecked her store and killed four people right outside.

"You don't think he's right, do you? You don't think we could make it in my car?"

"Maria, I think he's certifiable. Your car is how far away, fifteen or twenty feet? You go out there, it'll know. You take one step outside that front door, and it'll know. Even if we made it to your car it would crush us instantly."

Akecheta could sense the atmosphere change, and the temperature was dropping. The clouds were thickening, but it was still unlikely they would bring rain, not here, not now.

Maria smiled. "Thanks, Akecheta. I guess—"

Suddenly, they heard a loud banging sound, followed by muffled shouting.

"What was that?" asked Maria.

The ground began to shake, and they knew that the Goliath was on the move.

More shouting came from the back of the store, and then the building began to vibrate as the Goliath slowly emerged from its subterranean home. Maria watched as huge cracks appeared in the front wall, sending roof tiles crashing down around her.

"Let's move!" Akecheta grabbed Maria's hand, and raced toward the back store room. "That ass James has really done it now. He's killed us all."

Maria pulled her hand out of Akecheta's grasp.

"What are you doing?" he shouted. Akecheta balanced himself in the door frame. "Maria, come with me."

"Go." Maria knelt down beside the till. "I'll catch you up. Just go, Akecheta."

She put her hands on the box containing the gun and hoped to God she wasn't going to have to use it.

CHAPTER 14

"No, James, stop!"

Once Laurel had taken Alyce to the bathroom, Mackenzie had tuned out the background noise of the radio. Vic was busy fiddling with it, always trying to get a better reception, and Michele was sleeping, so there was little for him to do. It was a rare opportunity to get some time to think, and he was trying to devise a way out. It seemed like the silence only lasted a minute, and any plans in his mind evaporated when he heard the scraping noises begin. Mackenzie had been reclining, his back turned to the door, when he heard a whining sound, followed by a grunting. Thinking that Vic was up to something, he turned to see James climbing the shelving underneath the hatch to the roof. It was almost comical watching him climb. He did so quickly, but ungainly. In the dark corner, where the light struggled to penetrate, Mackenzie saw James holding something under his arm. It looked like a pile of rags, yet it appeared to be moving. At first, Mackenzie couldn't understand what was happening.

"James?"

As he reached the top of the shelves, James shoved a shoulder against the hatch, thrusting upward and sending the hatch scraping across the roof. The sunlight bore down on James, and Mackenzie finally saw what James had under his arm. But nothing made sense; what did James hope to achieve by going up on the roof? Surely he knew that there was no way out?

James shoved against the hatch again, opening up his way to the roof completely. He turned and looked back at the store room with disdain. His eyes swept across the room, noticing Vic but ignoring him like everything else of no value in the room. This was what he should have done a long time ago. He was finally taking action, doing something about their situation instead of waiting for someone else to. His eyes settled on Mackenzie's.

"See you later, Mac." James grinned. "Good luck."

Mackenzie watched as James climbed up onto the roof with Beers tucked under his arm, the little dog whining, unable to free itself from James' grip. As he said goodbye, only then did Mackenzie understand what James was doing.

"No, James, stop!" Mackenzie struggled to his feet. "Stop, you're going to get us all—"

The store began violently rocking, and the radio fell to the floor where the back panel fell off, exposing the batteries.

"Damn it," said Vic, "what the hell is going on?"

Mackenzie pointed a finger at the exposed access way on the roof. "your fucking boyfriend is about to kill us all, that's what," he growled.

"What are you talking about?" Vic bent down to the radio. "Once the quake's stopped, we can—"

Mackenzie grabbed a flashlight from the floor. He looked at Vic. "Come with me. Forget that damn radio, and follow me."

As Mackenzie navigated his way across the floor of the store room, feeling like he was trying to walk on jelly instead of concrete, he heard Michele call out.

"Alyce? Where are you?"

"She's safe. She's with Laurel." Mackenzie began to climb the shelving with trepidation. The last time he had gone up on the roof, Myles had died. Something had caused the Goliath to back off, but Mackenzie had a bad feeling they wouldn't get lucky twice. Going up to the roof was a bad idea, a *very* bad idea. He had to get James back down. He was putting all of them at risk.

"Mac?" Vic looked up as Mackenzie neared the roof's opening. The light that shone down through it was dim, gloomy, as if evening had fallen. Previously, the sky had been clear blue, but now as Vic looked up at the small square patch of sky, he saw dark gray clouds looming over them. "What should I do?"

"Just hold this still." Mackenzie felt the cut on his hand open up, and blood began to seep through the bandage. He had one hand on the lip of the roof now, but the shelves were rocking back and forth, making it difficult for him to get purchase and lift himself up. "Hold it still for a second, that's all. I've got to get your stupid…"

A huge booming sound drowned out the rest of Mackenzie's sentence, a horrible noise from outside the store that almost caused Vic to wet himself. It was the Goliath, no doubt. It was awake, and it was coming back. Vic stood looking up at the sky, wondering what to do. The shaking hadn't stopped, hadn't even paused, and the building was groaning as if it was about to come down around him. Maybe the best option was the roof. Perhaps James had it right. Had he known this was going to happen? Had he worked out what the monster wanted? But how come James had left Vic down there with the others? He had to know what was going on. He had to get up there and talk to James directly, before it was too late. Tentatively, Vic put a foot on the first shelf, and prepared to lift himself up.

"Hold it," said Akecheta. "I'm next. You stay here and keep an eye on the others."

Akecheta pushed past Vic and began to nimbly ascend the rickety shelving. Vic knew that arguing was futile. The man was on a mission. What did they all know that he didn't? Why was everyone suddenly so desperate to get up on the roof?

As Akecheta reached the top, Vic saw Maria enter the room, running awkwardly, as if she was trying to tuck something into her back pocket as she ran across the uneven floor. Her face was determined, though her eyes betrayed a fear that suggested their time in the store was up.

"What the hell is going on?" asked Vic, his fear growing exponentially. It wasn't just the shaking and rolling ground, or the booming noise from the Goliath outside, but something else was happening, something to do with James. "Maria, what the hell?"

Maria glared at Vic. "Stay here. Make sure Michele, Laurel and Alyce are safe. Stay here, Vic." Maria put her hands on the shelves, unsure if she could get up there. "Just…stay here."

* * *

"James. James, get back here," hissed Mackenzie. He stumbled across the shattered solar panels toward the front of the store where James was stood. Beyond him, the Goliath erupted from the ground, its dark form shifting within the shadows and cloud of dust until it emerged into the light and rose into the air like a plume of black ash spewing from a volcano. "*James*, for Christ's sake, what do you think you're going to achieve by—?"

Mackenzie was cut off by the monster letting out a roar as it planted a foot on the ground and stretched its head up to the sky. The air trembled as it roared, and Mackenzie clasped his hands over his ears. It was as if he was standing beside a jet plane as it took off, the roaring whooshing hot air almost deafening him. The monster's red eyes looked around and Mackenzie knew it was seeking them out. When the roaring ended, Mackenzie looked at James.

"Back off, Mac, this is my only chance. Maria's been holding out on us. She has a vehicle, a *car*, right down there on the southern side of the store. It's our ticket out of here, don't you see? It's not only the best chance of getting out of here, it's the *only* chance. Maria was saving it for herself. She was telling Akecheta about it, I heard her. I know what happens out here. Save your own neck before anyone else, isn't that about right?"

"James, I know you think you have no options, but you do. We all do if we stick together. Nobody is out to get you. We're all scared, but we're trying to figure this out like adults." Mackenzie noticed the looming storm clouds on the horizon. They were low and sullen against an ashen sky. The Goliath was approaching the store again, and it would only take a few seconds to reach them. Every step it took was like a thunderbolt charging through the ground sending vibrations up through the store, up through Mackenzie's legs, and into his racing heart. "James, *please*, listen to me. You wouldn't get more than a few feet in Maria's car."

James glanced over his shoulder. When he looked back at Mackenzie, his eyes were alive, his skin was bristling, and he knew what he had to do. The monster was close, closer than ever before, but it would work.

"You could come with me, you know? You and me, Mac. I've worked it out. I can get past it. I can beat the Goliath."

Mackenzie heard someone come up behind him, walking over the broken panels on the roof, grinding them beneath their feet. He remained focused on James and tentatively stepped forward. There was a cool breeze stirring up, probably from the edge of the storm that was flirting around the horizon looking for a place to land.

"James, you're not thinking straight. I couldn't leave my wife. What about the others? Look, come down and maybe we can figure out—"

"Fuck it." James grabbed Beers and held the tiny dog out over the edge of the store.

"James, don't you dare, don't you fucking dare." Mackenzie had seen him tuck the puppy under his arm as he'd climbed the shelving. All the time they had been talking, James had kept it there. Beers had been quiet, shaken perhaps, but not quite scared enough to know he was in danger. Mackenzie had hoped it wouldn't come to this and hoped that James was just bluffing. Instead Mackenzie came to the realization that James didn't want any help. He was psychotic.

James turned around to face the Goliath. He held Beers out with both hands, and Mackenzie could hear the dog begin whining and barking.

"James, let it go. Come back from there and let the dog go."

Beers was lifted high into the air. It was like James was offering the Goliath a sacrifice, holding the dog up as an offering, a token of submission.

"Don't get in my way, Mac," shouted James. "This is the only way!"

Though the air was humid, Mackenzie broke out into a cold sweat when he saw what happened next. Beers struggled to get free, his little legs pumping furiously but kicking only air. Then James stepped up onto the edge of the store and dropped the dog. With barely a sound, the puppy disappeared from view as James let it fall.

"No!" Akecheta pushed past Mackenzie. "What have you done?"

"I'm saving us all, you idiot." James looked at Akecheta. "While it's distracted going after that dumb dog, I'm taking Maria's car and getting the hell out of here."

"Like hell you are." Akecheta charged at James, his face a maelstrom of anger and hatred.

Mackenzie watched as Akecheta grabbed James, and the two men fell back onto the rooftop. All the time the Goliath was still advancing on them, and Mackenzie wondered for a moment if James' plan would work. He heard a faint whining sound and raced to the edge of the store. Leaving Akecheta to fight with James, Mackenzie knelt down and peered over the rooftop at the ground below. Beers was there on the dusty ground, limping slowly away from the shop front. It looked like one of his legs was broken, but the puppy was still alive. It began to bark as the Goliath came closer, and Mackenzie sank back, unable to watch, knowing the dog was about to become the monster's next meal.

Mackenzie saw James and Akecheta standing now, still grappling with one another, and then suddenly James twisted Akecheta around, holding one arm behind his back. Pulling his hand from his jacket, James pulled out a knife and held it to Akecheta's throat.

"Mackenzie, get the fuck up. Get away from there, and let the monster take the dog. I need to get to the car, and this is the only way. Give it what it wants. See? It's just a dumb fucking animal at the end of the day. A big one, I grant you, but an animal all the same. Feed it, and it'll be happy."

Mackenzie nervously got to his feet as James marched Akecheta slowly over to the eastern side of the rooftop. Mackenzie could tell Akecheta wasn't afraid. He had a cut lip, and sweat covered his face, but he wasn't scared of James. He looked angry, annoyed even at the inconvenience of having a knife held to his throat.

"James, this isn't right, this isn't you." Mackenzie glanced back at the monster. It seemed to have paused, and though it towered over them, its head was looking away. Something had drawn its attention elsewhere. Perhaps Beers was making a run for it. Even with a broken leg, the will to live was strong, and Mackenzie had no doubt that little pup would do what it could to survive and protect Alyce.

"James, drop the knife. Just think for a second. Any moment now that monster is going to see us all up here. There's no time for the car. There's no time for—"

"Shut up. *Just shut up.*" James ushered himself and Akecheta right up to the lip of the roof. He was perilously close to the edge, and Mackenzie could sense that James wasn't sure what to do next.

"This isn't how you thought it would happen, is it? Look, James, just let Akecheta go. This isn't helping you. You want the car? Take it. We won't stop you." Mackenzie wasn't lying. If James was suicidal enough to go out there in the car, then he'd let him. If it meant getting the others back inside and drew the Goliath away, then James was welcome to leave. "Just go, okay?"

"It's true," said Akecheta. "You can go. See how the monster's distracted? You were right, James. It went for the dog. You can make it."

They all looked at the monster. It was shuffling around in front of the store, looking around, and stomping its feet. Mackenzie knew it wouldn't take long to make a snack out of Beers. As they watched it, the monster bent down, and reached out a thick arm. They heard a snapping sound, and then the Goliath's arm retracted quickly. It dropped something into its mouth, and let out the bellowing sound of victory as blood dripped from its jaws.

"Fuck," said James, quietly. "I thought it would take longer than that. Stupid, slow fucking dog."

Another booming sound echoed across the desert, this time from away to the south. Mackenzie looked at James, the sour mood etched on his face matching the depressing gloom of the gray sky stretching out above him.

"Hear that, James? There's a storm coming. We need to move," said Akecheta. "You listening to me, boy?"

"Give me the knife, James, quickly, before it comes back." Mackenzie held out his hands, the palms facing upward and open. "You can do it."

James stared at Mackenzie, and then frowned. He shook his head. "No. There's not enough time. I need more time. The dog wasn't enough."

"What are you talking about?" Mackenzie watched as the frown left James' face. James closed his eyes, and when he opened them again, Mackenzie wished he had gone with Amy to San Diego, or stayed at home to watch the Brewers, or been anywhere but on that damn rooftop in the desert at that point in time. He wished he was anywhere else when that hideous smile crept across James' face.

"I need more time," said James calmly.

He drew the knife sharply across Akecheta's throat, cutting a deep line across from left to right, slicing open the skin and tissue to expose the oesophagus. Akecheta grabbed his throat as blood spewed out, trickling through his fingers. Surprise sprang from his wide eyes as his life gushed from his neck.

"I just need more time," announced James as he abruptly shoved Akecheta backwards and over the rooftop.

Mackenzie saw a bubble of blood rise up and burst from Akecheta's mouth as he fell backward, and that was the last he saw of him. There was a thud as Akecheta hit the ground and Mackenzie felt his knees go week. This was too surreal. He had no idea what to do next. Had that really happened? Did James just kill Akecheta? Mackenzie Brown was an ordinary guy who didn't so much as have a parking ticket to his name, yet now he was facing a dinosaur and a psychotic killer.

"That should keep it busy for a while. I'm outta here." James looked at Mackenzie. The knife in his hand glinted in the sun, and a droplet of blood dripped off the tip onto James' shoe. The alcohol had given him the confidence finally to take control. If anything, he felt relieved that it was over. Akecheta had been a thorn in his side from the start of the day, and he had no problem in disposing of problems. It wasn't the first time he had been forced to deal with someone in that way.

"I can't let you do that." Mackenzie straightened his back and stared at James. He had nothing to go on, no experience of how to handle someone armed and dangerous, but there was no way he could let James go now. The way with which James had so easily killed Akecheta told Mackenzie this wasn't the first time he had been in this situation. Was that any excuse to turn away though? Mackenzie hadn't had to face many dangers in his mediocre life, and whilst running his own business and raising a step-daughter had its own fair share of problems and pressures, nothing could prepare him for this. He could feel the monster's presence, and yet the Goliath was taking a secondary importance now that he was facing a killer. James had tricked them all, given them the illusion that he was nothing more than a spoilt brat, another whining tourist who came to hot places like the Mojave just so they could complain about the heat. James was using the guise of being a plain old traveler to fool them, to travel when he couldn't let the real man out. He was cold, selfish and cruel.

Mackenzie drew in a deep breath and steadied his nerves. He clenched his hands, and took solace in the thought that Laurel was safe, underneath the roof, away from this monster. And it occurred to him that it didn't matter he hadn't stood in front of a murderer before—how many times had James stood in front of someone prepared to stop him? Mackenzie owed it not just to Laurel but to everyone to stop James from escaping. He owed it to himself, to Amy, to Myles, to Akecheta and even Alyce's dog. Akecheta had quite literally saved Mackenzie's life earlier when Myles had been taken. The time to let James leave was gone.

James shrugged. "So be it." He raised the knife and pointed it at Mackenzie. "I'll just have to…"

"Stop right there, you motherfucking asshole."

Mackenzie heard Maria's voice, and kept staring at James. With the stress of everything his left eye was beginning to twitch, just beneath the lower lid, yet Mackenzie couldn't afford to take his eyes off James. He was only a few feet away, and any attempt to retreat or go to Maria would only allow James to attack, to gain the advantage.

"Maria, get out of here," said Mackenzie. As his eyes bore into James', he could see uncertainty there. The bravado was slipping, even if the mask wasn't.

"Maria, you've got to understand, there was nothing I could do." James softened his voice and lowered the knife slightly. Mackenzie noticed he still held it firmly though. "Akecheta was going to take the car. I was just trying to stop him. It was all an accident."

"Don't listen to him, Maria. James is a pathological liar. He's deranged. He threw Beers off the roof and then killed Akecheta." Mackenzie heard more booming noises echo across the desert. He couldn't tell what direction they were coming from exactly, as the noise just bounced around between the rocks and sparse trees, between the store and the Kelso Depot, so that it sounded like it was everywhere and nowhere. It didn't sound like thunder, yet he couldn't explain what it was. He just hoped they weren't about to be joined by a second Goliath.

"Maria," said James taking two steps forward so he was only an arm's length from Mackenzie, "Maria, you've got to see the only way out of this is to act quickly. Your car can save us. *You and me.* You can drive us back to Baker. I'll protect you. I'll help you. What do you say? You can save your store, save your sister, and get help for the others. Don't listen to Mac, he's been in the sun too long. I was trying to help Akecheta. I wouldn't willingly hurt anyone."

Mackenzie wondered how Maria was taking James' lies. How much had she seen? How much had she heard? The rooftop groaned and creaked and shuddered as if breathing its last breath. The loose solar panels jumped up and down as the store began to roll again, and Mackenzie suspected the Goliath was on the move. The sun was truly gone now, hidden behind a deep dark cloud. The store felt as fragile as James' state of mind.

"Maria, this place is turning into a glass coffin. Leave him to me." Mackenzie clenched his hands into fists. How dare James threaten his family and friends? How *dare* he do this? The Goliath was doing what it did because what else would an animal of that size do? If it found smaller prey, of course it would attack; of course it would try to kill them. James was the true monster here, killing for self-preservation, for motivations that were cowardly and greedy and baseless.

"No, Mac, I know what I'm doing." Maria's voice was closer now, behind Mackenzie's shoulder. "This asshole comes into my store and behaves like this? I saw what he did to Akecheta. He's a cold-blooded murderer and when this is all over, I'm going to make sure he's locked up for the rest of his pathetic life."

James sighed. "Well, I tried." He raised the knife, and lunged at Mackenzie.

Raising his arms in defense, Mackenzie prepared to feel the icy cold blade slice through his skin. He knew he had to stop James even if it meant getting hurt. His twitching eye had picked up the pace, to the extent that he could practically feel his eye pulsing. Although his stomach was doing somersaults, he didn't feel scared anymore. Mackenzie wanted it over. James could try to fight his way out of this, but there was no way he was going to win. Mackenzie would force them both over the edge of the roof if it came to it. He instinctively closed his eyes and waited for the impact, but instead there was nothing. Nothing touched him and no blade felt its way into his body. Suddenly, he became aware that James was gone. He opened his eyes and felt Maria's hand on his shoulder.

"Mac?" Maria whispered into his ear, and he knew what it was. He opened his eyes and looked up.

The Goliath had a massive claw wrapped around James and was silently lifting him up into the air. As the monster rose to its full height, Mackenzie could see James' face, a twisted, tortured mix of bewilderment and terror. He was wrapped firmly in the grip of the monster so only his head poked out of the top, and his feet from the bottom. Mackenzie saw the monster's head look from side to side, and then at James, at its prize. The dinosaur's red eyes had penetrating black orbs in the center, as black as midnight ebony, and although Mackenzie wanted to look away, he found he couldn't. It was peculiar. He knew James was finished. He knew there was no way to escape the Goliath, and he had no interest in watching any man suffer and die, yet somehow he couldn't take his eyes off James. Something inside of him was forcing him to watch, so he could see the end with his own eyes.

The Goliath squeezed its huge claws and roared. Blood oozed from James' eyes, and Mackenzie was thankful he was too far away to hear the man's screams. The Goliath roared again and Mackenzie watched in awe as its terrific power destroyed James. The pressure applied to his body was just too much, and as the monster squeezed tighter and tighter, James' head came off like a bottle top. His skull was ripped from his shoulders and his head fizzed into the air with a faint popping sound. A fountain of blood exploded from the monster's grip as James' body imploded.

Mackenzie and Maria stood on the rooftop as they were showered with the remnants of James' body, hunks of meat and a waterfall of blood cascading down over them like soft rain.

"Maria, let's get back in before it comes for us too." Mackenzie hoped the monster stuck to tradition and backed off. It had always stopped in the past when it had neared the rooftop. He didn't want to be around while pieces of James fell from the sky, nor did he want to wait to be next.

Without taking his eyes off the Goliath, Mackenzie slowly stepped backward toward the hatch. Maria still held onto him and shuffled back toward the hatch. The prehistoric creature lowered its head and looked at them. Mackenzie understood it was no more than luck that it had taken James first, yet he was relieved. He was relieved to still be alive and relieved that James was dead. Prison was too good for people like that.

Mackenzie heard a roll of thunder blanketed by thick clouds in the distance. The storm was closer now, tangible, charging the air with electricity; Mackenzie wanted the rain to come, to wash away the death that surrounded him, to wash away the bloody remains of James littering the rooftop, and to remind him he was still breathing, that he still had a foot in the real world.

"Maria. I don't think we're going to make it," Mackenzie whispered as the monster crouched lower over the store. Each time previously this had been the point at which it had backed off.

"We're almost there, Mac. Just a few feet more."

Mackenzie heard Maria whispering into his ear, felt her hand on his shoulder, but was unable to look at her. He wanted to keep his eyes on the Goliath and watch for any clues as to its next move.

The monster raised an arm and smashed it down upon the store, instantly causing the front to collapse and take with it a section of the roof. Shattered solar panels slid off the roof like glistening confetti, and Mackenzie barely managed to remain standing.

"It's not stopping. It's not stopping, Maria." Mackenzie noticed the shimmering solar panels reflecting back the monster, only now they couldn't show its whole face, just broken pieces of it: an eye, a tooth or a piece of bloody skin. What was it Akecheta had said about the Moerkhanee only being scared of each other? Had there been something about its reflection that had stopped it? Were the solar panels the only thing that had been stopping it from attacking? Chris had said something that registered now, about how it probably had poor eyesight from living underground. It just might be that it hadn't realized when it approached the roof it was seeing itself reflected back in the solar panels. It was scared of its own reflection. The problem now facing them was that those panels were smashed, and there was nothing else it was afraid of.

Edging around toward where it had smashed the front of the store, Mackenzie watched as the Goliath lowered its head and inspected the wreckage. The rubble and broken roof tiles were of no interest to it, and it swung its head around, taking off another few feet of the roof. There was an audible tearing sound as the eastern wall began to buckle, and a cloud of dust rose up into the stifling air.

"It's going to destroy the whole store. It's not stopping. It's taking us all." Mackenzie knew that the reason it had backed off previously had gone. The monster wasn't afraid, wasn't retreating underground, and wasn't going to stop until it had killed every last one of them.

Swinging its huge body around, the Goliath reached a muscly arm down and Mackenzie watched as it picked up Akecheta's limp body. Instantly, it threw him into its jaws and began to chew loudly, obliterating the body in seconds and swallowing the last of the dead tour guide.

Suddenly, Maria stepped in front of Mackenzie. She glared at him. "Get down that hatch and try to get the others to my car. Get away from here. Get as far away as you can."

"What are you doing?" asked Mackenzie as Maria turned back to face the monster.

"I'll be damned if I'm going to let it destroy my store without a fight."

Maria raised the gun in her hands and began firing at the beast. She unloaded the entire clip and the Goliath just stood there watching on bemused, as if nothing was happening. The bullets hit it, but had no effect. Mackenzie grabbed Maria's hand and pulled her toward the hatch, knowing they were unlikely to have another chance.

"Come on, Maria," he shouted as the Goliath smashed another leg into the store. "Hurry!"

CHAPTER 15

The storm clouds were making the light dull and had dampened the dry heat, but night was a long way off. "Down! Get down!" Mackenzie shoved Maria toward the hatch, but he could sense the Goliath behind him, still coming, still intent on attacking them and leveling the store. It wasn't stopping like it had before. Waiting for nightfall was no longer an option. "Last chance saloon," said Mackenzie.

He knew in his heart this was it. The thing wasn't going to stop now. Why should it? It had got the taste for blood. A few old bricks stood between them and the monster, and Mac knew it wasn't going to be enough stop it. He just wanted to get back down to Laurel. If he was going to die, if they were both going to die, he at least wanted the last thing he saw to be his wife's face.

"Yakazar-yakazaaaar!"

Mackenzie shoved Maria forward again as she neared the hatch. That strange calling noise the monster made was hideous. It signaled death. It signaled that *it* was in charge, that nothing could stop it. Quite what it meant to the monster Mackenzie had no idea. Was it calling for others? Was it something it did before charging? The things warm breath was on his back now. He could feel it, the warm sickly stench washing over him, cloaking him in the stench of rotten meat and the odor of something that should have died a long time ago. It was like being showered in warm sodden dirt. The roof was slowly being ripped apart, and it was buckling right underneath his feet.

Maria dropped through the hatch quickly, and Mackenzie got down on his knees. He looked through the hatch and saw Maria hit the floor. The shelves were gone, finally knocked over by the movement of the ground and the collapsing store. He slipped his feet in first, then lowered his body down and grasped hold of the roof. The monster towered over him now, and Mackenzie let go. There was no time for anything but to just drop and hope he didn't break a leg.

Landing on the hard concrete floor, Mackenzie felt all the air drain from his lungs. Invisible hands grabbed him and pulled him away from the opening, into the dark intestines of the store.

"Mac? Mac, you okay?"

Gasping for breath, Mackenzie muttered that he was and let Laurel pick him up.

"We have to get out of here," said Maria. Her legs were unsteady, but she was unhurt. It was no longer just the floor shaking but the walls and roof too. She couldn't quite believe she and Mackenzie had made it back into the store. She was caked in blood, her arms and face smeared bright red. She looked like she had coated herself in war paint. There was a bloodied hairy clump of James' scalp on her arm and she brushed it off quickly, sickened. Akecheta had fallen victim to the beast as had Mr. Stepper. Now they were all going to follow her two friends into the depths of hell, eaten by the Goliath. Maria put a hand on the wall to stop herself from fainting. She had shot it, blasted everything she had into its face, and it hadn't even blinked.

"Oh, Christ, only you two?" asked Vic. "What about the tour guide? James? Where's James?"

Mackenzie had blood all over him, clinging to his body and dripping from his hands as though he had washed in it.

"Mac, show me where you're hurt," demanded Laurel urgently as she pulled him toward her.

He plodded forward reluctantly, letting her lead him away from the hatch. He felt her hands running over him, searching for his injuries, running through his thinning hair, trying to find where the blood was coming from.

"Where are the others?" Laurel tried to catch Maria's eyes, but they never left the floor. Laurel pulled on Mackenzie's arm. "Mac? Where are they? Akecheta? James? Tell me."

Mackenzie just shook his head.

"Oh my God." Laurel took a step back and looked at her husband. He was drenched in blood. It was then that she understood. He wasn't hurt, or cut, or injured. The blood wasn't his. It was theirs. "*It* did this? It took them both?"

Mackenzie turned and looked at Maria. If she still had the gun, she hid it well. What did it matter anyway? It was no use against that thing.

"The Goliath. It was quick. It…" Mackenzie grabbed his wife's shoulders. "It took them all, ate them; I thought it was going to…"

Mackenzie looked up at the hatch. Where was it? The Goliath had been there, right above them, watching them disappear back inside the store, yet it had stopped. Maybe he was wrong. Maybe there was still a way out of this. The vibrations had stopped, suggesting the monster had too. The store was still standing for the most part, but he doubted they had long. They were going to have to try for Maria's car.

"Is it still out there?" Laurel looked for answers in Mackenzie's eyes, but all she saw was sadness and fear. "I think the front of the store is gone. I thought the whole building was coming down. Why did it stop?"

Shrugging, Mackenzie wiped a drip of blood from his nose. "I don't know anymore. All I know is that we have to get out of here."

"Where's Beers?" Alyce tugged at Mackenzie's leg. "Where's my dog?"

Mackenzie looked down at the quizzical expression on the young girl's face. "I'm sorry, Alyce, but your dog…ran away. It was scared. I think Beers ran away." He couldn't bring himself to tell her it had been eaten by a dinosaur, or that James had thrown it off the roof.

Alyce folded her arms. "He'll come back. If he's scared, he'll come find me. Can we go look for him? If he's outside, he might get lost. Actually, yes, let's go look for him."

Mackenzie watched as Alyce picked up her bag and began putting her things inside. Maria was busy shoving bottles of water into a backpack. The store wasn't built to withstand this sort of damage and would undoubtedly collapse soon. A huge crack ran through the western wall, and the floor was rippled as if huge snakes had crawled underneath it.

"Mac, where's James?"

Mackenzie looked at Vic. The mere mention of James' name brought a surge of anger to Mackenzie, but he had to accept that Vic liked James, maybe even loved him, and whilst the two were together, Vic hadn't been the one to lose it. "I'm sorry, Vic. There was nothing we could do." It was the best he could do. The truth wasn't going to help anyone. James was gone, and no amount of bitching about him now, and what he'd done, was going to bring him back from the dead.

"Oh, right." Vic looked crestfallen, and he put a hand over his mouth.

"I'm sorry, Vic," said Laurel. "We're going to—"

"Time to go," said Maria. "Right *now*." She shoved her car keys into Mackenzie's hand. "Once we get out there, we need to hurry. My hands are shaking so Goddamn much I'm not in the best position to drive right now."

"Where do we go?" asked Mackenzie.

"Anywhere that's not here," replied Maria.

"You really think we can make it?" asked Laurel. "I thought we'd decided it was too risky to go out there. You said yourself it's right there, waiting for us. Can we outrun it in your car, Maria?"

Maria looked at her and Mackenzie. She opened her mouth to speak, and then closed it again. What could she say? She didn't want to spell it out, but they were out of options. Stay and wait for the store to collapse in on them, or go outside and take their chances with the Goliath. At least out in the open there was a chance, however slim. Waiting inside was just waiting for death.

"Myles? Are you coming, dear?"

As one, they all turned toward the hatch. Michele had been so quiet since her husband was taken they had all but forgotten her. She was standing directly beneath the rooftop hatch, peering up at the opening.

"Michele? Come away from there." Maria handed the backpack full of water to Laurel. "Michele, we're leaving."

"Mom?" Alyce began marching over to her mother. "We're going to look for Beers. He needs our help. He's lost. Mom?"

Michele looked blankly at Alyce and then stared up at the hatch. She cupped her hands around her mouth and began calling out. "Myles? Myles, get down here now. Your daughter needs you."

"Michele, stop it. He's gone. Attend to your daughter," said Maria firmly. "Alyce is…"

With lightning speed, the Goliath plunged its jaws down through the roof, smashing through the hatch and snatching up Michele. As the roof tiles and broken solar panels began to cave in, Mackenzie saw Michele lifted up into the air, her head trapped in the monster's teeth. Her arms and hands pummelled the monster and her legs kicked wildly, but there was little she could do. It had her.

The Goliath shook Michele about like a toy doll, all the while smashing its huge head through the roof sending the building into freefall. With daylight now poking through more and more holes in the roof, and the Goliath threatening to tear the whole place down around them, Mackenzie knew it was time to go. Michele had stopped struggling, and the Goliath was pulling her up through the hole it had made in the roof. Seconds later, a shower of warm blood rained down on the place where Michele had been.

"Go, go, go!" shouted Mackenzie. Grabbing Alyce's hand, he charged from the back room, urging Laurel on ahead of him. From the desperate screams behind him, he knew Maria and Vic were following. He had no idea how they were going to get out. The front of the store had caved in, and the rear of the store had a giant dinosaur straddling it. The walls were heaving and rolling, and the ceiling above him was falling in. He would climb over every brick if he had to. If it cost him his last breath, he would get Alyce out of there. She was crying, begging him to go get her Mommy, but he pulled her with him, dragging her across the buckling floor.

Laurel suddenly began climbing over a pile of masonry, and Mackenzie saw light ahead. The dull sky blossomed above, and Mackenzie wasted no time in lifting the crying Alyce up and over the rubble. Laurel grabbed her, and Mackenzie began to scramble over the bricks behind them. The monster had knocked down a wall, meaning they didn't have to dig their way out, just use the gaping hole in the store where the front entranceway had once been. As Mackenzie stumbled onto the dusty ground, he saw Maria fall next to him. Vic followed her, and the ground shook as more booming thunderous noises echoed around their heads.

"Maria, where's your car?" asked Laurel.

"Mom! I want my Mom!" screamed Alyce.

Mackenzie felt a cloud block out the sunlight on his face, and he looked up to see the Goliath standing over them, one monstrous powerful leg now planted firmly in the middle of the store where they had been only moments before. The clouds were a long way off, clever enough to know to stay out of the way of the dinosaur that was leering over the remaining survivors.

"Fuck, we're dead," said Vic. He began to walk backwards, into the street, away from the collapsed store, away from the monster, and away from the others. "We're fucking dead."

"Maria, where's the car?" Mackenzie ignored Vic and looked around the street. He saw the charred remains of the bus, and the Kelso Depot across the road, but no sign of a car.

"There," said Maria quietly. She raised a hand and pointed to a huge mountain of bricks that had once been the south-western wall of her store. Underneath it, Mackenzie spotted a deflated tire, a shattered windscreen, and what looked like a car door. "There it is. He's right. Vic's right. We're f—"

A hail of bullets blistered the air, ripping through the sky above them and punching into the midriff of the Goliath. With a huge roar, the monster turned into the gunfire.

"What the hell is that?" asked Mackenzie. The thunder he had heard before was nothing of the sort. It was there again, a rolling noise that seemed to just roll on and on without pause. There was a pulsing sound behind the thunder, and more to it than just God's work. Mackenzie heard engines. He watched as more gunfire erupted overhead, shattering into the monster's body, tearing bloody holes in its thick hide. Drawn by the gunfire, the Goliath took a giant stride in the direction of the noise, away from the store. Mackenzie smiled. Maybe, just *maybe*, there was still a chance.

"I want to go home." Alyce yanked her hand from Laurel's and ran into the street kicking up dust with each step.

"Alyce, get back here." Laurel let Alyce slip from her grip, unable to hold onto her. She watched as she ran to Vic who was heading for the bus.

Catching sight of the movement below, the Goliath stopped and turned its head toward the two small figures below.

"Alyce, stop," growled Mackenzie. He noticed the monster's attention was drawn to her. They needed it to follow the gunfire, not them. "Just stand where you are."

A moment later, the monster resumed its march toward whoever was firing at it. Small bursts of gunfire reached the beast and tiny pieces of skin were shaved off its thick hide. Mackenzie could tell it would take more than a few bullets to bring it down.

"What is that? It sounds like an army," said Laurel.

"Maybe it is." Mackenzie beckoned Alyce over with promises to look after her. She came back to him slowly, her large eyes all the time staring at the magnificent creature towering above them.

"Out here? We should be so lucky." Maria ducked as a crackle of gunfire erupted. It was followed by an explosion, a muffled booming sound in the distance, and then nothing but the bellowing of the Goliath as it continued walking away from the store. "I don't think anyone out there's going to help us. With what's happened, I doubt we'll be seeing anyone else come through here today. Whoever it is, they're a fair way off."

"But the shooting…surely, that must mean rescue is coming?" Laurel hugged Alyce tightly to her as the girl returned to them. "The police or the army are close, you can hear them. They're going to kill it, aren't they?" She looked down at Alyce, at the orphaned young girl who seemed to finally comprehend that neither her mother nor her father were coming back to her. "They're going to kill it."

Maria licked her lips and then regretted it. She tasted blood. "I'm not convinced anything can kill that Goliath. You haven't seen it up close, Laurel, so close you can smell its breath rising from its stomach. You haven't seen how Goddamn *tough* it is."

Vic approached the group but hung back, staying out in the street. He preferred to be out in the open where he could see it and where he could see it was safe. He felt like an outsider, even though he had been cooped up inside with these people for the best part of the day. Was that his fault? Had he sided with James too much? It didn't matter now. James was gone, and these people were all he had left.

"What about your car?" Vic looked at Maria and then Mackenzie. "We can't just wait. This is our opportunity. We should make a run for it whilst it's fighting someone else."

"My car is gone, Vic. Just pray that whoever is doing the shooting can force it to retreat back underground. Maybe then we can make it back to Baker. Maybe then we can move on and get you all home. Maybe I can rebuild my store, maybe…"

Maria tailed off. Thinking about the future suddenly seemed almost a foolish idea. She was stuck in the desert with no transport with the last few remaining members of a tour group for company, whilst some unknown army fought a huge Goliath right outside. Her friends, Mr. Stepper and Akecheta, were dead. Glancing at the wreckage of the bus, she saw broken bones protruding from a mound of fleshy pulp. The only clue that Mr. Stepper had been there was the torch that lay on the blood-soaked ground beside the mangled body. Seeing it reminded Maria that Chris' body was now buried under the ruins of her store, the remains of James and Michele were spread over her walls and roof, and the Goliath didn't have a scratch on it. She hoped her sister was okay. Getting back to Baker was all she could think of right now. Short steps: get to Baker, get home, and go from there. Thinking beyond that was incomprehensible. Family came first, no matter what.

"Vic, help me with these," said Mackenzie as he began to gather things from the ground. Some of Maria's stock was mixed in with the crushed bricks and remnants of the store.

"I've got water, Mac," said Maria patting her backpack.

"It's not that." Mackenzie picked up two cans of fly spray and deodorant, and asked Vic to find some lighters or matches. "We have absolutely no weapons at all. I'm just trying to be prepared is all. We don't know for sure what we're facing, and in the absence of any real weapons, we may have to improvise."

Vic handed Mackenzie a dusty lighter. "Look, Mac, that's all well and good, but we need to find some way out of here, or at least a place to wait until the army show up. They can't be far."

Mackenzie looked across the street at the plume of thin dust being driven into the air by whatever it was that was shooting at the monster. There was probably a convoy of vehicles, possibly tanks and trucks loaded with soldiers; the Goliath was a hundred feet away, rampaging through the desert, crushing huge rocks beneath its feet as it headed into the fight. Mackenzie knew their only hope of getting anywhere was that convoy. Walking a hundred miles through the open desert was not an appealing prospect, especially with Alyce. Exposure, coyotes, and a huge fucking dinosaur meant it was a sure fire way of getting killed. Vic had a point about seeking shelter. They had to get out of the open and under another roof, one that was considerably stronger than Maria's small store. He looked across the street, remembering the backpacker earlier in the day, recalling the foreign girl who had unsuccessfully tried to run for cover from the monster.

"Maria, what is this Kelso Depot place? We never got around to seeing it for real before...well, you know."

Maria looked at the sky lit up with fire and lightning. Small yellow sparks crackled in the clouds, and she hoped that the Goliath was taking a beating. "It's the primary visitor center for the Mojave. There's a museum inside, some artwork, some really interesting stuff that you would've liked, and lots of information about the Mojave area and its history."

"Anything in there about how to deal with a hungry, marauding dinosaur?" asked Vic.

"Doubt it," said Laurel despondently.

"But it's still standing, right? It's the only thing around here that still is." Mackenzie hoped the building would hold. There were cracks in the façade and the red and white walls were coated in a fine dust, yet it *was* still standing. It could offer them a place to rest up and hide from the monster.

Mackenzie bent down to Alyce. "How are you, Alyce?" he asked. "What do you think? Shall we go to the Kelso Depot?"

"I'm okay." The young girl wiped her red eyes. "I know Mom and Dad aren't coming back. I want to go now. I don't like that

Goliath thing. It's horrible. I want to go. I've still got my bag, see?" Alyce held up her bright pink bag. "I took care of it. I've got my book and a sweater and a juice and a toy for Beers."

Mackenzie saw Alyce was trying to be strong. He was impressed by the girl's resolve. She was probably the calmest of them all. He wished he had that much courage. "What are you reading?"

Alyce lifted her book out of her bag to show him the cover. "Snow White. It's my favorite, remember? She looks like a princess." Alyce put the book away.

"So do you," said Mackenzie. "If anything, you're a thousand times more beautiful than any princess I've seen. And even though your Mom and Dad aren't here, I know they'd be proud of you. We're going to take care of you, okay? Stick with Laurel and she'll look after you. You know, we've got a daughter of our own. She's a bit older than you, but I think you'd like her."

"What's her name?"

"Amy."

"That's a nice name. Is she pretty too?"

Mackenzie smiled. "Yes, she is. Very pretty and brave just like you." Mackenzie looked at Laurel. "Let's go."

Together, they all walked across the street to the Kelso Depot. The fighting and the Goliath were out of sight now, taking place behind the large building. Although they could hear the fight, they couldn't see who was winning. The battle was close now, audible enough for them to hear the shouts of the soldiers, individual guns being fired, and the smacking sound of the Goliath as it planted each foot on the ground. It still felt like they were suffering from an earthquake. The monster's movements caused the whole area to rock and roll, and Mackenzie had to remind himself this wasn't a natural phenomenon. The disturbance in the ground was being caused by the Goliath. Only when the ground stopped moving would he finally feel safe. When the ground was still, that meant the Goliath was still. And he was confident that it would only be still when it was finally dead.

"Come on, princess," said Laurel reaching for Alyce's hand.

Mackenzie was thankful Laurel was still with him. Amy would be devastated if anything happened to her mother. Thoughts of

Amy were too much to take right now. He had to believe, to trust that John had taken care of her. Getting to her was a priority, right after they found a way out of this desolate desert. He looked around as they walked in silence. A dried-up creek ran away from the Depot and an old disused railway line stretched as far as he could see. Over in the distance from the west were small clouds of dust on the horizon. There were large undulating dunes and ridges in the desert, left behind by the Goliath. A blue-gray sky was settling over the horizon and to the west a faint orange glow suggesting where the sun was hiding. As the burning star disappeared from view, the sky above Mackenzie hushed and became a serene cobalt color. The air cooled as the twinkling stars emerged overhead. It would be night soon, which meant it was even more important to have shelter if they couldn't leave. He knew that a darkening sky meant the temperature would drop fast.

A booming sound cut through the air and he bristled. The sound ricocheted between the rocks until it was carried away on a faint breeze. Suddenly, the desert was quiet, unnaturally quiet; *too* quiet. There was no shooting, no shouting, no explosions or sound of fighting. It was eerie. Abruptly, the usual sounds of the animals that lived in the desert gradually rose. All manner of cries and whistles, squeals and yelps, screeches and shrieks rose up from the desert floor, all clamoring for attention. As he listened, he thought he might have even heard the faint howling of a hungry coyote.

"Is it dead?" Laurel had been leading them to the Kelso Depot, but stopped and turned to face her husband. The ground had stopped shaking, and the end to the fighting had caught everyone's attention. A grin broke out on Laurel's face. "It's dead."

"She's right. Listen." Vic held a finger up in the air, pointed toward the evening sky. "They got it. They fucking got it."

Even Maria broke out into a smile. "Well I'll be damned. I think...wait, what's that?"

From around the corner of the Kelso Depot, a figure came running, clad in khaki from head to toe. The figure held a machine gun and ran straight for them. Dark goggles dangled around the figure's neck, and when they came closer, it became evident it was a man, a soldier. He wore a pained expression on his face, and his upper body was covered in blood.

"What now?" asked Maria, as the soldier bore down on them. "What the hell is happening now?"

CHAPTER 16

"Look, just start over, you're not making any sense." Mackenzie hauled the soldier to his feet. After collapsing to the ground in front of them, the man had spoken so quickly that he had only been able to pick up odd words that made no sense.

"Private Randall, right?" Maria jabbed a finger into the man's chest. "Start talking. What the hell is going on?"

Mackenzie looked at the man he held in his hands. He was young, probably no more than twenty or so, and scared. He clung to his machine gun like a baby and sweat ran down his face. He had large eyes, a thick nose, and a face that could sink a thousand ships. Mackenzie imagined the man had signed up out of duty rather than any aspirations of a career. Panic was written all over the young soldier's face.

"Look, we were on our exercises when we got called up. I don't really know that much. It went underground, so we had nothing left to shoot at. I mean, I'm not sure the Goliath was even there to begin with. Right? What about LA? Who's in charge now? The Yucca Flats. Man, they messed up big time. Where's it gone? Is it here? I had to get out of there."

"Randall? Take a breath. Calm down." Mackenzie let go of the man, not wanting to antagonize him. He was visibly shaking, and Mackenzie had no idea if the gun was still loaded. The man was a mess. He was making no sense and getting all of his stories mixed up. "Just start from the beginning. Tell us what you can. It's all right. We're just like you, okay? We just want to be someplace safe. Talk to me, Randall. What's happened?"

The soldier looked around the small group of people, and his eyes settled on Alyce. "It's not the earthquakes that caused this thing to appear, it's the other way around," said Randall as he offered the girl a smile. "This thing, this Goliath, is *causing* the quakes. It tunnels underground, lives underground…it's hard to explain."

"Go on." Mackenzie tried to sound reassuring, to soften his voice so Randall wouldn't get spooked and then run off again, or do something worse.

"The tests out at Yucca. They messed up." Randall shook his head. "I've got a buddy in the Marines, stationed out at Twenty Nine. I managed to get hold of him before the shit started. Command wasn't telling us shit, so I figured I might be able to get more sense out of someone who actually knows what's *really* happening. He has a contact who told him the whole area is flooded with radiation. The mines, the tunnels, they…they knew what might happen, but…"

Randall tailed off and looked back over his shoulder. He winced at something visible only to him, and then looked back at the others.

When he didn't speak again, Maria prodded him. "But what?" she asked. "We know about the nuclear bombs. You saying the Goliaths are a result of that?"

"Sorta," replied Randall. "Well, yes. Look, there was a long hiatus between the last test in 1992 and a few months ago. According to my buddy, they thought the bombs might have been the cause of today's quakes. You know, open up a fissure underground or something? But that wasn't it. A couple of weeks ago, they started finding sinkholes opening up all over the place. The tremors got bigger and bigger, the reports of damage and injuries grew, and then animals started disappearing. Whole farms just vanishing, hundreds of livestock disappearing without a trace."

"They weren't just killed by the quakes? Landslides?" asked Mackenzie.

"No." Randall let out a long sigh. He knew he shouldn't say what he was about to, but there seemed little point in holding back now. Faced with imminent death, what was the point in hiding behind lies anymore? "You heard of Goodsprings?"

"Sure," said Mackenzie. "Couple of days back, the whole town fell into a big fucking hole. A lot of people died. It was on the radio. I think the news said the area was riddled with tunnels from some old coal mines. Before anyone had time to figure it out, the whole town fell into a sinkhole, destroying everything."

"Well, the whole town did fall into a big fucking hole, but that's where reality stops. We fed the media a line about the abandoned mines, to stop them going in and seeing what really happened."

"So what did happen?" Mackenzie was beginning to get angry. Private Randall might be wet behind the ears, fresh out of training, but he was clearly telling the truth. And now the truth was coming out, Mackenzie didn't like it one little bit.

"It was the Goliath," said Randall nervously. "The ground underneath the town was weakened by activity from the monster. Two days ago it popped up and destroyed the whole place. The town was decimated. There were a couple of buildings still standing, but nobody got out. It…it ate everyone."

Maria gasped and held her hand over her mouth, as if to stop herself from being sick. Vic said nothing but watched on with interest.

"She doesn't need to hear this," said Laurel to her husband as she took Alyce away.

"It *ate* everyone?" Mackenzie took a deep breath. "It ate hundreds of people?"

"Well, not quite everyone. There was one survivor," said Randall quietly. "Look I really need to get going. Let me—"

"No." Mackenzie stared at the soldier. "Say that again, please?" If he wasn't so angry he would pity the man. This soldier was just a grunt. He wasn't in charge of this sorry operation. He was just a messenger stuck in the shit with the rest of them. "You said there was a survivor?"

Randall nodded without looking up. He was afraid if he made eye contact with Mackenzie that he might freak out. "A woman. Sharyn something. I don't know her name. She saw the whole thing. She described it. The monster was real. She was the only eyewitness we had to what we were facing; to what we had created. The woman told the military after she escaped how Goodsprings was destroyed, just ripped apart by the sheer power of this thing. She was our most reliable source of information about what happened there."

"Jesus Christ." Mackenzie kept an eye on Laurel and Alyce. He didn't want them straying too far, but he was glad they weren't around to listen to Randall anymore. "You're saying just *one* of those things took down a whole town?"

"Yes. We encountered one outside of Baker, and another popped up in San Diego. Now they're coming up all over the freaking place like rats. The one that destroyed Goodsprings wasn't unique, or a rogue mutant; it's part of a whole new species, and from what I've seen, we're not top of the food chain anymore. We don't know exactly how many there are. People who see them don't tend to be around for long..."

Mackenzie instantly thought of Amy in San Diego. The radio reporter had told of the monster there, but he had assumed it had been dealt with. He had hoped when the monster that had been stalking them was dead it might be over, but there could be any number of these things. The Goliaths had caused the ground to shake; there was nothing natural about what had been happening at all. These things lived underground and had remained undetected, apart from human contact, for who knew how many years; yet now, thanks to the resumption of the nuclear testing, they were topside. Everything he knew, everyone he loved, was in danger.

"This Sharyn, where is she now?" asked Mackenzie. "Maybe she can help? What about your convoy. Are they still heading this way?"

"I don't know. I...I got lost. I think so, but..." Randall was obviously covering up for the fact that he ran. He was itching to go before he was discovered. "As for Sharyn, the witness, well according to my buddy, she wasn't much use to us. She was in no fit state to—"

"You keep saying *was*," said Mackenzie. "Where is she now? Why haven't we seen *her* on the news? Why did the military say nothing about what really happened to Goodsprings? They could've warned us."

Randall shrugged. "It's not like I was there, but you know how it is. We couldn't have her causing panic. Imagine what would have happened if it had gotten out the military had covered up what happened in Goodsprings. She wasn't an asset once we learned the truth, she was a liability. Look, I should get back to my unit. They'll be looking for me. I've already said more than I should."

"Let me guess, she succumbed to her injuries?" Mackenzie had a headache growing that would not go away, pushing to the front of his eyes. This whole sorry situation could have been avoided. It was a complete mess, a shambles from the very beginning.

Randall nodded. "What's done is done."

Not thinking what he was doing, Mackenzie punched the soldier in the gut. Randall doubled over and immediately pointed the machine gun at Mackenzie. "You want to go?" he wheezed. "You think you know better than me? I'm not a decision maker, I just do my job."

Maria glared at Mackenzie. "Stop. This is a waste of time. We need to figure out a way out of here, not fight. You heard the man. The Goliath is gone. It's dead. It's dead, Mac."

Mackenzie saw the gun pointing at him, but ignored it along with Maria's advice. "Your *job* is to protect people. Seems to me that you're part of a jigsaw that just doesn't fit anymore. I'm sick of being fed a pack of lies. My family are in danger, and as far as I can see, the blame lies with you and yours. You caused this mess."

"Mac, stop," pleaded Laurel. She had one arm around Alyce, the other down by her side. Her hand was curled up into a ball, the fingernails digging into her palm as a measure to control her fear. She could see her husband was angry. He wasn't thinking straight. Behind the anger in his eyes, she could see fear too. He didn't want to fight. He just wanted to protect her, to protect them all.

"Let him do it," said Vic. "The sniveling bastard deserves it. I lost James because of people like him."

Mackenzie swung at Randall who ducked easily, leaving Mackenzie swiping at nothing but air. Randall retaliated and threw a punch back at Mackenzie, connecting with the side of his head.

Mackenzie stumbled backward, shocked. Laurel began screaming at them to stop, but neither of the men were listening. She knew Mackenzie was going to get hurt if it continued. He wasn't a fighter, and he was taking on a trained soldier.

"Stop this, Mac," ordered Maria. "This isn't going to help. This guy is no more to blame than anyone else. The Goliath is gone. Focus your energy on how we're getting out of here. We need to find this man's convoy. We need their help. We can apportion blame later. Just…"

Mackenzie was blinded by rage, by frustration and grief. He charged at Randall. He was quite sure that the soldier wasn't about to shoot him, and Mackenzie succeeded in grabbing him. Both of them grappled like bears, twisting around and around each other until they tripped and slammed into the hard ground. Randall thrust a fist into Mackenzie's face, and blood spurted from his broken nose. Quickly, the soldier grabbed Mackenzie, rolled on top of him, and pushed him down on the ground, bouncing Mackenzie's skull off the road. Mackenzie yelped in pain and saw stars.

"Fuck you. I was trying to help," the soldier began screaming in Mackenzie's face. "You should listen to your friends. Who the fuck are you? What's your problem?"

"Enough," said Maria as she pulled them apart. "Enough of this shit, both of you." Maria hauled Randall off Mackenzie, and pushed him away. "Get out of here. Go find your friends and tell them you have five civilians stranded out here who need transport."

As Mackenzie dusted himself off and stood up, Randall began trudging away. "Fucking asshole," muttered the soldier.

The man's footsteps were the only sound that Mackenzie heard as he wiped the blood from his nose. Then he looked up and realized everyone was looking at him. Maria looked like she was about to take his head off, Vic had a wearied look on his face, and Alyce was snuggled up to Laurel's side. His wife was crying, and when he started to approach her, she took a step back.

"No, Mac," said Laurel as she shook her head. "What were you thinking? That wasn't like you."

"I'm sorry, okay?" Mackenzie rubbed the back of his head, finding blood where the soldier had slammed him into the ground. "What he was saying, what he said about the testing and the monsters and how all this could have been avoided. I just saw red. I just…look, I'm sorry. Laurel, can we just—"

"No, Mac, look at the state of you. Alyce is scared. You need to calm down."

Mackenzie sighed. She was right. He had lost it. Randall had only been the messenger. They did need the army's help, and his unit had to be close by. What had he been thinking? He knew that he had let his judgment be clouded. The truth was he had been thinking about Myles, about Akecheta, about Amy, and what happened next. Laurel would come round, he knew that, but he should've listened to Maria. She was right. They did need the soldier's help. They needed to get home.

"Hey, Randall?" Mackenzie called after the soldier. The man was looking around nervously and seemed in no hurry to get back to his unit. Mackenzie suspected he was deserting, but in the middle of the desert found himself unsure where to turn. "Randall, wait up. We can vouch for you. We'll tell them you were helping us. Just wait. I'm sorry, but don't…"

Mackenzie heard a faint noise, almost like a muffled explosion. It echoed across the desert and mountains in the distance, trickling through the scrub and cacti before it reached his ears. His leg twitched as the dirt beneath his feet started to vibrate. At first just slowly, then more insistently until it was jumping around like fresh popcorn on the stove.

"Laurel?" Mackenzie looked at his wife with confusion. Was he imagining this? Had he hit his head that hard? The look on Laurel's face told him this was real. The ground started shaking then, rippling like waves that knocked Maria off her feet. Mackenzie saw Vic begin to run back to the store, as if he could find shelter inside the ruins of the old place.

"Laurel!"

Mackenzie began to run toward her and Alyce before the uneven ground knocked him off his feet too. It was impossible to stay upright, like trying to walk a tightrope in a hurricane, and he saw Laurel and Alyce go down too.

The Goliath emerged quickly, exploding from underneath the Kelso Depot with a deafening roar. Its magnificent body climbed up through the building at speed, bringing the walls down around it. It was like a bomb going off, and the huge building was reduced to rubble and a cloud of dust in seconds. Mackenzie heard the familiar booming sound of the monster and watched as it clambered from the ground, appearing from the ruins of the building with frightening speed. He watched as the Goliath reared its head and let out its familiar call, its bulbous head silhouetted against the dark blue evening sky.

"YAKAZAR-YAKAZAAAAR!"

Before he could say or do anything, Mackenzie saw the Goliath step forward, out into the open, and seize Randall. The man had dropped to the ground and begun firing at the monster. The bullets had done nothing though except to draw the creature's attention. A huge foot stamped on Randall, and gallons of blood splashed out from underneath the monster's leg, decorating the road with the soldier's blood. When the Goliath lifted its leg, there was little left of the soldier except an untidy pile of clothes and bones, all tied together with stringy flesh and sinews of flesh. The monster roared again, and Mackenzie knew it wasn't going anywhere. The army might have scared it into going underground, but now that it was back, it wasn't leaving. It wasn't dead. It didn't even look hurt. Maybe it was a territorial thing. Maybe it had claimed this area and was clearing it out. Unless Randall's unit appeared, armed with a lot more guns, they weren't getting out of this one.

Mackenzie began to crawl along the ground toward Laurel and Alyce. The destruction of the Kelso Depot had been quick, yet the dust that had blown up around it lingered in the evening air, and Mackenzie had to frequently wipe his eyes so that he could see. The air was thick with the dust now, and he couldn't call out to them, to let them know he was coming. Every time he opened his mouth, it was filled with warm air and sand.

"Don't let it take me. Oh God, it's coming, I can hear it. It's coming!"

Mackenzie heard the voice somewhere to his left. It wasn't male, and he would have recognized it if it had belonged to Laurel or Alyce immediately. That only left one option: Maria.

With the ground still shaking and the sandstorm swirling around him, Mackenzie got to his feet. He cupped his hands around his mouth and called out. "Maria. Maria, where are you?"

Mackenzie became aware of a shadow in the cloud of dust that had yet to disperse. It was the monster. It was moving, fast. It was getting closer to them.

"Maria?" he called out again and got little answer.

She knew it was coming. It was heading in her direction, and she had no choice but to run. Her store was gone, the Depot was gone, and there was nowhere to run to. The desert was her last chance. Perhaps she would be able to hide so that it couldn't find her in all the dust?

Maria ran. She ran faster than she had for twenty years. Something snagged on one of her feet and she tumbled down, smacking sharply into the road. Her hand sliced open on a piece of wreckage from the tour bus, and she jumped up quickly. In the maelstrom, she could see the Goliath, its hideous form reaching into the sky like a terrifying obelisk. It was going to hunt them all down, and right now, it was hunting her. Maria was thrown into fear as the head of the giant beast loomed over her. It came closer and closer through the sand, its deep red eyes becoming clearer the closer it got. Soon, she saw its teeth and jaws, dripping with blood. It snorted and stomped a foot on the ground sending shivers over her body. It could see her now, smell her, practically taste her; Maria felt dwarfed by its size and power, and she was caught in a no-man's land. She could stay and fight, but hadn't the strength to repel it, or she could run and hope to outwit it, hide in the desert or the ruins of her store.

Maria turned and ran. No way was she giving up that easily. She heard Mackenzie calling for her, but couldn't see him. She was running away from the voice, not wanting to lure the beast any closer to him or the others. She ran, hoping it would get lost, give up the chase, or go and find something with a little more meat on its bones. She didn't look back, but ran in what she thought was the direction of the open desert. The thunderous footsteps of the Goliath echoed in her ears. She wasn't about to waste time in looking back for it. She just ran.

Maria was drenched in sweat, and though she was under the shadow of the beast, she could feel warmth on her back. It was sickly warmth, moist and oppressive, as if she were being coated in boiling paint. She recognized this wasn't like the usual dry heat of the sun. The creature was undoubtedly right above her now. She could smell it. It was the same hideous smell she had experienced on the rooftop with Mackenzie. A smell like rancid meat engulfed her, and she tried not to think about how close the thing probably was. Her legs were beginning to feel like jelly and the rocking motion of the ground as the Goliath pounded over it was unsettling. Maria stumbled over a large rock that jumped into her path and she was unable to stay upright. Her legs tangled together, and as she fell, her face caught the side of the rock which tore a deep gash across her cheek.

"Take my hand."

Maria looked up and saw Mackenzie's face appear. Frantically, she grabbed his outstretched hand, and he pulled her away from the rock.

"Mac, you have to get going. It's…" Maria saw Mackenzie's eyes drift upward and widen in terror.

"Quickly!" Mackenzie shoved Maria out of the way and stepped forward. He held out a large pressurized can and lighter, and just as the Goliath came in for the kill, he ignited the burst from the can, spraying the Goliath's face with flames. He had been lucky to find the bag with them in and hoped it would work just like in the movies. As he stood there burning the creature's face, he wasn't sure if it would do anything. In the next three seconds, either it would snap its jaws around him, or he might get lucky and scare it off.

The monster recoiled as the fire licked its face, singeing its eyelids, and Mackenzie let out a sigh of relief. Mackenzie knew it wasn't enough to really hurt it, but was probably enough to surprise it. He had bought them no more than another thirty seconds, but it might be all they needed. He kept the fire burning until they were in the clear and only when he saw the Goliath step back, wiping an arm across its face as it disappeared once more into the sandstorm, did he toss the can and lighter aside.

"Maria, get to your store. Hide in the wreckage. Stop running and making any noise, and it might not find you. Laurel and Alyce are there too. Just go, now, before it comes back."

"What about Vic?" she asked.

"Haven't seen him," said Mackenzie. "I don't think the Goliath has either though, so we just have to trust he's okay. I figure if we play dead, maybe that thing won't be able to find us. This dust storm is clearing, so we don't have much time. Go that way, now. To the store."

Maria ran and Mackenzie heard the Goliath thundering across the road under the darkening evening sky. He heard gunfire and engines again, and he reckoned Randall's unit must be close. They must have heard the monster resurface. He hoped his plan would work. Movement and noise only attracted it, so their best option was to be still and hope the army would deal with it. With all the noise they were making, the monster would probably go after them, which would make it easier to hide in the store. He couldn't see the monster anymore, so it may have already gone for them. As he turned to run after Maria, Mackenzie heard a distant voice calling for help.

"Vic?" Mackenzie listened and heard it again. It was close. "Vic, where are you?"

A shadowy figure stumbled through the dust, and when it emerged, Mackenzie recognized Vic.

"I got lost in all this shit."

Vic looked scared but unharmed. He approached Mackenzie cautiously. "Where is it? I thought I saw it a moment ago, but then it disappeared."

"It's going after the army. Come on, Vic, we're heading back to the store. We're going to…"

Mackenzie stretched out his arm to offer Vic a hand, and then felt the sand and dust in the air shift slightly. It was almost imperceptible, but it was there. Just behind Vic, there was a disturbance in the swirling air. Mackenzie looked up and froze. It was still here. The Goliath hadn't gone anywhere. It was stood right there, not moving, hiding in the storm, watching them. It was happening just as when it had started attacking the store. It was toying with them, letting them think they were hiding from it, when *it* was just hiding from them. They had been foolish to think they could outsmart it. The monster might be a big brute, but it certainly wasn't dumb.

"What is it?" asked Vic as a frown spread across his face.

Mackenzie didn't know what to do. He had been outwitted. Outrunning it was impossible. He had nothing left to fight it with, and it was slowly, quietly, lowering its head right over Vic. Mackenzie said nothing. He opened his mouth to tell Vic to run, but what was the point? Where would he go?

"Fuck," said Vic quietly as he looked up at the monster above him. The snarling jaws of the monster were directly above him, close enough that he could count its teeth and reach out and touch them. The front incisors were dripping with saliva that left patches of oily liquid on the ground. As the monster opened its jaws wider, foul air overwhelmed Vic, and something dislodged itself from between the creature's teeth. An arm fell, landing beside Vic on the ground. The fingernails were manicured and painted red, and a gold bracelet was still wrapped around the wrist. The arm had been ripped off with such force that the bone had been severed neatly, and only a few straggly veins and thin muscle tissue remained.

It was then that Vic lost control of his bladder. He opened his mouth to scream, aware that Mackenzie was calling out to him, but there was nothing he could do. The Goliath lunged and snapped up Vic in its powerful jaws, breaking his spine instantly as it closed its jaws around him, squashing his fragile body. Vic's blood was forced to find an exit route, and it spurted from every orifice, showering Mackenzie in gore and viscera, splattering his face with brain tissue and warm blood.

He was barely six feet away. Mackenzie took a step back from the monster. Vic hadn't cried out once he was inside the thing's mouth. He was probably killed quickly, and Mackenzie watched in awe as the monster suddenly reared up, threw back its head, and swallowed Vic whole. The Goliath opened its mouth, and Mackenzie noticed its whole body quivered as it roared.

"Yakazar-yakazar…"

The dust was clearing quickly now, and Mackenzie could see the ruins of the Kelso Depot and the store, the burnt-out bus, and the splattered remains of Randall and Mr. Stepper. If he ran to the store, Mackenzie knew he might lead it to the others. It was too risky. He was a dead man, and he knew it. At least he wasn't going to lead it to his family, and Mackenzie began running in the opposite direction, waiting for the creature's bloody teeth to snap around him.

CHAPTER 17

Mackenzie could hear the gunfire from the still invisible army as he ran, and the ground in front of him exploded as a grenade missed its target. There was shouting as soldiers behind him closed in, and the rumble of engines grew in volume.

Mackenzie snaked a shaking hand across his face, wiping the blood away as best he could. He was in awe of the monstrous thing that was slowly picking off the tour group one by one. It truly was the ultimate killing machine and he despised it with every inch of his soul. Knowing it was there, right behind him, made him feel sick. His knees felt weak, and he wanted to go back home. He wanted to take Laurel and Amy back home to Milwaukee where dinosaurs didn't exist, and he led a mundane but satisfying life selling second-hand cars. It wasn't an exciting life, but he had a good life, and a happy family. Why did this have to happen now, to him? Why was this happening at all? What Randall said bounced around his brain. They had created this. They had messed with things they shouldn't have and boy, were they paying for it now. Everything was fucked up. It was so confusing. Everything was mixed up in his head; the bodies, the military, Amy, the Goliath ripping Vic apart. The only thing he could hold onto was Laurel. All day her face had been so full of worry and fear that it broke his heart. He had to get her out of here. She would get to Amy, take care of her. That was what he had to do. It was something he could control, something he could make a plan about. Being bait for the Goliath was about as useful as he could make himself right now.

A fiery crackle of bullets flew past his ear and ripped into the ground to his left, narrowly missing him. A cactus was shredded into pieces, and Mackenzie kept running. He could feel the beast behind him; he didn't need to look. He knew it was there. It wanted him. Mackenzie felt pleased, not at his own impending death, but that he had given Laurel a chance. There was satisfaction mixed in with all the guilt and grief and fear. If she made it out of this alive, then it hadn't won completely.

The monster let out a bellow, and Mackenzie jumped over a large rock as more bullets whistled past him. The dust had really settled now, and he was out in the scrub, off the road, and well away from the store. There wasn't much more he could do. He could tell from the noise the monster was making that it was only a few feet away. It was now or never. Mackenzie slowed to a jog, and saw a jeep in his peripheral vision. It was going fast, and on the back were men firing at the monster. Mackenzie wished they had gotten here just a few minutes earlier. He stopped, out of breath, and sank to his knees. He couldn't run anymore. He was exhausted. Collapsing to the floor, he wrapped his hands around a small sharp rock. If the Goliath was going to eat him, he would make it as painful as possible. He could smash a lot of teeth with that rock.

Mackenzie turned and found the beast standing right over him. Its upper jaw was peeled back in a snarl, and its thick skin covered in bloody holes. Evidently not all of the army's bullets had missed their target. Saliva and blood cascaded down from the vicious creature's jaws, showering Mackenzie in a gentle rain of viscera that sickened him. He looked into the monster's red eyes, into the black orbs at their center.

"Come on then, you bitch," shouted Mackenzie. "You want supper, come and get it."

Mackenzie lifted the rock in his hand knowing he was unlikely to get to use it. The monster could destroy him right where he was; squash him like a bug on a windshield. The Goliath opened its mouth letting out another roar, its stinking breath engulfing Mackenzie.

A burst of gunfire behind him made Mackenzie duck, and he saw a six-foot gash open up across the monster's forehead as the bullets tore through the skin. Another round of gunfire caught the monster off guard and Mackenzie saw one of its front incisors shatter under the pressure. Suddenly, the monster backed up and reared up to its full height.

"Get the fuck down!"

Mackenzie didn't see who had said it, but knew when the time was to follow orders. He dived behind a rock and made himself as small as possible, pressing his body up against the rock. Five soldiers ran past him, their weapons hot and letting out an endless parade of gunfire. The men shot at the dinosaur as they ran, and Mackenzie felt the ground shaking as they ran past him. Looking past the men, Mackenzie saw a convoy of trucks, jeeps, even a tank, and soldiers; lots and lots of soldiers. Mackenzie looked around to see another convoy on the other side of the monster, and smiled inwardly. They were trying to flank the beast, take it down from both sides so that it had nowhere to go.

The sound of gunfire was deafening, and Mackenzie wondered how the thing was still standing. Making sure to keep his head down low, he peered over the rock. It was war in a microcosm; destruction wrought real on a miniature scale, as if a world war was taking place in a snow-globe filled with sand. The soldiers still standing were firing their automatic rifles as the Goliath moved around the desert trying to dodge them. It was like a dance, a twisted ballet that could only result in death. Mackenzie thought about trying to get to the store, but there was no safe path such was the barrage of bullets whizzing through the air. He wondered how long the men could keep going. One got too close to the monster, and it took him down easily. Even with the man firing his weapon at point blank range, the Goliath snapped him up in its jaws and crushed him, before swallowing the remains. Another repeated the same mistake and the monster simply stood on him, killing him instantly under its powerful, heavy legs. A missile of some sort whistled through the air above Mackenzie's head and punched into the monster's mid-riff, exploding with such force that Mackenzie expected to see the monster torn in half. When the fire and smoke dispersed, he could see the monster was still standing, attacking the platoon now despite the bloody hole in its side.

Swiftly, the Goliath charged at the men, mowing them down with ease. It ignored their guns, ignored their shouts, and simply ran them down where they stood. It punched a hole through its attackers, and rushed one of the jeeps. It was no more difficult than kicking a football and Mackenzie watched in amazement as it smashed through the jeep, causing it to explode in a fireball and scatter the men surrounding it. Turning back quickly, the Goliath swept up the standing men in its jaws, smashing them under its feet, and carving a deadly path through the men who were struggling to contain it. The Goliath raced over the desert ground and headed for the other convoy of vehicles. It raised a foot over a truck and brought it down on the front of the vehicle so that the engine was crushed under its weight. A huge claw extended from the creature's foot and dug straight through the armor plated metal. Then it tossed the truck from side to side, ignoring the hail of bullets still pouring into it from all sides, and tore the truck open. The driver was thrown clear and hurtled through the air before being caught in the creature's snapping jaws. Its teeth shredded the man, and his dying screams were drowned out by the roaring noise of the magnificent creature as it frenziedly ate the unlucky soldier.

Mackenzie sensed the monster was angry. It could have retreated underground, gone far from the battle to lick its wounds, yet it stayed above ground to fight. This was going to end one way or another. Mackenzie watched as another truck drove straight at the beast. The flashes of gunfire from it suddenly ceased when the monster bent its head down and smashed into the truck's side, sending it tumbling over and over through the desert. Several men were thrown clear of the truck as it came to a halt and the Goliath tried to pick them off one by one, hunting them down like dogs as they fled the burning wreckage. Mackenzie saw limbs flying in all directions as it ate them. One soldier was pinned down under its claws, unable to escape. The monster's head hovered briefly over the man before sinking its sharp incisors into the man's torso and plunging right through him into the ground. Mackenzie heard the poor man call out in pain before choking on his own blood. Then he was gone, swallowed up like so many before him, into the belly of the beast.

A massive fireball erupted into the crisp air as a shower of grenades fell onto the monster's body. It let out what Mackenzie could only describe as a howl, before straightening up. The monster took an unsteady step forward, almost as if it was dizzy. Was it actually hurt? Were they finally making an impression on it? Mackenzie had to take his chance and get to the store. He had to make sure Laurel was still all right. Creeping forward carefully, ensuring he didn't catch the monster's attention, he made his way toward the ruins of Maria's store, scarcely able to believe he was still alive.

"Yakazar-yakazar."

The vicious sound erupted from the Goliath's throat like a sword cutting the air, slicing through the very atoms and sending a chill over Mackenzie's body.

"Yakazar-yakazar."

It moved sluggishly, as if it was weak or drained of energy. Mackenzie watched as the Goliath stumbled, swung its arms at another jeep, but missed. It looked cumbersome and heavy, and Mackenzie started to believe it was finally going down. He watched as the tank he had seen earlier took aim and fired a shell into the side of the monster. The explosion took a huge chunk out of the Goliath's torso and sent massive chunks of sizzling flesh flying through the air. As the dinosaur sank to its knees, he couldn't help but grin. The monster was dying. It had killed numerous soldiers, but it appeared to be succumbing finally to the battering it was taking.

"Mac? Oh God, Mac, I thought…"

Laurel came running from the shelter of the ruined store and grabbed Mackenzie.

"Are you okay?" Mackenzie hugged Laurel and looked her over. The fight was still raging behind him, and he didn't want to risk them getting caught up in it, so he rushed Laurel back to the store. A truck sped past them, crunching over the dry ground as it raced toward its target. Several soldiers ran after it, all firing at the Goliath.

Sheltering under a collapsed wall of the store, Mackenzie hugged Maria and Alyce. "Is everyone okay?"

"Considering we're in the middle of World War Three, we ain't doing so bad," replied Maria. "Oh, and we picked up someone else hiding in the rubble of my store."

Mackenzie watched as Beers poked his head out from underneath Alyce's backpack. He laughed as it sniffed around, and then hid when Alyce whispered to the dog.

"I thought he was tucker. How on God's green Earth did you find him?"

"He found us. Just sniffed us out, poor little thing. One of his legs is broken, and he's half scared to death, but I think if we can get out of this, he'll be fine."

"You had us worried, Mac," said Maria. She coughed as a plume of powdery dirt swept past them.

Suddenly, a soldier stopped and knelt down right beside them. Dirt coated his face. Grime and sweat mingled to form an oily complexion, and he looked at them all quickly as a tank rumbled onwards behind him. It bounced across the road as the ground continued to swell and subside as the Goliath crashed around. To Mackenzie, the explosions and roars of the dinosaur sounded like they were in the final stages of the battle.

"Incoming! Stay down!" ordered the soldier.

"Wait, what?" Mackenzie put the others behind him, forming a barricade between him and the soldier.

"Airstrike. Sixty seconds out. We're taking this animal down. Stay behind this wall, and *don't* move." The soldier rapped his knuckles across his helmet and grinned. "We're going to take its head off."

"But what about…?"

"When this is over, get the hell away from here. The Mojave is no place to be right now." The soldier spotted Alyce cowering behind Mackenzie and stood up. "Especially for a kid. Jesus, man, what the hell are you guys doing out here? This was supposed to be a clear area."

"Can you help us?" asked Mackenzie. He ducked as a mortar shell exploded to the right of the store, showering them all in masonry and dirt. "We could use a ride."

"Sorry, man." The soldier shook his head. "We've got no time to be giving civilians a lift. We're getting out asses kicked out here."

The soldier abruptly left them and raced away to rejoin his platoon. Mackenzie knew the soldier had thought Alyce was his, but his mind instantly thought of Amy.

"Laurel, Maria, get down and cover Alyce." They needed more cover. Spotting one of the doors that had been ripped from Maria's car, Mackenzie reached out and grabbed it. It wasn't going to do much, but with all the bullets and shrapnel flying around, anything felt better than nothing. He took what he hoped would be a last look at the Goliath. It was pounding at the ground, clawing at the dirt with its stubby nose and claws, obviously aware it was losing the fight and needed to retreat. It was sending a massive amount of dirt into the air as it attempted to dig a hole to freedom. Flashes and explosions ripped through the air around it as the military tried to keep it confined and above ground. Fire flashed everywhere and rockets hurtled through the air at speed toward the monster.

"What's going on?" asked Laurel as Mackenzie ducked behind the wall, dragging the car door with him.

"It's nearly over," he said as he shuffled forward, trying to get as close to her as possible. "Just keep your head down, say your prayers, and this will all be over soon."

What if the Goliath managed to dig itself underground before the airstrike hit? What if the monster, that had survived so much, escaped the blast? How would they manage to get away then, to get back to civilization, or whatever was left of it? Mackenzie heard the approaching jet planes. The time for questions was over.

"I love you, Laurel." Mackenzie wrapped his arms around her. Maria was huddled in close, while Alyce and Beers were beneath them. There was literally nothing left to do now but wait.

It was a few seconds later when they felt the airstrike hit. The resulting blast sent shockwaves through the air, knocking them off their feet. The car door was wrenched from Mackenzie's grip. Even with their eyes closed the darkness was lit up, and the fireball was visible for miles around. The sound of the explosion was enough to make their ears ring, and though it was over in a second, it was a while before any of them felt brave enough to stand up.

"Is everyone all right?" asked Mackenzie as he brushed himself down. They had tumbled from their hiding place, but the wall had done its job and protected them from the blast.

"We're good," said Maria as she stroked Alyce's hair. The little girl held Beers in her arms, and the dog was shaking.

"Are you?" Laurel wiped her husbands' face. He was covered from head to toe in gore that caked his face.

Mackenzie nodded. "I'm fine." He stepped out into the road and began to march toward the crackling fire that surrounded the store.

"Mac, get back here, it's not safe."

"I need to know, Laurel. I need to know it's over."

As he advanced towards the point where he had last seen the Goliath, he became aware of how quiet it was. The battle had finished, the screaming had stopped, and even the ground was still. It didn't shake or tremble, not even the slightest. It was eerily quiet. Up ahead was a massive fire, burning wildly. Dark smoke drifted into the air and something in the fire popped and sizzled.

As he walked closer, he saw movement through the smoke. Obscure figures were jogging away toward a jeep that roared away as soon as the last of the men had gotten on board. He saw a tank in the distance, a circle of soldiers walking around it. Then he saw a lump of flesh in the road ahead with dark red blood congealing around it. The thick meat was scorched, and the black skin on the outside was at least five inches thick. The piece of burnt meat was at least ten feet across, and had to be from the Goliath. There couldn't be any other explanation. It wasn't a man, nor from any coyote or snake; something that big could only be from one thing.

Mackenzie wafted away the smoke that permeated the air and choked his airwaves. The smell was disgusting, but he had to know. He had to see it for himself. He walked past another hunk of meat, this time even bigger, long enough to block the entire road. There were long deep welts down the skin, and the meat had turned black. Mackenzie broke into a jog. The fire was welcoming him, encouraging him to see what it held. The flames rose high into the air, and the pall of smoke seemed to reach the stars. Mackenzie's spirits sank when he saw the hole. The ground was beginning to slope down, and he knew it was the Goliath's tunnel. It had escaped. It had clearly been injured, but it must have somehow managed to dig a tunnel and escape the airstrike. The loose dirt beneath Mackenzie's feet was difficult to navigate, and he began to slip as he walked down. Nothing was going to stop him from continuing into that dark hole though. He wanted to know for sure. He wanted to see it, to find proof what had happened to it.

"You there, hold up."

Surprised to hear another voice, Mackenzie spun around to find a soldier walking towards him. The man had a pistol pointed at Mackenzie. He was tall, with a shaved head and thick black eyebrows. He wore khaki from head to toe above his black boots.

"Name and rank?"

Mackenzie held up his hands. "No, sir, I'm not with any unit. I'm just a civilian. We were—"

"You shouldn't be here. What's your business?"

Mackenzie lowered his hands. "What's my business? Well I'd like to know first of all that you killed that fucking thing."

The soldier stared back blankly. Mackenzie could feel his nerves fraying. After everything they had been through, he had no inclination to get involved in any discussion about what he was doing here. He had precious little energy left and didn't want to waste it on this man. At the same time, Mackenzie knew he couldn't afford to piss him off. He remembered what had happened to the last witness, the woman in Goodsprings who had become a liability once they had used her.

"Look," said Mackenzie approaching the soldier, "I brought my family here for a vacation. This was supposed to be a nice day out, you know? Visit the Mojave, see the sights before joining my step-daughter in LA." Mackenzie couldn't keep the exasperation from his voice. He had reached his limit and just been pushed over the edge. "I'm just a used car salesman from Milwaukee. I'm on vacation with Laurel, my wife. She always wanted to see the Grand Canyon, the Salt Plains, the Mojave—she'd always been into that stuff. Personally, I'd have settled for a cold Coors in front of the flat-screen watching the Brewers, but I'd do anything for my wife. If you've got someone special, you'll know exactly what I mean. So I decided I'd take my wife on her dream vacation. Only problem is, she never dreamed about seeing a Goliath. I guess we got lucky. A big fucking dinosaur went and interrupted our pleasant little vacation. It killed just about everyone else on the tour group. It killed and ate several people right in front of me and damn near killed me too. So you want to know what I'm doing here? I'm going to make sure it's dead. I want to see its dead body with my own eyes. I want to dance on its grave and spit on its fucking corpse."

The soldier took a step forward and eyeballed Mackenzie. Smiling, the soldier raised an arm and pointed in the direction of the massive fire that still burnt nearby, a few feet below. "Why didn't you just say so? Take a look, just be careful."

Mackenzie nervously turned his back on the soldier, half expecting him to put a bullet between his shoulder blades. Nothing happened though, and Mackenzie slid down the declining ground a few more feet until his feet hit a large rock. Standing carefully, Mackenzie peered through the smoke. It took a moment for his eyes to focus, but when they did a large smile spread across his face.

The Goliath's body lay in a crumpled heap at the bottom of the pit. The tunnel it had dug itself to escape hadn't gone deep enough, and the crater had only served to help contain the fire. Evidently the airstrike had been a success.

The monster's extended abdomen was swollen and carved open to reveal brightly colored entrails that wound down over its belly like magnificent snakes. The creature's innards were coated in a dark green slime that gave off a foul stench. Mackenzie looked at the monster burning, its entire body consumed by fire. It was dead. Searching for the head, Mackenzie carefully picked his way over the ground, until he saw it. There, split in two, was the Goliath's head. Most of the skin had been burnt away exposing its white skull, dripping with crimson blood. One red eye remained open, and Mackenzie stared into it. There was no life there. It was soulless. The Goliath was dead. Finally, it was dead.

Mackenzie began to laugh. He laughed at the sight of the dead beast, at the absurdity of it all, and then noticed the soldier approaching him. He forced himself to stop, to get his feelings under control. His laughter was threatening to turn to tears, and there was still a long way to go. He couldn't afford to give in now.

"So what now?" asked Mackenzie.

The soldier turned up his nose at the repulsive odor coming from the rotting beast. "It's only one. We have a lot more work to do yet. We're pulling out. Next stop is wherever they send us. Plenty more of those bastards out there."

Mackenzie had to try, even though he suspected he knew the answer. "Look, I don't suppose you've any room for..."

The soldier shook his head. "Sorry, sir. We lost a lot of men, and a lot of vehicles in the fight. We can't take you anywhere. I'll call it in, see if there's anyone nearby who can help. Honestly, you're better off staying put tonight. There's going to be a lot of fighting. You'd be better off waiting and calling for assistance in the morning."

"Right." Mackenzie thought about it. "Maybe we can shelter here tonight. There are supplies in the old store we can use."

"Very good. Take care of your family." The soldier turned and trudged away, leaving Mackenzie alone, thinking about what he'd said.

Take care of your family.

How the hell was he supposed to do that? The Goliath was dead, but now they had new problems. It would be getting cold soon and putting a roof over their heads was going to prove difficult. Was there any water? What would they do about Alyce? Mackenzie steadied his hands and headed back towards the others. He heard an engine in the distance and knew the army was leaving. They had a job to do, and he couldn't hold it against them for not giving them a ride. That didn't make it any easier though, knowing they were on their own for now. Being out here alone was almost as scary as being out here with the Goliath. He didn't know how to survive out in the exposed desert at night.

When he reached level ground and had cleared the worst of the smoke, Mackenzie took a couple of deep breaths. He had to keep it together. Laurel needed him. Amy was still out there, probably scared shitless that her parents were not coming. Well, he had no intention of dying out here in the desert. He was going to take Laurel and the others, get to Amy, and get home. The more he thought about the future, the less worried he became. The shaking stopped and he knew he had to focus on what he could do, not on what he *couldn't* do. Laurel and Amy were his whole world and if the Goliath couldn't split them up, then nothing could.

"Well?" asked Maria as Mackenzie returned to the destroyed store.

Mackenzie let out a chuckle as he saw her, Laurel and Alyce. "It's dead. I saw it."

Maria nodded and tears welled up in her eyes. "Thank God."

"You hear that?" Laurel bent down to Alyce and smiled. "The monster's gone. You're safe now honey."

"And Beers?" Alyce looked up at Laurel and Mackenzie as she held the whimpering dog in her arms.

"*And* Beers," replied Laurel.

Mackenzie heard the distant echo of the army convoy disappearing across the desert. The few men left were headed for the bigger cities. They were going to need all the firepower they could muster to take down more of those Goliaths.

"It's a long way back to Baker," said Maria. She bent down and picked up a crushed water bottle. All around her lay the contents of her store, including the walls and roof. It was all gone, every last piece. The Goliath had decimated the building and everything around. If they looked carefully, they might be able to find a couple of blankets, but anything approaching a decent shelter for the night was out of the question. "How are we going to make it?"

"We have to," said Mackenzie looking at Alyce as she tenderly stroked Beers behind the ears. "We just have to. A soldier out there said he'd call in some help for us, but I think they've got bigger problems. I wouldn't expect help anytime soon. We're going to have to use what we have."

Laurel looked despondent and took Mackenzie's hand. "What about Amy? Are we supposed to spend the night out here? With that thing out there? I need to know Amy is all right. I need to…"

Laurel's eyelids fluttered and Mackenzie saw her head spinning. He gripped her hand tightly and waited for the dizzy spell to pass. "Don't worry, okay, I'll figure it out."

Laurel opened her eyes and smiled, but Mackenzie knew it was forced. She was worried about Amy. She was worried about making it through the night, and he had to admit so was he. With the Goliath rotting out there, it would attract rodents, coyotes, maybe even snakes. It wasn't a pleasant thought of having to spend the night with a creature they had just spent all day trying to get away from. He suspected the temperature dropped quickly once the sun set, so they were going to have to work fast to find protection from the elements too.

"Laurel, we'll get to Amy as soon as we can." Mackenzie wished he could say something more reassuring, but nothing came to mind. He was trying to avoid confronting his fears that not only would they not make it to Amy, but that she had come upon trouble herself. At least one of those monsters had been seen in San Diego.

"Don't know about you folks, but I'm getting cold." Maria stood behind Alyce and put her arms around the girl. "Whatever we're going to do, we're going to have to do it soon."

Mackenzie stared out at the burning body of the monster. The fire was dying out, and the stars were dancing above it, shimmering through the fading smoke. How ironic would it be to die from exposure having survived the Goliath's attacks all day? Mackenzie wished he had pressed the soldier more. Maybe if he had shown some urgency, demanded help instead of asking for it, maybe he could have persuaded one of them to give them a ride. He had been so relieved that the Goliath was dead he hadn't really thought about much else. He knew that questioning himself wasn't achieving anything, but where should they start?

A distant boom was followed by the crack of thunder. Once it had passed, Mackenzie thought he heard the familiar rumbling of an engine. "Hey, does anyone else hear that?"

They listened. Laurel heard it, then Alyce, and finally Maria.

"I think they've come back for us," said Laurel hopefully.

Maria rubbed Alyce's shoulders and back, trying to get some warmth into the girl. "Amen to that."

It was definitely an engine, and it was getting closer. They waited impatiently until they finally saw it. Mackenzie doubted the army would send anyone for them, but soon enough he spotted a vehicle coming down the road. It managed to avoid falling into the pit where the Goliath lay and appeared through the smoky haze on a direct course for the Kelso Depot.

Laurel gasped. "Mac, is that…?"

"Okay, now I'm seeing things," said Maria in disbelief.

As the school bus pulled up to a stop beside them, Mackenzie approached it. The door swung open, and a man behind the wheel yelled out.

"What the heck are you folks doing out here?"

"That's a good question. We could fill you in if you could give us a lift." Mackenzie edged closer to the bus, intrigued as to who would be driving a bright yellow school bus out in the Mojave at night. "We ran into some…trouble."

"I can see that." The driver put the bus into park, jumped down from his seat, and stood in the doorway. "Don't suppose any of you happen to know the way back to the West coast? I'm lost as hell out here. Every direction looks the same. Saw the fighting a way back and thought I might be able to get some help."

"If it's the coast you're looking for, you're going the wrong way," said Maria.

"Tell you what," said Mackenzie brightly. "If you can give us a ride, we'll get you on the right road. Mister…?"

The driver jumped down onto the road and held out a dusty hand. "Norman. Been a hell of a day. *Hell* of a day. Hop on up."

Mackenzie introduced himself, and ushered the others on board. Once Maria, Laurel and Alyce were safely sat down, he thanked the man again.

"Please, no need for that," said Norman smiling. "Just get on up and make yourself comfortable. It's a long way back to LA, and boy have I got a story to tell you."

THE END

ACKNOWLEDGEMENTS

My fantastic publisher Severed Press regularly produce good quality novels, which you can find at www.severedpress.com

The Goliaths are fictional creatures of course, but with technological advances, nuclear weapons still available, and so much of the planet still unexplored, are we *really* sure of what is out there waiting for us? Imagine if man wasn't the dominant species on Earth…

If you have enjoyed reading this, then please consider leaving a review and pay a visit to my website www.russwatts.co or look at my other titles:

The Afflicted
The Grave
The Ocean King
Devouring the Dead
Devouring the Dead 2: Nemesis
Hamsikker
Hamsikker 2
Hamsikker 3

SEVERED**PRESS**

CHECK OUT OTHER GREAT KAIJU NOVELS

KAIJU SPAWN
by David Robbins & Eric S Brown

Wally didn't believe it was really the end of the world until he saw the Kaiju with his own eyes. The great beasts rose from the Earth's oceans, laying waste to civilization. Now Wally must fight his way across the Kaiju ravaged wasteland of modern day America in search of his daughter. He is the only hope she has left . . . and the clock is ticking.

From authors David Robbins (Endworld) and Eric S Brown (Kaiju Apocalypse), Kaiju Spawn is an action packed, horror tale of desperate determination and the battle to overcome impossible odds.

KUA MAU
by Mark Onspaugh

The Spider Islands. A mysterious ship has completed a treacherous journey to this hidden island chain. Their mission: to capture the legendary monster, Kua'Mau. Thinking they are successful, they sail back to the United States, where the terrifying creature will be displayed at a new luxury casino in Las Vegas. But the crew has made a horrible mistake - they did not trap Kua'Mau, they took her offspring. Now hot on their heels comes a living nightmare, a two hundred foot, one hundred ton tentacled horror, Kua'Mau, Kaiju Mother of Wrath, who will stop at nothing to safeguard her young. As she tears across California heading towards Vegas, she leaves a monumental body-count in her wake, and not even the U. S. military or private black ops can stop this city-crushing, havoc-wreaking monstrous mother of all Kaiju as she seeks her revenge.

SEVEREDPRESS

 twitter.com/severedpress

CHECK OUT OTHER GREAT
KAIJU NOVELS

ATOMIC REX
by Matthew Dennion

The war is over, humanity has lost, and the Kaiju rule the earth.

Three years have passed since the US government attempted to use giant mechs to fight off an incursion of kaiju. The eight most powerful kaiju have carved up North America into their respective territories and their mutant offspring also roam the continent. The remnants of humanity are gathered in a remote settlement with Steel Samurai, the last of the remaining mechs, as their only protection. The mech is piloted by Captain Chris Myers who realizes that humanity will not survive if they stay at the settlement. In order to preserve the human race, he leaves the settlement unprotected as he engages on a desperate plan to draw the eight kaiju into each other's territories. His hope is that the kaiju will destroy each other. Chris will encounter horrors including the amorphous Amebos, Tortiraus the Giant turtle , and the nuclear powered mutant dinosaur Atomic Rex!

KAIJU DEADFALL
by JE Gurley

Death from space. The first meteor landed in the Pacific Ocean near San Francisco, causing an earthquake and a tsunami. The second wiped out a small Indiana city. The third struck the deserts of Nevada. When gigantic monsters- Ishom, Girra, and Nusku- emerge from the impact craters, the world faces a threat unlike any it had ever known - Kaiju . NASA catastrophist Gate Rutherford and Special Ops Captain Aiden Walker must find a way to stop the creatures before they destroy every major city in America..

CHECK OUT OTHER GREAT DINOSAUR THRILLERS

WRITTEN IN STONE
by David Rhodes

Charles Dawson is trapped 100 million years in the past. Trying to survive from day to day in a world of dinosaurs he devises a plan to change his fate. As he begins to write messages in the soft mud of a nearby stream, he can only hope they will be found by someone who can stop his time travel. Professor Ron Fontana and Professor Ray Taggit, scientists with opposing views, each discover the fossilized messages. While attempting to save Charles, Professor Fontana, his daughter Lauren and their friend Danny are forced to join Taggit and his group of mercenaries. Taggit does not intend to rescue Charles Dawson, but to force Dawson to travel back in time to gather samples for Taggit's fame and fortune. As the two groups jump through time they find they must work together to make it back alive as this fast-paced thriller climaxes at the very moment the age of dinosaurs is ending.

HARD TIME
by Alex Laybourne

Rookie officer Peter Malone and his heavily armed team are sent on a deadly mission to extract a dangerous criminal from a classified prison world. A Kruger Correctional facility where only the hardest, most vicious criminals are sent to fend for themselves, never to return.

But when the team come face to face with ancient beasts from a lost world, their mission is changed. The new objective: Survive.

CHECK OUT OTHER GREAT DINOSAUR THRILLERS

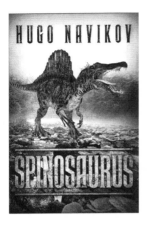

SPINOSAURUS
by Hugo Navikov

Brett Russell is a hunter of the rarest game. His targets are cryptids, animals denied by science. But they are well known by those living on the edges of civilization, where monsters attack and devour their animals and children and lay ruin to their shantytowns.

When a shadowy organization sends Brett to the Congo in search of the legendary dinosaur cryptid Kasai Rex, he will face much more than a terrifying monster from the past.

Spinosaurus is a dinosaur thriller packed with intrigue, action and giant prehistoric predators.

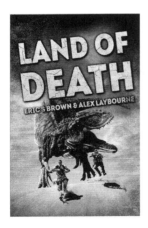

LAND OF DEATH
by Eric S Brown & Alex Laybourne

A group of American soldiers, fleeing an organized attack on their base camp in the Middle East, encounter a storm unlike anything they've seen before. When the storm subsides, they wake up to find themselves no longer in the desert and perhaps not even on Earth. The jungle they've been deposited in is a place ruled by prehistoric creatures long extinct. Each day is a struggle to survive as their ammo begins to run low and virtually everything they encounter, in this land they've been hurled into, is a deadly threat.

CHECK OUT OTHER GREAT KAIJU NOVELS

MURDER WORLD | KAIJU DAWN
by Jason Cordova
& Eric S Brown

Captain Vincente Huerta and the crew of the Fancy have been hired to retrieve a valuable item from a downed research vessel at the edge of the enemy's space.

It was going to be an easy payday.

But what Captain Huerta and the men, women and alien under his command didn't know was that they were being sent to the most dangerous planet in the galaxy.

Something large, ancient and most assuredly evil resides on the planet of Gorgon IV. Something so terrifying that man could barely fathom it with his puny mind. Captain Huerta must use every trick in the book, and possibly write an entirely new one, if he wants to escape Murder World.

KAIJU ARMAGEDDON
by Eric S. Brown

The attacks began without warning. Civilian and Military vessels alike simply vanished upon the waves. Crypto-zoologist Jerry Bryson found himself swept up into the chaos as the world discovered that the legendary beasts known as Kaiju are very real. Armies of the great beasts arose from the oceans and burrowed their way free of the Earth to declare war upon mankind. Now Dr. Bryson may be the human race's last hope in stopping the Kaiju from bringing civilization to its knees.

This is not some far distant future. This is not some alien world. This is the Earth, here and now, as we know it today, faced with the greatest threat its ever known. The Kaiju Armageddon has begun.

Printed in Poland
by Amazon Fulfillment
Poland Sp. z o.o., Wrocław